W9-BFE-399

SOUL OF A NATION
A Historical Novel

Written by P.E. Chute

© 2014 P.E. Chute

© Cover photo by Spider Martin

All Rights Reserved.

No part of this publication may be reproduced, stored in a retrieval system, or transmitted, in any form or by any means, electronic, mechanical, photocopying, recording, or otherwise, without the written permission of the author.

First published by Dog Ear Publishing
4010 W. 86th Street, Ste H
Indianapolis, IN 46268
www.dogearpublishing.net

ISBN: 978-1-4575-3267-2

Library of Congress Control Number: has been applied for

This book is printed on acid-free paper.

This book is a work of fiction. Places, events, and situations in this book are purely fictional and any resemblance to actual persons, living or dead, is coincidental.

Printed in the United States of America

Dedicated to

Jimmy Lee Jackson
Reverend James Reeb
Viola Liuzzo

⁓

They gave their lives for equality
and the right of all citizens to vote

⁓

SOUL OF A NATION

PART ONE

NOTIONS OF HOPE

ONE

I t was a new year. 1965. Like many who mark a new year with resolutions and hope, the Steering Committee of the Dallas County Voters League (DCVL) of Selma, Alabama, fervently resolved it would be their year to move mountains; they would attain voting rights for all. It helped enormously that Dr. Martin Luther King, Jr. granted lending his name and organization to their struggling voting rights campaign that had limped along for years.

Mother Nature acknowledged the New Year by blowing in a January of unseasonable freezing rain that forced all citizens of Selma, both black and white, to shudder and take notice. Gone was Selma's genteel Southern façade, replaced by frost bitten shrubs, beleaguered yellow-poplar trees, and plugged up sewer drains unable to handle the excess water. Unpaved streets in the Negro neighborhoods were ribbons of mud. Some blacks fortunate enough to own cars parked them blocks away from their homes to insure they wouldn't get stuck.

Dr. Martin Luther King, Jr. came to Selma to preach on January 2, 1965 at the urging of Amelia Boynton, a founder of the DCVL. By arriving at Brown Chapel African Methodist Episcopal Church, he was defying an injunction issued by Circuit Judge, James A. Hare. The injunction forbid "no more than three Negroes to assemble" with Dr. King or any one of his lieutenants from his Southern Christian Leadership Conference (SCLC) in order to talk about registering voters. King, after receiving the Nobel Peace Prize the year prior, had become the South's greatest threat to the status quo. Gatherings with this influential Doctor would certainly cause trouble.

But Amelia Boynton didn't frighten easily and ignored the injunction when she paid Dr. King a visit and convinced him to come to Brown Chapel. She knew King's fame would help their cause. While Amelia herself was a voter, it irked her that Selma systematically suppressed the black vote while whites simply signed their name to register and then remained on the registry rolls year after year, even if they were dead. Somehow, through Southern wizardry, their votes still counted from the grave.

The newly appointed Director of Public Safety in Selma, Wilson Baker, also ignored the injunction when King spoke on January 2nd because the gathering was termed an "Emancipation Proclamation Celebration." It fell on the 102nd anniversary of Lincoln freeing the slaves. Baker could call the service a commemoration not a voter rally and thus avoid a confrontation which he sought to avoid whenever possible. Semantics mattered.

King took full advantage of this latitude and preached forcefully, stirring the black community to again believe in their cause. His fiery words infused energy into the demonstrators who were sorely discouraged. After years of struggling in obscurity, Dr. King shined a light on the prevailing voter suppression and resuscitated their commitment.

Every person in the congregation was devoted to the DCVL cause, but it was the Steering Committee members who were most in awe of being in the same building with such an international celebrity. By the end of 1964, the whole world wanted a piece of Dr. King, wanted his name associated with their cause. Yet he came to the small town of Selma, Alabama, to battle for voter equality. The Committee was profoundly honored King had chosen them.

It was at this propitious occasion that Annie Lee Jones, a Steering Committee member of DCVL, enraptured by King's preaching, sat in a pew with her stout legs relaxed, her feet resting on top of her shoes to give her toes a respite. After a long day of cleaning someone else's three-story house, her feet needed the rest. Annie Lee had considerable girth and constantly pushed her body to go beyond weary. For years she devoted herself to fighting for the right to vote even though she still was disenfranchised. She never met a demonstration she didn't like and was one of the Committee's most faithful members. She resolved that one day she would become a voter like Mrs. Boynton or die trying.

Born and raised in Selma, Annie Lee's hometown continually thwarted her by passing declarations that kept Negro voters to less than one percent of Selma's population even though blacks made up fifty-seven percent of the town. Known for her quick temper that lasted no longer than her equally famous ready laugh, Annie Lee could draw herself up and pull energy from those broad toes when she needed to speak with authority. She was a natural leader. Other Committee members respected her unwavering resolve and rarely questioned her suggestions. With little formal education, her fifty plus years had schooled her ability to know when to speak and when to hold her tongue. Except for those times when her mad got the better of her, which admittedly and regrettably was a bit too often.

Next to Annie Lee sat Elverse Turner, another active DCVL Steering Committee member, with his beautiful wife, Mandy, and their fifteen-year-old son, Carlton. It was a rare Saturday the family got to be together as Mandy often worked extra hours as a nurse at Good Samaritan Hospital.

Elverse was a tall, impressive man in his forties with a soft nature that dispelled any fear one might have that his stature posed a threat. In fact, when his handsome face broke into a smile, women melted and men shook his hand agreeably and slapped him on the back. Had he been less humble he might have realized the affect he had on others and used it to his advantage. Instead, he remained true to his modest nature.

Mandy had a beauty that made people think she should have been a movie star. She was cast in a few high school plays and usually played the lead, but she was not a frivolous woman and wanted no part of the kinds of roles generally relegated to black women in Hollywood. So instead of chasing a starlet dream, Mandy studied medicine.

Son Carlton already gleaned the politics of change in the South. He could hardly contain himself that he was actually hearing Dr. King speak in person and took in King's every word. A leader in his school, Carlton wanted to be able to quote his hero's words to his classmates when they returned after Christmas break. Carlton was so motivated by Dr. King that he couldn't get to sleep that night for thinking how he would convince his parents to allow him to march, too.

With King's challenge ringing in his ears, Elverse silently vowed he would go beyond politely waiting in lines, obeying the Southern voting rules that applied only to blacks. How, he did not yet know. In the meantime, he would make certain he was in every protest registration line.

In bitter rain, at the delivery back door of the Dallas County Courthouse, a registration line formed. Elverse Turner was among those who stood in it. He had closed his hardware store to go through the useless exercise of expecting Alabama to bestow upon him his right to vote. The wind whipped rain in all directions and seemingly through those bodies assembled. More than a few were soaked to their black skins. Elverse turned up the collar on his water repellent jacket as he cogitated on King's words to go beyond passive compliance. The downpour seconded that opinion.

Elverse waited more than two hours before he reached the radiator warmth of the courthouse lobby while whites scurried freely through the main entrance, careful not to slip on the slick marble green steps. He strode to the voting registrars office and removed his dripping cap. The registrar, a bored white woman, addressed him patronizingly without bothering to look up from her oversized, carved mahogany desk.

"Name?"

"Elverse Turner."

She snapped her head up and latched onto his gaze with her own. "Why do you bother to keep coming back? Your poor brain done flunked twice by my count. And watch your drips—you're getting my things wet." She pulled the large ledger back an inch from the edge of the desk.

Elverse shifted his cap behind his thighs and responded with his best cat shit grin. "Each time I get better acquainted with the questions I'll be asked, and it inspires me to study the Constitution harder." He willed his voice to remain pleasant without a trace of enmity.

The woman "humphed" and pointed to a line in her huge registration book. "You can answer them all right. It won't matter if they don't approve you."

"Don't I know it," Elverse agreed.

She tapped her red polished nail on the page. "Sign here on this line. That's your number. Come back when registration opens next month and wait for it to be called."

Elverse signed his name with the ballpoint pen lying in the crease of the book while the registrar studied his handsome face and tightly crossed her legs to deny any rising attraction her body might entertain. He removed a small grocery receipt from his pocket and began to record his number when she snatched the pen out of his hand.

"This here's state property! Use your own."

Elverse was lucky. As soon as he left, the registrar closed the office door, flipped the sign hanging on the door knob that said "Gone To Lunch," and those remaining in line would continue to wait to no avail. "Lunch" would last all afternoon.

One month after his rousing New Year sermon, Dr. King returned to Selma on February 1, 1965, with his good friend, Dr. Ralph Abernathy, who was vice president of King's SCLC organization. They led some two hundred and fifty people through the streets of Selma to the Dallas County Courthouse to protest the slow voter registration process. They were quickly arrested and King and Abernathy spent four days in the county jail. Once released, King encouraged the DCVL Steering Committee to keep up the pressure, to remain in touch, and then departed to fulfill other commitments. All

DCVL members, especially Anne Lee Jones, took King's charge to heart and responded as if they had taken a solemn oath. The Committee immediately set about organizing more marches.

February not only brought the return of Dr. King but more merciful weather as well. The sun displayed a rare burst of clemency by shinning down upon their latest registration line. Elverse was again waiting at the rear door of the courthouse, grateful for the warmth of the sun's gentle solicitude. His Committee buddies, Annie Lee and Moses Washington, accompanied him.

Moses was a slight man who looked even smaller next to Elverse. His wiry build resembled that of Sammy Davis Jr., a comparison he loved because he too danced and utilized that talent in his classroom. Students adored Mr. Moses, as he preferred to be called. He didn't just turn to write something on the blackboard; he would shuffle backwards and quick twirl around, the chalk held high over his head like a drum major. He was a steadfast counterpoint to timid country teachers who fearfully sat on the sidelines rather than bear witness to inequity and teach their students self-determination.

Yet, it wasn't easy being such an example for every time Moses missed a day of teaching he was docked a day's pay. When asked how he could afford it, he replied his principles gave him no choice.

A Federal Marshal was walking the line this early morning, counting heads. Teacher Moses chimed in with the Marshal and counted along under his breath as the officer drew closer.

"Ninety-eight, ninety-nine, one hundred." The Marshal stopped and raised his voice. "All right," he said. "Everybody in line after this here person is under arrest." The Marshal pointed to the man directly in front of Moses. Moses was indignant and flashed an angry scowl at the Marshal. Annie Lee was immediately in the Marshal's face.

"And why is that?" she demanded as she put her hands on her ample hips and created a wide stance for him to encounter. "We have a right to be here," she argued. "Today is our day to register as well you know. And if we are willing to wait, you should be willing to protect our rights."

The Marshal waved her aside with a dismissive hand. "There is a court order and it limits the number of those waiting to register to one hundred. Not one hundred and one, one hundred. I intend to carry out the law." The Marshal had raised his voice and was demanding that everyone in the line heed his rules. "You will turn your line around and walk to the county jail."

Elverse shook his head at the absurdity of yet another court order barring them from the voting booth. Posse men appeared and led the threesome away along with every other person after Mr. One Hundred. The participants mildly groaned at being arrested simply for standing in a line to register to vote or, as their opponents would claim, loitering.

Elverse took out his wallet, an Italian kid leather Christmas gift from Mandy, to make certain he had enough money to make bail. Annie Lee concentrated on the billfold and watched him count the bills.

"I'll need a loan, Elverse," she said dolefully. "I left my pocket book behind this morning and only tucked a dollar in my bosom."

Elverse smiled and nodded. "No trouble. I think I've got us covered."

"In that case, I'll owe you, too, brother," said Moses gratefully, aware his teacher's meager paycheck was still one week away. "Guess we have to do our part to keep the jail lights on."

"You got that right, brother," snickered Annie Lee. "They should make us a neighborhood park for all the money they've collected off our movement."

Registering to take a test was only the first step in the Southern multi-step registration process. There were lots of ways black Selma citizens could be denied voter status even if they passed their voting test. The all White Citizens Commission charged with interviewing potential black voters could find an applicant "not qualified" without giving much of a reason, or could use their power to dismiss the hopefuls if they couldn't recite whole sections of the United States Constitution.

Uncle Parker was a man who had been on the White Citizens Commission for so long, no one remembered his full name. He often employed his favorite tactic of verbally asking questions from the application forms rather than allowing applicants time to think and write their answers down. The seeker had to stand and listen as Uncle fired off queries and demanded immediate answers. Uncle would start off easy.

"OK, boy. State your name, the date and place of your birth, and your present address." Even so, sometimes an aspirant would be so nervous he or she would forget the order of the question and be immediately disqualified. For those who could answer correctly, Uncle Parker would continue.

"I want them to think it's going to be a piece of cake so I throw them a real easy question. I say, 'If you are self-employed, state the nature of you business.' Sure most don't even have a real job but I act as if I gave a rat's whisker," he bragged to his friends. "Then I ask my personal favorite from an application test that says, 'Are you now or have you ever been a dope addict or a habitual drunkard?' Course, I couldn't care less to hear their lame ass answer so I immediately follow up by telling them to step outside the exam room to think it over. After about fifteen minutes they're brought back in and asked to repeat the question exactly as I asked it. I just love the lost look on their faces when they stumble to try and remember exactly how the question was posed. Of course they can't do it. That's when I kick 'um out. Works every time."

But like Gandhi and his protesting followers, these rejected applicants simply started the registration process all over again. The would-be voters kept showing up and the overburdened system finally bogged down. The Committee's constant registration demonstrations wore a hole in the fabric of the system until, with the help of a Federal Judge, it was ordered more people had to be registered.

There were also efforts to go door to door to register people, mostly by dedicated workers from SNCC, (the Student Nonviolent Coordinating Committee), that people nicknamed "Snick" rather than pronounce the acronym. It was a hard working organization with boots on the ground that walked the neighborhoods to move people beyond their fear and sign up. It was dangerous work. You could be thrown in jail if you registered people. You could be beaten for registering people. Your life could be threatened if you didn't get out of town. You could be killed.

Lines at the courthouse picked up but still the processing of applicants was too slow. Of necessity, registration lines became a daily occurrence.

Leading the line this day was John Lewis, the young Director of SNCC. Lewis was no stranger to protesting. By the time he arrived to assist the black community of Selma, he had already known beatings, jail cells, and humiliation. He had been a freedom rider in 1961, participated in lunch counter sit-ins, and managed voter registration drives all over the Deep South. He was a devoted believer in non-violent action and had the strength of purpose to remain so. He could not be dissuaded from applying pressure on the powers that be regardless of the consequences.

So it was not out of character that John Lewis led an enormously long registration line well over the 100 person limit. Not only that, he led the demonstrators down Lauderdale Street to the *front* doors of the courthouse. At the head of the line were the faithful: Elverse, Annie Lee, and Moses.

"We're already pushing the law by being over the limit. I don't know if it's such a good idea to march up the front steps, too," Elverse remarked softly.

"Why not?" Annie Lee shot back. "We pay our taxes. We should be able to walk in the front door just like everybody else."

"Right," agreed Moses. "As a citizen, why am I going through the same door where they deliver the toilet paper?"

Elverse grinned. "You got a point there, brother."

They walked on, closing in on Selma's remodeled courthouse that looked more like a bureaucratic unemployment office than a gracious Southern government building. Newly remodeled, its square, basic façade was devoid of any ornamentation except for two oversized lanterns that hung on either side of its ordinary entrance.

John Lewis was not a tall man but he was a giant in his conviction. He walked with sprightly intention. "Walk tall, now,"

Lewis called out to the several hundred Negroes following behind him. Elverse, Annie Lee and Moses knew being up front was a dubious honor since attempting to go through the front doors of the courthouse would surely cause an ugly confrontation. Sheriff Jim Clark was the Dallas County Sheriff in charge of policing the courthouse since it sat on county property, and Clark was always quick to rage against any Negro disobedience.

In fact, Sheriff Clark was one of the main reasons movement organizations joined forces in Selma. Not only were the black citizens already organized and protesting voter suppression, here was Sheriff Jim Clark, a hotheaded avowed racist who did everything in his considerable power to keep them from succeeding. It was a winning combination for confrontation and publicity. What Bull Connor had been to Birmingham, Jim Clark was to Selma. These savvy civil rights groups understood Clark would bring attention to their cause with his brutal tactics that were sure to make the papers.

Clark unwittingly obliged the marchers by playing out his designated role. He burst through the Courthouse doors, his face flushed, livid that black demonstrators dared challenge him and the Southern way of life.

Annie Lee watched him warily. "Here comes the volcano," she said barely under her breath.

"Keep it cool, Annie Lee," Elverse warned in a whisper.

Two deputies attempted to restrain Clark but he easily shook them off. His rotund body charged down the steps like a snorting bull as he began to bellow.

"Where the hell do you think you're going? Git around back where you belong and wait to be called!"

"We want to wait in the lobby!" Lewis shouted back.

"Ain't nobody scared to demand our rights around here," Annie Lee chimed in.

Clark rushed the line, swung a mighty arm at Lewis who ducked, and then pushed Annie Lee hard on her breasts. As the line turned around to retreat, Clark shoved the back of Annie Lee's neck with his nightstick. It was one insult too many. Her nonviolence training evaporated like water drops testing a hot griddle and she whirled around and clocked him with a right hook. Clark fell to the ground, dazed. His eyes bulged with enraged indignation and disbelief.

The deputies rushed Annie Lee, grabbed both her arms and wrestled her to the stubby winter grass. The blood vessels strained in the deputies' red necks as Annie Lee fought back fiercely, her legs kicking the air. Clark jumped to his feet then plopped on top of Annie Lee, his face contorted in a sneer, and straddled her stomach like a cowboy riding a horse. As his men held each of her arms, he raised his billy club over her head. It happened so fast there was nothing Elverse, Moses, or John Lewis could do except witness the take down. A camera flash went off.

"You going to hit me, scum?" Annie Lee asked defiantly. She yanked an arm free and grabbed for his baton but she was no match for three men. Clark easily retained his club and responded by whacking her over her skull. It made a hollow, cracking sound not unlike a batter who splits his bat after connecting poorly with a baseball. The stunned marchers gasped, hardly believing their eyes and ears. Clark rolled off Annie Lee's belly, rose, and hitched his pressed pants back into place.

Elverse and Moses rushed forward to help Annie Lee where she lay motionless. A third deputy stepped in and edged them back menacingly with the butt of his nightstick.

Clark brushed himself off and straightened the creases of his impeccable khaki uniform. He adjusted the small button on his lapel that read "Never."

"I jus' love this nonviolent stuff," he crowed.

The posse men roughly pulled Annie Lee to her feet, clamped handcuffs on her wrists, and led her away, her legs wobbling underneath her body. A bleeding gash on her forehead trickled blood onto her frayed black wool coat collar, now badly torn.

An FBI agent dressed in a dark suit and scribbling notes on the small note pad he always carried rushed up to Clark. "Who was that woman?" he asked.

"Annie Lee," the sheriff answered.

"Miss or Mrs.?" he asked, thinking her last name was Lee.

"She's a nigger woman, Mr. FBI big shot. Ain't nothin' in front of her name."

 TWO

I t was an early grey school day morning in Flint, Michigan that required the kitchen lights to be on. The Cole family was in full get-ready-for-school-breakfast mode. Leslie May Cole stood at her yellow gold speckled Formica kitchen counter efficiently making tuna sandwiches in an assembly line for her three children's lunch bags. She was dressed in a candy striped hospital volunteer uniform and white flats that made her look even more girlish than her mid thirty years. She thought about her day's schedule as she automatically plopped tuna salad on every other slice of bread. In back of her bread line stood three open brown paper bags like waiting sentinels.

"Annie!" Leslie called. "Come to breakfast. Are you dressed?" She pushed her short blond curls back with her forearm and proceeded to place a slice of cheese on top of each tuna portion.

Her husband, David Cole, a dignified man several years her senior, leaned against the counter watching her efficiency as he sipped coffee from a ceramic mug with his union's logo on the front. He had worked his way up in the Teamsters and now wore a business suit and sat behind a desk. His conservative ties were usually one solid color, nothing flashy; he was careful to blend in with his new status. He was proud how he had risen in the ranks to provide for his wife and family. David loved Leslie dearly and would do anything to make her happy. He fell in love with her china doll appearance—delicate, fair, a classic beauty—only to discover he had actually married Eleanor Roosevelt. After years of adjustment, they finally achieved an easy, comfortable marriage. He accepted that Leslie needed space to be her own person and came to realize it was support, not resistance to her independent streak that made their relationship work. She was too restless to remain a homemaker now that all her children were in school, so in addition to volunteering at Genesee Memorial, she enrolled in a political science night class at Flint Community College.

Alex, their ten-year-old son, sat at the oak breakfast table spooning down a bowl of Cheerios. Without breaking concentration on his math homework he piped up, "Don't forget, Mom, two sandwiches. Growing boy and all that."

Leslie grinned as she nodded and took out two more slices of bread from the Wonder Bread wrapper, adding tuna salad and more cheese. She then began to separate leaves from the head of an iceberg lettuce and ran them under the tap.

The front door slammed and their oldest son, Justin, jogged into the kitchen with the morning paper, shaking snow off the wrapper. He was a handsome, intense boy who often wore a thoughtful expression on his fourteen-year-old face. He sat down at the table and spread the paper open at the opposite end from his brother and began reading the stories on page one.

David topped off his coffee from the stainless Sunbeam electric pot and ambled over to his son to take the front section but Justin held on.

"Sorry, Dad. Current events today."

David nodded and began to read over his son's shoulder.

"Jeez," David said as he read. "They imposed martial law in Saigon. Monks are still demonstrating."

Alex gleefully slammed his math book closed as Annie, his adorable six-year-old sister, bounded into the kitchen with her lower lip stuck out in frustration. Alex tickled her as he bolted past. Annie marched up to her mother. "I can't find my other stupid polka-dot sock," she pouted.

"Oh, dear," said Leslie. "Call out the sock patrol. Where could it be?"

"But I really want to wear them," said Annie, hanging her head for dramatic affect.

Leslie stopped her sandwich production, wiped her hands on her apron, and took her daughter's tiny hand. "OK, sweetheart. Let's go see if we can find it. But if not, wear your pink ones. They'll look pretty, too." Together they headed for Annie's bedroom.

The toast popped and David slid the pieces onto a plate, buttered them, took one for himself, and placed the plate on the table.

"Mom!" Justin shouted.

"What?" Leslie called back from little Annie's room.

"The Selma sheriff clubbed a woman named Annie Lee who was demonstrating at the courthouse!"

"What?" Leslie rushed back into the kitchen and over to the table.

"There's an article about Selma and it says the sheriff clubbed a woman named Annie Lee."

"Oh, no," said Leslie.

She peered over Justin's shoulder and David joined her while chewing a mouthful of toast. Justin turned the page and there was a large, slightly blurry picture centered at the top. Leslie froze.

"It sure looks like it could be Annie Lee, but it's hard to tell," said Justin.

Leslie glanced at David who was trying to fathom the photo of a large woman being held to the ground whose face could not be seen. Justin leaned back so his parents could read over his shoulder. Leslie's hands flew to her mouth and she began holding her breath. David dumped his toast and slipped his arm around Leslie's waist as they continued to read the accompanying article.

"Good god!" David said. "That's the idiot sheriff sitting on top of the woman?"

All three tried to decipher the halftone dots making up the grainy photo.

"I think it's her," Leslie whispered, the color draining from her face. "He hit her with his nightstick... and then arrested her? Oh, good heavens. She's... she's probably in a hospital right now... or jail." Leslie turned to her husband and began to tremble.

David put his hands on his wife's shoulders. "Leslie, hold on. We can't assume anything until it can be verified. It might not be our Annie Lee. They don't say her last name is Jones."

Leslie shook herself loose. "Of course it's her. I can feel it. Oh, what if it is? I was afraid something like this would happen. I've got to go down and get her out of there. These demonstrations are just stirring things up. She thinks the South will change? The only thing that's going to change is how much worse the violence will get. I hate Alabama!"

Leslie sprinted across the kitchen to the wall phone. Justin and David followed her.

"Are you calling her, Mom?" Justin asked.

"Yes sweetie. And if there's no answer, then I'll know it's her."

"Leslie, if she doesn't answer her phone that doesn't prove anything. She just might not be home," reasoned David.

"At this hour? Of course she'd be home."

David considered other possibilities. Could there be more than one hefty black woman named Annie Lee living in Selma? And demonstrating? And willing to fight the Sheriff? Probably not.

"If there isn't an answer I think we should call Jackson." David suggested.

"If I don't get an answer then I will call Jackson and… and the police if I have to. Somebody's got to know if it's our Annie Lee and where she is," Leslie said. Her hand shook as she began to dial the number she knew so well. David stood next to her for support and tried to think things through.

"Justin," David said, "Get our telephone directory out of the drawer."

Justin opened a deep drawer and searched under multiple loose papers, take-out menus, and maps for their personal directory. Little Annie ran back into the kitchen holding her socks aloft and swinging them like a lasso over her head.

"Found 'um, Mommy," she announced proudly. No one replied so she lowered her socks and looked bewildered from her mother to her father to her brother.

"Hey," she said and frowned. "What's going on?" No one answered. She searched her mother's face. "Mommy? Are you crying?" Leslie patted her daughter's head and took her hand.

"It's ringing," Leslie announced.

Alex also returned to the kitchen as he pulled on his down jacket and saw his family huddled around the phone.

"Mom?" he said. "Our lunches?"

"Oh, lord, right," said Leslie and hung up. "I'm sorry."

"OK, kids," said David taking charge. "Get your coats and jackets and the things you need for school. We don't want to be late."

They all hustled out of the kitchen except Alex who went and got the box of Twinkies from the pantry. Leslie rapidly slapped the top pieces of bread onto each of the sandwiches, wrapped them swiftly in wax paper and tossed them in the bags.

"I'm sorry, honey," she said to Alex. "I didn't have time to put lettuce on your second sandwich." He shrugged. From a wicker basket filled with apples that sat on her counter, she grabbed three and tossed one into each beg.

Alex followed her down the line adding a Twinkie to each bag—two for his own. Leslie ran to the pantry and retrieved a strawberry pop tart.

The family returned all bundled up in wool coats, scarves, and hats. She kissed and hugged each of her children as she handed them their lunch bags. She gave Annie the pop tart since Annie missed breakfast.

"Good-bye, my darlings. Have a good day at school."

David gave her a quick kiss. "Find out what happened first before you get all upset. I'll call you later as soon as I'm out of my meeting. Try not to worry. And if it is her? Just remember she's tough. She's going to be OK."

"Who's tough?" asked Annie.

"Tell you later," said David. "Let's go," and herded the children toward the door of their attached garage.

Justin broke away and ran to the table and tore out an article on Churchill's funeral arrangements from the front page then rushed to catch up. He gave his mother another quick kiss as he passed. "Bye, Mom. Love you. Hope she's OK," and scooted out the door, which slammed, the hydraulic closer still broken since Christmas.

Leslie immediately dialed again. She stretched the cord to the Frigidaire and removed a quart of Hudsonville ice cream from the freshly defrosted freezer. Keeping the receiver cradled to her ear with her shoulder, she opened the carton and got a spoon from the silverware drawer. She took a bite of Rocky Road. The phone kept ringing.

✍

THREE

The White Citizens' Council (Annie Lee called them the Klan in neck ties) and the actual Ku Klux Klan threatened any DCVL progress by creating an environment of fear through economic pressure and violence. Activists could lose their jobs if it became known they were involved, or worse— be hurt or burned out of their homes. Judge Hare had no problem issuing his injunction against Negroes assembling anywhere in the county since he considered such edicts necessary to keep Negroes in their place. And with Sheriff Clark enforcing his orders, the two men created an environment as repressive as any dictatorship.

But they couldn't stop Amelia Boynton. Amelia continued to use her modest clapboard home to meet with civil rights leaders and DCVL members to strategize about how they would increase the voter rolls. At one of these clandestine meetings the Steering Committee considered expanding their protests beyond Selma into other nearby towns to create even bigger unrest and attention. When the town of Marion was raised as a possibility, however, the meeting grew quiet.

"That's where Brother James Orange was arrested," said Moses softly. People nodded their heads and looked down at the floor.

"There's talk he might be lynched," said Amelia. More nodding of heads. Such conjecture had spread through the community like an airborne disease.

"They're mean sons-of-bitches," said Elmira, Moses' wife. She rarely minced her words and made plain what everyone was thinking.

"If we go there, we would be sure to find trouble," said Elverse. There was a pensive silence.

"Well then, trouble is what we'll meet," claimed Annie Lee, fresh out of jail. Members looked up. "We'll kill two birds with one stone. We'll demonstrate for the vote and we'll make sure nothin' happens to James."

People gazed at Annie Lee who looked so resolute. No one spoke. She met their gaze. "Well?" she asked. "Are we gonna let Marion's reputation overcome us or are we gonna stand up for what we know is right and protect our brother James at the same time?"

Elverse sighed. He knew there was no arguing with Annie Lee's dare. He silently asked the Almighty to give him courage. As a man originally from the North, he had heard of Marion's reputation but had never so much as stepped one foot in that town. Downtown Marion was not a town where any black human being chose to be. He saw no reason to visit, ever. Period.

But with James Orange sitting in Marion's flimsy jail where death threats circled his cell, the Committee reluctantly chose the town they feared. It was located in the next County of Perry. James Orange, a field secretary for King, had remained in the town to continue registering black voters after King had left. His actions of helping people fill out voter registration forms got him arrested and it was unimaginable that he would be given a fair trial. The Committee decided they would hold a rally, starting at Zion Chapel Methodist Church where C.T. Vivian, another assistant to King, would speak on the right to vote. The assembled would then march through the center of town to the jail and thereby ward off any lynching attempts.

Marion wasn't that far from Selma, but if Selma could be considered the rim of a frying pan, Marion was the searing bottom. Here the demonstrators would test just how hot that skillet would hiss.

Over three hundred chanting black marchers poured out from Zion's Chapel Methodist Church after Vivian's inspirational preaching, led by two men who carried the ends of a very long banner. It read,

"THE RIGHT TO VOTE IS A CONSTITUTIONAL RIGHT"

Annie Lee, Moses, and Elverse held up the middle section of the banner. The street lamps along the street burned brightly, lighting their way. A chant rose up from the parade, filling the night air, and was repeated over and over like an insistent musical mantra.

"We want the vote. Amen! And we're walkin' to the jail to see our brother, Jim. We want the vote. Amen!"

The marchers following the banner lustily sang out into the frosty dark night and clapped in rhythm as they ambled toward the Town Square and jail. Annie Lee's forehead sported a bandage from Sheriff Clark's club, but it did not interfere with the determined look on her face or the power of her voice. Moses equally joined in with gusto and stepped to the rhythm of the singsong phrase. It was Elverse who barely mouthed the words and instead assessed the crowd that had assembled on both sides of the road. The bystanders were jeering, taunting faces that initiated an involuntary shudder down his spine. Elverse hadn't grown up with such institutionalized hatred. It still rattled him.

Town whites had come to heckle the black marchers who dared walk on their town streets and head to the center of their town square. When the marchers did reach the town square they abruptly stopped at the sight of a tight knot of blue helmeted state troopers. Some wore guns on their belts; all had their nightsticks drawn. The singing quickly faded away and the clapping ceased. A sense of dread was palpable. Alarmed, Elverse scanned the crowd for a possible clearing and tried to formulate an escape route if it became necessary.

As if by signal, the streetlights blinked off and troopers tightened the straps on their helmets that glimmered faintly in the dark, catching what little light there was from storefronts and the moon. Waving their batons, they charged the marchers.

"Yahoo!" they hooted as if they were rodeo cowboys eager to rope a steer.

Pandemonium broke out and Elverse, Annie Lee, and Moses dropped the banner and spun around to run back to the protection of the church parking lot where Elverse had parked the car. Troopers trampled over the banner as they crossed into the crowd and began swinging their clubs at the retreating backsides of demonstrators who desperately tried to out run their assailants. Adrenalin pumped through the troopers' bodies; many were deputized volunteers who gloried in their unrestrained power over their victims who dared not fight back.

Elverse became separated from Annie Lee and Moses as he bobbed and weaved through the crowd. Having been a wide receiver in high school, his footwork came back to help him. Then a man named Skinny Eddie tripped, fell, and blocked his path. Elverse reached down to help Skinny to his feet. A club swung down hard on his shoulder. Elverse winced in pain. The trooper barely slowed down as he stomped over Skinny and wielded his nightstick like a windshield wiper, hitting bodies on his right and then on his left as he moved down the street.

"Grab my hand," Elverse yelled to Skinny. He pulled the terrified man to his feet but Skinny remained frozen in terror, his legs refusing to engage. Elverse pushed him forcefully and the two staggered forward. Elverse towed Skinny toward a café called Mack's where Elverse hoped they could get off the street and hide.

Annie Lee and Moses continued to dash for the car. Annie Lee was panting hard. She looked over her shoulder to see if troopers were still in pursuit and stumbled on the man running in front of her. She tumbled forward, skidding her face along the pavement. She felt street grit grind into her cheek. Moses grabbed under her arms and heaved with all his might.

"Get up, Annie," he shouted, "Get Up!"

Elverse and Skinny Eddie reached Mack's Café and swung the door open only to see troopers were already inside beating up patrons. The two men turned to run elsewhere but a trooper trotting up the sidewalk closed in and blocked their escape. Elverse and Skinny were forced to duck into the restaurant and take their chances. The trooper broke into a sprint to catch the swinging door and followed them in.

Inside was bedlam. People were shrieking and pushing to exit the café's back door. Elverse witnessed one young man trying to shield a woman and elderly man with his own body from a crazed trooper bashing them. The young man screamed for the trooper to stop. "These people are old!"

Instead, the trooper threw the man up against a cigarette machine and drew his gun. At close range the trooper shot him in the stomach. Elverse rushed forward and fished out a handkerchief from his jacket, waded it up, and pressed it against the man's wound. The man took his free hand, now bloodied, and grabbed Elverse's jacket to try and pull himself up. Another trooper drew his gun and shot out the overhead lights, creating almost total darkness. Glass rained down on the hysterical crowd. Elverse panicked thinking the troopers would shoot more people and forced the wounded man's hand open to let go of his jacket. He pulled away and raced to the back exit and pushed his way out with the others.

At the curb in the Square whites were whooping and heckling the live action show. An unruly pack surrounded a television crew filming the melee. One brazen man slugged the TV cameraman who swung his heavy camera toward his assailants like a pendulum in an attempt to protect himself. A policeman standing next to the crew merely turned his back, signaling a free pass for any irate bystander who wanted to join in the attack with impunity. Men quickly became a frenzied mob and kicked and punched the media crew and shot out their filming lights. Guns seemed to be everywhere.

Among the crowd watching this skirmish were Sparky Wilkerson and Choice Thompson, two KKK members from Dallas County who heard about the march and drove to Marion to watch what they hoped would become trouble. When Sparky saw the law wasn't going to stop the assault, a broad grin crossed his ruggedly handsome, youthful face.

"Well, well, well," he marveled and punched Sparky's arm. "Let's go get us a nigger!" With that he ran off, leaving Choice to hobble after him as best he could.

Sparky caught up to an elderly Negro man and his grandson and pulled on the old man's coat, hoping to drop him to the ground. But the young boy rammed Sparky and it was Sparky who stumbled to his knees. Grandson and grandfather escaped, the grandfather's coat pulled halfway down his arms but still intact. Sparky was livid and quickly rose to his feet and slapped his jeans at the knees to brush himself off.

"Damn you coons," he screeched. "I'll Kill You!" But the twosome had melted into the crowd and disappeared.

Choice shuffled up to Sparky, careful to avert his eyes to pretend he hadn't witnessed his buddy fall and fail. Instead he looked around as if searching for a victim in the crowd.

Sparky spit and without a word took off in pursuit of another target. He captured a slender middle-aged man and gripped his arm. Sparky kept spinning him around in a circle like a windmill until Choice caught up and grabbed the other arm. Together they tossed the man to the ground like a bronco.

"I'm gonna brand you," Sparky howled, falling to his knees. Hot excitement surged through his veins all the way up to his blond crew cut where every hair stood on end. He whipped out his pocketknife but had to let go of the man's arm to open it, all the while damning the knife for not being his automatic switchblade. Why hadn't he come better prepared? Choice had yet to drop down onto the street and couldn't hold the man from a bent over position. The man easily squirmed away from Choice's grip and ran off. Sparky was insane with rage.

"Shit, Choice! Why didn't you get down to hold 'um better? Christ." He brandished his knife toward Choice's nose, rose, and kicked Choice lightly with the point of his cowboy boot.

"You're worthless."

"Sorry, Sparky. You know my legs don't bend so easy as they used to. And I gotta watch out for my foot."

"Shit, you ain't no cripple," Sparky said as he pocketed his knife, knowing his opportunity had passed. "You're just milking the system."

The crowd had already thinned and Sparky watched them disappear as he stood there, steaming. Troopers always got to have all the action.

Annie Lee and Moses made it back to Elverse's shinny Rambler and nervously sat waiting for their friend to return. Cars all around them were racing to the exit and they felt like sitting ducks as spaces by their car became vacant. Annie Lee sat in the back seat, rocking back and forth as she held a handkerchief to her bloody cheek. The bandage, once on her forehead, was long gone. Moses sat in the driver's seat, drumming his fingers on the steering wheel and searching the dark night for any sign of Elverse.

"Come on, come on, please, god," Moses mumbled over and over.

A head popped up at the passenger's front window and both Annie Lee and Moses screamed. It was Elverse. Moses flipped up the door lock and Elverse scrambled in, tossing the ignition key to Moses.

"Lord have mercy, let's get out of here," Elverse cried, slamming his door and pressing down the lock all in one motion.

Moses fumbled to put the key into the ignition. The engine sputtered, then caught. Moses threw the car into reverse and pealed out of the lot, the tires squealing. "This town's a devil town," he exclaimed. "I sure am glad we live in Selma."

"I just want to live, period," Annie Lee cried. "Step on it!"

Moses drove with a heavy foot as if he was driving a getaway car in a bank robbery. Elverse's little green Rambler streaked along the dark country road, shaking under the unaccustomed speed as they sought out a safer Dallas County.

Annie Lee and Moses lived in the George Washington Carver Projects. The "Carver" as it was known was tidy red brick affordable housing located in the all black section of town that included Brown Chapel.

After Annie Lee and Moses were dropped off at the Carver, Elverse took to the wheel and drove on to his house on the outskirts of town and gratefully turned into his own driveway. The pebble gravel made a crunching sound beneath his tires, announcing his arrival. Mandy tore back the living room curtain and peered out. Seeing it was her husband, she flew out the front door and shot out to Elverse who was locking the car. Already dressed for bed, her robe flapped open as she ran, displaying a body every bit as beautiful as Dorothy Dandridge. Mandy threw her slender arms around her husband's neck and squeezed.

"Elmira called and said there was big trouble. Oh, baby, are you all right? I've been so scared." Mandy's voice was shaking with concern and she wanted to hold her husband, proof that he was there and safe.

Elverse removed her arms, took her hands in his and kissed them. With their arms around each other they walked into the house.

Carlton stood waiting, worry written all over his young face. All he and his mother knew from the phone call was trying to march in Marion had been a disaster. He studied his father as Elverse closed and bolted the front door, something Carlton had never seen him do unless they were going to bed. Sometimes they didn't bother to lock their door at all. Watching his father slide the bolt scared Carlton and his heart began to beat double time. He surmised his dad had witnessed something really bad. Suddenly he didn't feel secure in his own home. Was someone after his Dad? They lived out in the country where there were few lights. When it was night, the complete darkness always reminded him that they were on their own. Now he felt a terrible vulnerability.

Mandy also watched Elverse and waited anxiously for the details of whatever ordeal her husband had just been through. Elverse began to pace, unable to form words. The floorboards squeaked. Then Mandy noticed smears on Elverse's jacket sleeve.

"Elverse," she said looking more sharply at the stains. "What's that on your jacket?" Recognition clicked in and she gasped. "Elverse, that's blood on your jacket!" Elverse waved off her observation.

"Elverse, talk to us. What happened? How did you get blood on your jacket? Are you hurt?" Mandy pleaded for an explanation.

"I'm mighty thirsty," he said finally.

"I'll get you some water," Carlton volunteered and leapt to the kitchen, not wanting to miss a single word. Elverse stopped pacing once his son was out of the room and stood before his wife and looked deeply into the eyes he loved so very much.

"Mandy," he said quietly. "They shot a man tonight." Mandy's hands flew up to his face and cradled it.

"Oh, Elverse. No!"

"Right in front of me they did. Our march was stopped by troopers just waiting for us to reach the town square. Obviously they somehow found out we planned to march and called in extra men. They just started to attack and beat people. I ran for a café but they were already attacking people in there, too. It was a crazed free for all. People screaming and trying to get out? And… and this trooper… he just draws his gun and shoots this young guy. Right then and there in front of my eyes. Didn't care who witnessed it. Oh, god!" Elverse's teeth began to chatter; he took a deep breath.

Carlton returned with a glass of water that Elverse downed in one gulp. He handed the glass back. "Another one, son. No, wait. Put some water up for tea. Why's it so cold in here?"

Carlton sprang back to the kitchen and Elverse could hear him filling the kettle as he lowered himself into their worn Morris chair. Mandy snatched the knit afghan off the back of their couch and tucked it around her husband. She commenced to rub his shoulders but he flinched and waved for her to stop.

"What's the matter, baby? You *are* hurt. Elverse? What did they do to you? Honey, answer me."

Elverse remained silent as he replayed the shooting in his mind. With a quaver in his voice he began to find words for the haunting images filling his scrambled brain.

"They shot him at close range. For no reason." He shuddered. "And I ran out the back. Just like everybody else. I left him."

"Well, of course you did, Elverse. Anybody in his right mind would get out of there. They had guns. But are you hurt? That's what I want to know."

"Just my shoulder. It tangled with a billy club."

"Let me see."

Elverse shook his head. "Not right now."

Mandy crouched on the floor and hugged her husband's legs, holding on to them as if she could stop them from ever marching again.

"Elverse, promise me you won't march anymore, baby. You can't vote if you're dead. The movement isn't nonviolent if they be shooting at you."

Elverse shut his eyes but the images continued to play across his lids. The pleading eyes of the man shot haunted him. "It certainly has changed things," Elverse agreed. "They crossed a line tonight."

A phone rang in a room at the Ramada Inn in downtown Selma. The same FBI agent who had asked Sheriff Clark about Annie Lee fumbled to turn on the brass lamp next to his bed. He hated this assignment. What a waste of time, taking notes but not having the power to do anything. The Bureau understood nothing would happen in Washington while Southerners controlled the budget and all major Committees in Congress. FBI manpower was one quarter the size of the New York City Police force, and without the cooperation of local police departments, the FBI had no chance to make any kind of case, particularly if it involved police brutality. Not that he really cared; the agitators were probably Communists anyway. The phone's incessant ringing stopped when he lifted the receiver and put it to his ear.

"Hello," he said groggily. Instantly he was very much awake and reached for his trusty pad and pencil from the nightstand drawer as he listened. "Marion, you say?" There was a long pause to which he answered, "Holy shit," and "yeah." He whistled softly. "You sure it was a trooper?" He started making notes, more from habit than conviction. "OK," he said and ended the call. He immediately began to dial a number and pulled the covers up around his neck as he waited to disrupt another government worker's sleep.

An emergency DCVL Steering Committee meeting was called to respond to the violence in Marion. The distraught leaders decided to immediately initiate another march on the streets of Selma to protest the shooting in Mack's Café. Like many movements, protests were being heaped upon protests in reaction to calamities that erupted beyond the original reason to demonstrate. Protests became less and less about the original cause and more and more about the grievances that piled up. Blacks were outraged troopers had opened fire on peaceful demonstrators who hadn't carried a single weapon. They were determined to show the police power that bullets would not stop them. They would not be intimidated. The Committee, sworn to nonviolence, knew they had to create a visible outlet for the outrage if their movement was to be kept under control and managed within their nonviolent philosophy.

It was night and Selma was ablaze with anticipation. There were heavily armed posse men lining the roads. Sheriff Jim Clark strolled smugly along the sidewalk followed by an entourage of even more posse men. Whites were gathered at street corners, hoping to see more action like the kind they'd heard about in Marion. It would be more exciting than TV.

Sheriff Clark reached the corner, stopped, and leaned back on his heels as he crossed his athletic arms over his immense belly. He surveyed the scene. To his deputies he said, "We'll show that shit Dallas County Improvement Association what needs to be improved. We'll be glad to improve their own damned nigger selves." The deputies nodded appreciatively and chuckled in agreement.

"I believe these communists call themselves the Dallas County Voters League now," one deputy offered meakly.

Clark glowered at him. "Whatever the hell they call themselves. Don't make no difference," enjoined Clark. "They're all darkie Sambos bent on breaking the law."

Across the street another circle of deputized state trooper volunteers stood by, waiting for orders and killing time by exchanging jibes.

One trooper waved his hand into the brisk night air authoritatively like a Greek orator and barked, "If we put a diving board up top Pettus Bridge and hang a sign, 'No Niggers Allowed,' we can watch all them fools jump off." The men laughed so hard at his little joke that one trooper began to have a coughing fit; he had swallowed his own spit from his chewing tobacco.

Behind a wooden street blockade, a cluster of white teenage girls laughed shrilly. Despite the cold, they hoped to be noticed by wearing tight straight pencil skirts that accentuated their slender bodies or new bell-bottom trousers worn below their waists with wide leather belts. They'd seen these new trends modeled in the latest Seventeen Magazine.

A shiny black Cadillac cruised by them, driven by an older, craggy faced man. It was Uncle Parker. It was not especially hidden that Parker was the hardened face of the KKK cell in their town, yet, because many people feared him, he enjoyed a certain status and respect, like being appointed to the White Citizens Commission that ran the voting interviews. Much less harsh was the face he presented to his church where he was admired as their most generous tithing elder. The congregation called him "Uncle" because, to them, he was their Uncle Sam, the man with the money. No one dared ever ask him how he made it. Not even his wife, Allie April, knew.

Sparky rode in the car with Uncle and hung out the passenger window all the way down to his silver belt buckle as they passed the girls. He stuck two fingers between his lips and gave a piercing, long wolf whistle. The girls shrieked giddily as he waved at them and they waved wildly back.

"You got a girl now, Sparky?" Uncle inquired.

"Nah, not really," Sparky answered, dropping back into the car seat. "There are so many to chose from I don't see any need to settle for just one. Besides. I like to keep my time loose. Be my own man; keep to my own schedule. You take Rusty? Good god, I know he's your nephew and I don't mean no disrespect, but he's so tied down with a wife and kid and payments and shit that he might as well be Paul Bunyan."

"Paul Bunyan?"

"Yah, you know, the giant guy they tied down so he couldn't move?"

"Oh. Right. That fella in literary books."

"Right."

"Well, we all get tied down sooner or later... unless you're one of them queer fellas." Uncle laughed. "You're not queer, are you?"

Sparky threw him a disgusted look. "Shad-up," he said.

All the people on the streets of Selma were waiting for what the Negroes were deciding inside Brown Chapel. The shooting had rallied many more sympathizers from the black neighborhood, and the church pews were full to overflowing with several hundred in attendance.

Annie Lee sat toward the back of the church so as not to draw attention to her swollen scraped cheek that had turned a very deep purple. Next to her was her male friend from childhood, Jackson Dupree. Jackson loved Annie Lee with a deep, abiding love that was as comfortable as an old pair of slippers, and his easygoing nature was the perfect counter-balance to her intense, fiery temperament.

All were listening to Hosea Williams lead the group in prayer. Williams was one of a handful of leaders on loan from King's organization; James Bevel was another. These two men, along with John Lewis, quickly became an integral part of the DCVL Selma protest, and the community now turned to these seasoned leaders for their organizing expertise. Hosea stood at the podium wearing his blue denim work overalls, the identifying field uniform of the Southern Christian Leadership Conference that they sometimes wore in place of business suits. If clothes make the man, under-dressing keeps him self-effacing.

"Bless Jimmie Lee Jackson," Williams prayed aloud. "Let his courage be our courage as he lies in his hospital bed and fights for his life. Bless Jimmie Lee's grandfather, Cager Lee, and his mother, Viola Jackson, who were also beaten that fateful night. Help us to comprehend how officers of the law could beat an eighty-two year old man and an unarmed woman. A mother and a grandmother. And we humbly pray to give comfort to Jimmie Lee's little girl, Brenda, whose life has been turned upside down by ineffable violence."

The man shot in Marion now had an identity. He was the youngest deacon ever to be ordained at St. James Baptist Church in Marion, and he had been seeking to register to vote for the past four years. In Mack's Café, Jimmie Lee was struggling to protect his Mother and Grandfather. Annie Lee shifted in her seat, smoldering with indignation, but kept her head bowed. Williams continued.

"He was stricken by an evil force but we will not strike back. Even though troopers chased Jimmie Lee out of the café and beat him after he had been shot, and even though Jimmie Lee was not immediately taken to a hospital, the love our Lord Jesus taught us is stronger than any trooper or any gun or any disrespect for his life. It is with that love, a love that fills our entire being that we march tonight. We will sing our hymns of praise and our music will rise to the heavens and stir the angels to maintain peace in the streets.   Give us courage and strength to march peacefully with Your loving countenance. In Jesus' name we pray. Amen."

Amens echoed throughout the sanctuary.

Elverse sat near the front with Moses and Elmira; Mandy was home making sure Carlton finished his homework. He pictured Mandy's face as he was about to rise to confront obvious peril.

Elverse met Mandy at a clinic where she was interning her last semester of college. He was down from the North to help his Aunt and Uncle move off their farm. Uncle had severe asthma and could no longer tolerate the dust in the fields. Uncle and Elverse were carrying a box of sharp farm tools to the rented moving van when Uncle seized up with an attack and dropped his end of the box. A knife slid out and somehow improbably sliced Elverse's left ring finger almost to the bone. But before Elverse drove himself to the clinic, he raced into the kitchen, put a pan of water on the stove to boil, took a dish towel and wrapped it tightly around his finger and hand in a kind of tourniquet, then yelled for his Aunt packing boxes upstairs to come quick to help Uncle.

Elverse arrived at the clinic light headed; the towel was now soaked with blood. Mandy took one look at him and shouted for the doctor while she rushed Elverse into their small examining room. She assisted the doctor as he stitched Elverse up, and she brought him a glass of orange juice when the ordeal was over. As Elverse sat and weakly drank the juice, Mandy patted his bandaged hand and said, "Well, at least you'll still be able to wear a wedding band."

Aunt and Uncle departed the following week but Elverse never left. Elverse and Mandy were married the following year and Carlton was born the year after that. Now, sixteen years later, their love enabled them to adjust their schedules so Elverse could commit time and energy to voting protests.

Hosea stepped down from the altar. The congregated lifted their heads. The moment was tense. Everyone in Brown Chapel recognized the danger of knowingly marching past people who wanted to hurt you. Hosea nodded to his aides and walked down the center aisle toward the front doors. People rose up, some defiant, others hesitant, to file out behind him. Elverse clasped the pew in front of him to steady his trepidation then followed somberly. Moses and Elmira took each other's hands and solemnly walked next to Elverse in the procession. When they got to Annie Lee's pew, Jackson crossed himself but didn't move toward the aisle. Annie Lee gave him a disapproving nudge.

"Hey, woman? Don't be poking me," he said. "I'm working up to moving. Jus' give me a minute. Where's your love?"

"Well, excuse me if I can't find my love jus' now when those racists are lyin' in wait for us outside," Annie Lee huffed. "So if you please, just move your big self on out so we can get this over with."

The chapel doors parted and Hosea Williams stepped out into a blast of raw night air. On the bottom church step facing him stood Wilson Baker. Newly elected Mayor Smitherman created Baker's post in the hope a cooler presence would prevail within the city limits to counteract Sheriff Clark. Dressed in his signature conservative blue suit, chewing on a cigar, Baker was a large, imposing man, slightly older and slightly more trim than Sheriff Clark. Lining the curb behind him, standing at attention, was the entire Selma police department. Hosea took in the show of force and took a step forward.

"Hold it right there, please, Mr. Williams," Baker said.

Hosea stopped and cocked his head. "Why, Wilson Baker, what an unexpected pleasure. Nice night for a stroll, wouldn't you say?"

"No, Mr. Williams, I wouldn't," Baker countered. "And I can't let you. Anyone who steps past me will be arrested."

"Brother Jackson is lying in a hospital bed, maybe dying, and—"

Baker cut him off. "He's exactly the reason you can't march. Can we talk, Mr. Williams?"

Williams barely nodded and the two men climbed into Baker's big white fin tailed Chrysler parked at the curb and slammed the doors shut. Hosea's aides stood near the car and smiled at the line of skittish policemen. Inside the car the men dropped their mannered courtesy and got down to business.

"What's the problem, Wilson?" Hosea asked. "You gave us assurances we could march in Selma."

"Those were day marches, Hosea. Night marches are a whole different kettle of fish."

"They're effective," countered Williams. "More people can come."

"That's for sure," agreed Baker. "All the slime and trash crawl out of their holes, protected by the night. You're inviting trouble. Somebody will get killed."

"Give us more protection. You're the Police Chief."

"What? Those same troopers who cracked heads last night in Marion are here with Clark and his goons. It's real ugly out there. All they need is an excuse to go on another rampage."

Williams looked out his window at his aides and the growing number of demonstrators beginning to ring the car.

"I can't tell my people our protest for Jimmy Lee is off. They're angry. They've had it with Southern justice. They know he was unarmed and was shot for no good reason."

"Look," Baker placated, "King doesn't want anybody killed. Roughed up a little, maybe—makes for good press, I'm aware of that—but not killed."

Williams studied his hands. "I need an alternative."

Baker reflected a quick minute. "OK. Give me a list of demands. I'll deliver it to Mayor Joe. I'll promise to improve conditions for future day marches. Hell, I'll petition President Johnson if it'll cool things down."

The two men looked at each other. They both appreciated how tenuous each other's position was. Hosea played out Baker's scenario in his head. Backing down could look like weakness. It could embolden those against them to keep attacking. Worse, every violent act perpetrated on them made it harder to justify maintaining a nonviolent stance. He studied the dashboard as he considered the strong possibility of more violence and whether his own members would split off from their commitment to nonviolent action. It was so much harder to remain disciplined and nonviolent. So much harder.

Hosea said finally, "All right. Deal." He let out an exasperated sigh, knowing he would have to figure out how to appeal to patience without appearing weak. He noticed a small mob had formed around the car.

Baker, too, saw several Negroes glaring into the car while his police line shifted nervously, unsure of what they were supposed to do if the crowd grew surly and started rocking their boss' pride and joy.

"Looks like people are getting edgy and wondering why I'm in your car so long," Williams said.

"Don't let me keep you," Baker agreed.

They both got out and Baker barked orders for his police to line both sides of the stone steps while Williams shouted to his followers to turn back into the church. He had new information to tell them. While a few swore under their breaths and glared at the police, all turned back.

Elverse was relieved. He'd already seen enough violence to last him a lifetime. He had witnessed the festering sore of racism explode open and had little confidence it would heal.

The evening ended with disappointed town folk and volunteer deputies returning to their cars or strolling on home to see what was on TV after all.

In the Cole kitchen in Flint, Leslie was still up marking one more dinner dish that she covered in aluminum foil. She took her masking tape, wrote "Spanish Rice" on it and attached it to the foil. Yawning, she carried the dish to the refrigerator freezer, adding this casserole to other tightly wrapped dishes filling the freezer compartment. She returned her scissors and tape to their drawer.

David padded out to the kitchen in his flannel pajamas and slippers and regarded his wife forlornly. "Sweetheart," David said. "Do you know what time it is? Come to bed."

Leslie glanced up at the yellow clock shaped like a teapot that little Annie had picked out and given her for Christmas. The knife and spoon hands showed it was past midnight.

"Sorry, David. I was just trying to cook a few more dinners for you before I leave."

"I still think it's a bad idea to drive alone all that way in the dead of winter. Please reconsider. Wait until spring when we can all go."

"You know what happened to her. She's in too much danger. It can't wait."

"But we could go down over Spring break—it's not far off. We could take turns driving and the kids will get to see your hometown again. It makes more sense."

"David, we've already been over this. I have to go. I can't just sit here while Annie Lee's playing Russian roulette with her life. I checked the weather and there aren't any storms predicted all next week."

David took his wife in his arms and held her tight against the night chill. He kissed her cheek. "Leslie May, Leslie May," he whispered. "And you believe the weatherman?"

She smiled ruefully and kissed him. "I'll be fine, darling. Really." David just shook his head. Leslie shrugged. "She raised me."

Arm in arm they left the kitchen, turning off the light as they passed and headed for their bedroom.

The Steering Committee held clandestine meetings frequently to discuss strategy and how to work with the national organizations now attached to their efforts. But while they were the local voice that understood the community and acted on the community's behalf, they were not necessarily in unison. Believing in the cause didn't mean the Committee always agreed among themselves about tactics.

Thus, after the Marion attack where Jimmie Lee Jackson was shot and their Selma night protest march was stopped, Dr. F. D. Reese, the current president of DCVL, called the Committee together the following week. Yet, first on their agenda was not their own struggle. Two days after being turned back by Baker, the world learned Malcolm X was assassinated. In Harlem, a public viewing of his body was taking place. Many attending the Committee meeting had not approved of Malcolm's tactics, but others saw the evolution of the man and wanted the group to pay their respects. John Lewis held this view and would attend the funeral later that week. The Committee agreed to hold a moment of silence.

It wasn't long after the silence, however, that voices grew loud and heated. Talk became very animated about how to proceed. Reverend Lowry offered, "Let's reach out to the white churches and appeal to their Christian spirit. We could ask to speak at their Sunday services and explain how they could amplify our movement and help us create the equality and justice we seek."

His suggestion created an uproar. And was mocked.

"Right," replied Annie Lee sarcastically. "Just like those white ministers in Birmingham who all signed that letter complaining to Dr. King who was sitting in the Birmingham Jail that his tactics were all wrong. They were real helpful Christians, weren't they?"

"Still," defended Elverse, "we need to think beyond color and look to people of faith to do the right thing. Give them the chance to respond with their better selves."

"I wouldn't hold my breath," said a dubious Elmira who looked over at her husband. Moses nodded. Ultimately, no decision was made to appeal to the town's white churches that so far had shown no interest in their cause.

This meeting was one of the rare times Mandy attended because she wanted to express her opinion about the shooting Elverse had witnessed. When the conversation turned to thrash out the merits of night marches, Mandy disagreed with Amelia Boynton who was dogged about marching day and night.

"Baker was telling us the score last week when he stopped you from marching" Mandy insisted. "We should forget—"

"—For years we've been mounting this campaign," Mrs. Boynton declared. "We need to keep up the numbers. Keep up the pressure. At night more—"

"—That's right!" cried Mandy. "And you can watch those numbers disappear if they be shooting, Amelia."

Elmira, who had been listening to their argument, stated blandly, "I'm not afraid to meet my Maker."

"Well, now, a lot of folks is," Jackson reasoned as he walked out from the hallway with an armful of coats. "Or, at least we're not in any hurry." He hoped everyone would go home, get some rest, and cool off. He didn't like to hear fighting among the members.

"There's something to be said for marching in broad daylight. It is much safer. We've got to set some limits, what with our children marching and all," said Elverse, pleased he could support his wife's position.

But his comment backfired as Mandy shot back, furious, "If they're shooting there shouldn't be any children's marches. Period. I swear!"

"The point is to keep up the pressure without endangering any lives. They wouldn't dare hurt children. They're not that stupid," said Moses.

Elverse took a deep breath. The coats were handed out and he helped Mandy on with hers. Everyone was frustrated that they were leaving with no plan. Jackson put his arm around Mandy as they walked toward the front door but she was not backing down.

"I wouldn't count out how reckless they are," she said. "I wouldn't put anything past Clark. He's an evil man who doesn't even see our children as human. To him they're no different than halfwits. If you're not white, you're not bright."

"Well, let's all sleep on it," said Jackson kindly.

Annie Lee nodded in agreement. She, too, wanted the group to be united and saw they needed more time to think through their next crucial step after the shooting.

"We're no lost ball in the high weeds," she said. "We'll figure out what's workable. Let's see what Brothers Bevel and Lewis have to say before we rush on any decision. They definitely have more experience in these matters than any of us."

Annie Lee opened her front door so the Committee could leave and there stood Leslie Cole, her arm raised, ready to knock. Caught by surprise, both women let out a little shriek. Annie Lee was the first to recover.

"Well, bless my soul. Sweet Jesus, it's Leslie May! I wasn't expecting you till tomorrow next."

Annie Lee stepped out onto her poorly lit covered stoop and threw her arms about Leslie. They hugged a long while. When they parted, Annie Lee turned to those who had formed a circle at the doorway.

"Some of you may remember Leslie May Cummins as a child? She's Leslie Cole, now? Came down to visit a few years back with her whole family when her dear pappy passed? She's just driven all the way down from Flint, Michigan to pay me a visit. Lordly, child, you must have kept your foot pressed to the gas pedal and outwitted sleep."

"I am pretty tired," admitted Leslie with a rueful grin.

Elverse stepped forward and pumped Leslie's hand.

"So you're from Flint," he said enthusiastically. "I'm from Detroit myself. So nice to meet you. That's quite a hard trip and I ought to know. I make it myself every couple of years. I don't envy you that drive. Did you run into snow?"

"Just when I was leaving," said Leslie, laughing. "I was so glad to see it in my rear view mirror. I really got lucky there weren't any new storms all the way down. And the new interstates are fantastic."

"Well, welcome," said Elverse warmly as scenes of Michigan flooded his head. "I guess we'll be seeing you around town with Annie Lee."

"Thank you. I'm glad to be here. I've missed seeing my Annie Lee."

Elverse and Leslie shared a smile as Mandy feigned being busy buttoning her coat. Elverse exited and Mandy passed with a simple nod and a mumbled good evening.

"Good night," Leslie called after them.

"That was Mandy, Elverse's wife," whispered Annie Lee.

People murmured kind introductions as Leslie continued to greet each member who passed through the doorway to head for their cars or walk home in another section of the Carver Projects. She shook their hands and said, "Hi! Nice to meet you," or, to a few, "So nice to see you, again." She giggled. "I feel like a governor running for reelection. Good night."

The group chuckled good-naturedly as they stepped into the night air. Jackson was the last to leave and gave Annie Lee a quick kiss as he passed.

"Good night, sugar. Talk to you tomorrow." He then turned to Leslie and gave her a big bear hug. "And you, you little June bug, it's great to see you again. That's such a long drive. Mighty glad you made it here safe and sound. Good night now."

"Good night, Jackson. It's great to see you again, too. We'll catch up with you tomorrow most likely."

Jackson departed with a wave and Annie Lee picked up Leslie's suitcase and pulled Leslie into the warmth of her home and closed the door. Once inside where the light was brighter, Leslie gasped, shocked to see Annie Lee's bruised, scraped face.

"Oh, Annie Lee," she exclaimed. "Look what they did to you. My god! I didn't think it would be this bad. You look awful."

Annie Lee laughed her deep laugh. "Now ain't that a fine way to greet me after not seeing me for years. I ain't that ugly! Come on, honey. Let's get you settled."

Annie Lee turned to head down the hallway with the suitcase but Leslie grabbed her shoulders and wrestled the suitcase out of her hand and set it down.

"Don't joke," Leslie said. "These people are lunatics down here. I am so glad I came to get you out of this. They could have killed you. When I think what you've been going through."

Annie Lee crossed her arms and looked directly at Leslie.

"Whoa, whoa, whoa, child. I'm not goin' through anything I don't want to be goin' through. You're just tired which makes everything look worse than they really is. I just tripped when we was demonstrating over in Marion. I did this to myself."

"Oh, good heavens, you were in Marion, too?"

"Of course, honey." Annie Lee chuckled. You should have seen my face last week. You would've been right to call me ugly then."

Leslie grasped Annie Lee and hugged her tight. "No, Annie Lee. This isn't funny. You're too close to all this to see it clearly. You're in danger. Nobody should be marching, least of all in Marion. Next you'll be marching to Hayneville in Lowndes County for god's sake."

Annie Lee broke their hug and patted Leslie's head. "Leslie May, we're not that crazy! Honey, I can take care of myself. Come on, now. Let's get you settled in."

Annie Lee picked up the suitcase again and headed down the hallway. She was glad the national press hadn't picked up on Jimmie Lee being shot. Leslie definitely would have boiled over her pot with that news. Leslie followed, removing her wool car coat.

"But why, Annie Lee? Why do you need to keep demonstrating? I don't get it. The Civil Rights Act passed last year. Isn't that enough?"

"No, sweetie, it ain't. The Civil Rights Act was a good thing as far as it went but we still can't vote."

"Not here, maybe," Leslie agreed. "It's the South. What do you expect?"

Annie Lee banged down the suitcase as she turned back to Leslie. "I expect to have the same rights as white folk right here where I live!"

Leslie flinched but didn't back down. "But that will take years down here no matter how many laws Congress passes."

"That's what President Johnson said when Dr. King went and visited him in Washington to tell him we need the vote. Johnson said to give it a few years so Congress could get used to the Civil Rights Act."

"Right."

"Wrong. Know what Martin said back to the President?"

"No."

"He said, 'then we'll do it ourselves.' And we are."

Annie Lee set her jaw and picked up the suitcase again and headed for her tiny guest room, Leslie following.

"You wouldn't have to wait if you came up North," said Leslie. You could vote up in Flint this very day. You, know? What better reason to come and live with us for a while. I'll make you a party to celebrate the first time you cast your ballot."

"Oh, honey." Annie Lee shook her head. "It ain't a party I need. It's equality and no cake and ice cream is gonna make that happen. No. We got to keep pushing to change things here."

They reached the bedroom and Leslie studied Annie Lee's face. Quietly, Leslie said, "There's no point in pushing against a brick wall, Annie Lee."

Annie Lee laughed her deep laugh again.

"Ever hear of Jericho?"

⁓

Part Two

DEEP IN THE YELLOWHAMMER HEART

FOUR

A bone tired Leslie slept in until the Selma sun was high above the horizon the next morning. Annie Lee was already up and as soon as she heard Leslie stir, she fixed a simple breakfast of grits, eggs, and coffee—lots of sweet coffee—before they washed the dishes and set out for the cemetery in Leslie's red Ford Galaxy sedan.

Annie Lee put on her torn coat and Leslie regarded it with disapproval. "What happened to your coat?" she asked.

"I was wearing it when I tussled with the sheriff," Annie Lee answered nonchalantly. Leslie shook her head.

"When we go to town, I'm buying you a new coat."

"Now, Leslie May," objected Annie Lee.

"No objections. If you're going to march, you have to look good," said Leslie firmly. Then they both laughed.

It was a spectacular day, clear and bright and crisp. Leslie drove along the streets that were still vaguely familiar yet needed Annie Lee's guidance to remind her of some of the turns. They made a quick stop at a florist shop before heading for the cemetery gates.

When they arrived at Old Live Oak Cemetery, Leslie parked the car, and they each carried a small bouquet of roses, asters, and chrysanthemums to lie at the gravesites. They reached the first gravestone and Annie Lee bent over and laid her flowers in front of the stone after brushing away a few dead leaves. The simple grave marker read:

CAROL LEE CUMMINS
Beloved Wife and Mother
7/14/1900 – 2/5/1935

Annie Lee's knees creaked as she rose and stood respect-fully in front of the stone. "Your Mama was the nicest lady I ever worked for," she said softly. "I was still just a baby myself and was so scared to hold you. Like Prissy, (she went into a falsetto voice), I didn't know nothin' about babies."

Leslie grinned. "I don't know how you did it, Annie Lee. At fifteen all I thought about was boys. No way could I have cared for a baby."

"Oh, I had thoughts about boys, too, Leslie May. They was heavy on my mind if I recall, especially one in particular named Jackson Dupree."

"You've known Jackson that long?" Leslie asked, surprised.

"Honey, I think Jackson and me shared the same Mammy's milk. I've known him forever."

They walked over to the adjoining marker.

"So he was your beau? I always thought he was more like a brother."

Annie Lee hooted. "If he was my brother then I'll be going to hell for sure!"

Leslie kneeled down and placed her bouquet at her father's gravestone and traced the words on the marker with her finger as she considered this surprising new information about Annie Lee. Her father's grave read:

DABNY JUSTIN (D.J.) CUMMINS
Beloved Husband and Father
May he rest in peace 2/1/1897 – 4/9/1961

Leslie remained crouched by the stone, thinking. "When Mama died and Daddy came to you and begged you to come and live in with us, I bet you didn't know then that you'd stay until I was grown and went off to college."

"No, honey. I had no idea it would be for that many years. No idea at all."

"But why, Annie Lee? Why did you do that when you had your whole life ahead of you? Why did you stay on in our house instead of marrying Jackson and starting your own family?"

Annie Lee looked across the cemetery headstones and smiled. "I loved you, honey. I loved you and your brother. I had to see you both through. Besides. Jackson wasn't available at the time."

"Oh?" Leslie asked innocently as she rose, "He went into the army?"

"Another woman," Annie Lee said simply.

Leslie put her arm around Annie Lee as they headed slowly back to the car.

"Annie Lee," Leslie marveled. "How come I never knew all this?"

"And there's no need to know it now, Leslie May. It's in the past. Jackson and me have it all worked out now just fine."

"But—"

"—No buts, Missy. Jackson and I have always loved each other and always will. End of story."

Leslie didn't press the point. She knew it did no good to coax Annie Lee to tell anything more than Annie Lee was willing to share. She only told you what she wanted you to know. She had always kept secrets, which was what made her so damn intriguing.

They walked down the path in silence when Leslie remembered the newspaper clipping. She stopped and fished out her wallet from her purse and removed a folded article tucked in the bill side. She handed it to Annie Lee. Annie Lee took the clipping, unfolded it and frowned when she recognized the picture.

"That is what we saw in our paper back home," Leslie explained. "It was so shocking."

Annie Lee scrutinized the clipping of herself about to be clubbed by Sheriff Clark. "Humph," she growled. "Some way to get famous with that pig sitting on top of me."

Annie Lee handed the article back to Leslie who tucked it back into her wallet. The photo side flopped open revealing a picture of Leslie's children. Annie Lee took the wallet and studied the picture, gazing at little Annie the longest.

"My, how they're growing up. And little Annie, my sweet namesake. Isn't she the bee's knees? She's not a baby anymore." Annie Lee kissed the picture then handed the wallet back to Leslie. "I don't know how you could leave such beautiful children and drive all the way down here by yourself."

Leslie replaced the wallet in her purse as they walked on.

"Now don't you start. David said the same thing, as if time wasn't of the essence."

"He was right, you know."

"David's mother is staying with the children. They'll be fine. Coming down here couldn't wait. I was so worried about you," said Leslie.

"Well you can stop worrying because I'm just marching."

"Just marching."

"Yes. Just marching. So send your worries off to bed."

"Annie Lee, listen to me. The entire family wants you to come to Flint. We all think you could be really happy with us? Just for a year or two. Justin and Alex are dying to bunk together again so you would have privacy when you take over Justin's room. And David said we could take a closet next to that room and make it into a private bathroom for you. You'd have your own suite. Justin especially wants you to come. He loves you so much and wants to know you better. It would be wonderful to have you be close and part of the family - all of us under one roof. We could start packing you up today and be gone in no time."

"Gone. In no time."

"Yes. You could come and try it for a time, just until all this trouble blows over."

Leslie assessed how her words were falling on Annie Lee's ears and adjusted her proposal as deep frown lines formed on Annie Lee's resistant face. "Well, maybe staying for a year would be too long but you could come for at least a month to try it out... whatever. You could stay forever for that matter, although even I know you won't do that. But don't you think it could be groovy? Think of it as an extended vacation. Watch little Annie grow. Teach Justin how to make corn bread. Tell the children stories about what it was like growing up in Alabama. Right now Justin is very keen to understand what it's like to live in the South. He's real interested in history."

Annie Lee remained silent. They ambled toward the car.

Encouraged that perhaps Annie was considering her proposal, Leslie continued. "And if you think it would be too hard to be away from Jackson, maybe David could get him a job and then you could both try out the North. Of course, if you weren't happy, well, you could always return. But how will you know unless you try it?"

Annie Lee took a deep breath. Her grip tightened around her pocket book. "I'm part of the movement here, honey. One of the founding members of the Dallas County Voters League. Try to understand. I can't just leave. Besides. I don't want to leave. It's sweet of you to offer but this here's my home. So you need to get this idea of me goin' North out of your head."

"But I came down here to take you out of these troubles," Leslie objected. "You knew that's why I wanted to come when we talked on the phone."

"I did not," Annie Lee corrected. "I listened as you described your concern, but I didn't comment any on going North."

"Did so."

They arrived at Leslie's car and Leslie unlocked the door so Annie Lee could climb in.

Annie Lee raised her voice. "Did not! I just said I'd love to see you. Didn't say nothin' about any going back up North with you so you might as well—"

But Leslie had closed the door. She didn't want to hear any more objections.

Leslie pulled away from the cemetery and headed toward the downtown business district where Brother Moses who had called in a sick day was turning his attention to almost five hundred excited youngsters gathered in the Selma churchyard. He high stepped as he paced in front of them and spoke into a megaphone. Carlton stood near the front of the group looking tall and proud and every bit the image of his father.

"What kind of children are we?" Moses danced back and forth as he shouted out his questions.

"Disciplined," the children shouted back.

"What kind?" Moses asked again.

"Disciplined," the children repeated with more enthusiasm.

"Louder," insisted Moses.

"DISCIPLINED!" shouted the group.

"That's right," continued Moses. "And how we gonna march?"

"Proud."

"How?" Moses tested.

"PROUD!" yelled the kids.

"And what's in your hearts?" queried Moses.

"LOVE!"

The children were now dancing along with him.

"That's right!" Moses acknowledged gleefully. He twirled and pointed at them. "And if they hurt you, you gonna hurt them back?"

"NO," shouted the children with force.

"Why not?" Moses sounded incredulous, teasing.

"Because we are the children of God," the group replied in unison.

"And He loves you!" The voice of Moses bounced off the exterior church walls. "And He wants you to be the future voters who will vote for what's good, and fair, and equal."

"Right on! Yes," the children screamed.

"We will march for justice—not for violence. Violence leads to Darkness. But justice leads us to the Light. And love sets us free!"

The children were all jumping up and down now, pumped and ready to march. "AMEN!" they shouted. "AMEN, AMEN!"

Leslie and Annie Lee drove to a well-established children's shop on Main Street and, as luck would have it, found a parking space in the same block. They hadn't spoken the short drive from the cemetery to Main Street and both felt bad that they were already arguing on the first day of Leslie's visit. They parked, crossed the street and entered the store, talking small talk about the children as they passed through the wide entrance. Then Leslie circled back to the topic, hoping to lighten up their disagreement.

"Sometimes, I think Annie inherited more than just your name, Annie Lee," Leslie said with a smile. "She can be so stubborn that when she gets something into her head, it's hard to get her to change her mind."

"Well, those traits should serve her well in life," said Annie Lee grinning. "After all. Ain't hurt me none."

Both women laughed, easing the tension. They walked down an aisle, glancing at merchandise. "After we find something for Annie, let's go try to find you a coat," said Leslie.

The shopkeeper pirouetted around the glass counter and eyed them darkly.

"I promised Annie I'd send her something as soon as I got here. What do you think? A little blouse, maybe? She already loves clothes. Or a toy?"

The shopkeeper stepped up to them. "Yes?" she questioned, as if she couldn't comprehend why they would be in her shop.

"Good morning," Leslie said pleasantly. "We're looking for something for my six year old daughter, but we don't really know what yet. We'll just browse a little first, if you don't mind."

The shopkeeper stiffened. "All right. But don't let your nigger touch anything."

"Excuse me?" Leslie said, her ears burning. "This woman happens to be my mother. I'll thank you to show her some respect." The three women stared each other down.

"Come on, Leslie," Annie Lee said. "This shop don't need our business."

"Fine," retorted the sales clerk.

Leslie and Annie Lee linked arms and waltzed toward the front entrance. Annie Lee turned back to the clerk and called out, "Some day you're gonna die for my business!"

Once outside a fuming Leslie turned to Annie Lee.

"I can't believe some people still use that terrible word. How dare she. It's criminal how ignorant some people are."

"I've been called worse, Leslie. Names don't matter none. Sticks and stones may break my bones but names will never hurt me—if I don't let them. No, it's you saying what you said in there that bothers me more."

"Me? What do you mean?"

"Why'd you call me your mother in there? You know I done told you never to call me that."

"Oh, Annie Lee, come on. I did it to get her goat. Did you see the look on her face? It was priceless... the racist old witch."

"Child, she can't help not keeping up with the times. Why two years ago I couldn't even step inside that store. But don't change the subject. You have a mother even if she be gone to her grave and that title don't belong to this here colored nanny walking right beside you."

Leslie stopped and regarded Annie Lee who was visibly upset. "Why, Annie Lee, sometimes I don't understand you. You're defending that woman who just called you a nigger and are ticked off at me. Why would you do that? And what do you mean by calling yourself a nanny? I never called you that. No one ever called you that in our house. You know you were much more than that to all of us. You were a mother to me, my substitute mother."

"To the South I was your nanny and we need to leave it at that," Annie Lee insisted and increased her step.

"But why? Why do we need to leave it at that?" Leslie persisted, catching up with her. "This is 1965. When do I finally get to say out loud what I've always felt?"

"When we get some respect. Do you remember when we took bus rides? You sat up front and I had to sit in the back of the bus with all the other colored folk. I sat back there and worried myself sick that somebody might snatch you up every time the bus made a stop and the doors opened."

"Really? Good grief, and I thought I was such hot stuff to be able to sit up front all by myself. It never occurred to me I was causing you worry. I'm so sorry. I just never thought about it from your perspective, I guess. I'm really sorry."

Annie Lee didn't answer but her pace slackened to a stop. She and Leslie faced each other.

"Oh, Annie Lee. I knew things weren't equal then, really I did once I was older. But in our own house, when we didn't have to deal with the stupid laws, we were equal, weren't we?"

Annie Lee didn't answer.

"Well?" pressed Leslie. "Didn't you consider yourself equal in our house?"

Annie Lee took in Leslie, the child now a woman she'd known all her life.

"Leslie May. You came here to Selma thinking you needed to save me from the South and what you found is a colored woman fighting for her dignity."

Leslie returned Annie Lee's gaze. "You have plenty of dignity, Annie Lee. You just need to come north where you don't have to prove it. Come home with me where you'll be safe, and where you'll be with family that loves you. Don't be so stubborn."

"Me, stubborn?" Annie Lee rocked back on her heels. "Look who's calling the kettle black? You're so stubborn you could argue with a wall and win. It ain't me little Annie's taking after, it's you!"

Annie Lee began to chuckle. It grew to a laugh.

It became Leslie's turn to scold. She pursed her lips. "Don't start with the old games. I won't join in."

Annie Lee nodded and just kept forcing her laugh. "Come on, honey. When things got too hot, we'd make ourselves laugh. It always helped."

"No. This is too serious."

Annie Lee had a twinkle in her eye as she watched Leslie soften. She pretended to agree. "Of course, it is. Come on. Ha, ha, ha, ha, ha, ha! HA! HA! HA! HA! HA! HA!"

Annie Lee was now belly laughing and her whole body shook. Leslie couldn't help but grin. When she could no longer hold out, she finally joined in, just as she did when she was a little girl. Soon they were laughing like they'd heard the funniest joke in the whole world.

"HA! HA! HA! HA! HO! HA! HA," until tears sprang to their eyes.

Singing voices intruded upon their silliness and became louder and louder. They abruptly stopped and cocked their heads to listen.

"What is that?" Leslie asked. "What do you suppose is going on?"

Just as she finished asking the question, hundreds of children rounded the corner and came into view singing, "We Shall Not Be Moved." The women's eyes widened as they took in the scene. Sheriff Clark and his posse men were on horseback herding the children who had gathered at the AME church with Moses. They were being forced to run through town right in the middle of the street. Cars braked and had to pull over to avoid hitting a child.

Everyone gazed in bewilderment. Two white women shopping across the street stared in disgust. "My lands, what is going on now?" Asked the older of the two.

"Those poor, pickaninny darlings," said her friend, shaking her head. "What could that fool sheriff be up to?"

Annie Lee spotted Carlton in the group and quickened her pace to cross the street and get back to the car.

"Hurry," she cried over her shoulder. "We got to go tell Elverse."

But Leslie was dumbstruck. She saw posse men had nightsticks drawn and a few had whips. Then she saw some had cattle prods. She snapped and ran to the gutter.

"HEY!" she yelled. "What do you think you're doing?"

A man on a horse rode over to her and tipped his hat.

"Ma'am. These burr heads are all truant, Ma'am. We're taking 'um in. They got to learn the importance of going to school and gettin' educated." With that, he grinned and turned his horse around and rode off. Leslie screamed after him.

"STOP IT! THEY'RE ONLY CHILDREN!"

Leslie saw Annie Lee waiting at the car and ran across the street to unlock the door. As they got in, both were smoldering.

Through her teeth, Annie Lee said, "That posse dude wouldn't have bothered to turn his head let alone his horse if I had asked him the same question you did. We're gonna change that, too."

Annie Lee directed Leslie to Elverse's hardware store where they quickly parked and bolted inside. Elverse was high on a ladder straightening light bulbs when they barged through the swinging door. He looked down and greeted them in his friendly way.

"Well, hi y'all, ladies. What a nice surprise. Be down in a jiffy."

"Better make it right now, Elverse," Annie Lee instructed. "There's bad trouble. And we need to alert the Committee."

"What is it?" he asked as he took in their anxious faces and quickly descended the ladder.

Annie Lee answered. "Clark and his hoodlums are running children out of town who gathered to march with Moses today. Didn't see him anywhere but did see your son Carlton in the group."

Elverse jumped the last step and rushed to the counter to grab his cap as Leslie added, "A posse man said they were truant and were being taken in."

They hastened for the door.

"But they wasn't heading to the city jail or the school," said Annie Lee. "They was heading out into the country toward your place."

Elverse flipped his "Open" sign to "Closed" and locked the door while Leslie and Annie Lee returned to Leslie's car. Elverse jumped into his Rambler and the two cars roared out of the small dirt parking lot.

The children reached the edge of town where few people could witness what was occurring. The march had slowed from a run to a fast walk and became ragged with long spaces between those children able to keep up in front and those slowest bringing up the rear. The mostly volunteer posse seemed to relish herding the children onward and scaring them with threatening shouts to move faster. Any child seen straggling got a nightstick blow to their back or a whip cracked over their head, terrorizing the children even more. As the march lost its precision, the posse was forced to spread itself thin.

Carlton was keeping up but spied a very young girl in pig-tails who was not. He knew Carla Grace from church. She was half running, half stumbling, and wholly exhausted. Tears streaked her cheeks. He jogged over to her side and bent down to comfort her. She stopped and regarded him with her big, woeful brown eyes.

"It's OK," he said soothingly. "Don't cry, Carla Grace. They're just trying to scare us. They won't really hurt us."

He took the sleeve of his jacket and wiped the tears from her face. Her eyes grew wide as she saw over Carlton's shoulder a posse man ride up and reach down to prod Carlton on his back. The prod sent an electrical shock through his body. He yelped and jumped upright. Carla Grace screamed and the horse balked and neighed toward her. She felt its breath on her face. The posse man laughed.

"Get moving, you monkeys," he hollered then rode off in pursuit of another boy trying to run toward the trunk of a huge Sycamore tree that he hoped to hide behind. Yet another boy looked over his shoulder as a horseman closed in on him.

"God see you," the boy cried. The horseman smacked the boy with his billy club and blood spurted from the little boy's mouth.

Older children in the lead began to split off, some running to the right and some running to the left, as Negro farmhouses began to appear. As they escaped in all directions, most of the posse was pulled to the front to chase them. Carlton saw his chance to flee and pulled Carla Grace by the hand. They ran up a narrow path between two pastures, ducked under a fence, and jogged up yet another lane. The shouts and commotion became distant and faint. They arrived at a second road where they kept running until they reached Carlton's house.

Carlton and Carla Grace burst inside and slammed the front door closed without the latch quite catching. They moved away from the door, both gasping hard as they bent over and held their aching sides and tried to stop panting. A puff of wind widened the crack in the door. Carlton looked at Carla Grace and grinned, proud that he had brought her to safety. Just as they began to inhale normally they heard the whinny of a horse. They sucked in their breath.

"Quick!" Carlton whispered and indicated toward his parent's bedroom. They tiptoed into the bedroom, and he pointed for Carla Grace to crawl under the bed. The bedroom door squeaked as he pushed it partially shut before scrambling after her. They each held their breath as they heard footsteps on the front porch.

The front door creaked open. A slightly built posse man with his nightstick hanging at his side stood at the threshold, surveying the room. Carlton could just make out his boots. The man took a tentative step inside the living room when all three heard a car screech to a stop on the gravel driveway. The man froze and quickly stepped back. A booming deep voice addressed him from behind his back and he jumped.

"Looking for something, sir?"

The posse man whirled around and saw Elverse standing in the yard a full head taller than himself. He quickly stepped back further from the door. Elverse found it easy to summon his courage and confront this trespasser who was on his property, invading his home. He stood there, his hands having formed fists even though they still hung at his sides. The posse man assessed the much taller Elverse before he answered. He calculated it was not the time to retort with an insult.

"Some kids. They run away from school."

"This here's private property, sir," Elverse said in a low, even voice. "I suggest you check the park."

The posse man walked past Elverse with an unconvincing swagger to the rail fence where he unhitched his horse and rode off without another word.

Elverse rushed into his house, closed and locked the door.

"Anybody here?" he called out. The hair on his neck prickled when he heard a commotion in the bedroom.

"Yah, it's me, Dad," Carlton called out as he and Carla Grace wriggled out from under the bed. "It's me and Carla Grace."

"Thank God," Elverse said as he dropped to one knee and opened his arms to accept the two trembling children who ran to him. He held them close. Carlton had been so brave but now was shaking. Little Carla Grace openly bawled. Elverse held them tight and patted their backs.

"Shh. It's OK now. He's gone. Shh. We're all safe. He won't be coming back, not with me here."

On the dirt road where the children had been forced to run, private cars and taxis mostly driven by black drivers formed a line. In that line was Leslie's red Ford and Police Chief Baker's white Chrysler. A photographer ran toward the Chief who was helping children into his back seat. Leslie also approached him but the photographer reached Baker first.

"Mr. Baker," the Photographer said. "What's the Chief of Police doing taking nigger kids back to town like a cabbie?"

Baker looked at the photographer with distain. "I'm also a human being and these are children."

Baker turned his back on the photographer and returned his attention to the children while the photographer snapped his photo and hurried off, leaving Leslie to catch Baker's eye.

"Chief Baker, I want to thank you," Leslie began. "You are a great role model for the right kind of law enforcement in this town. You have fairness and foresight."

"It's not foresight, ma'am" Baker allowed. "It's my job."

Leslie regarded this lawman and decided not to argue the point. "Still, I know your job isn't easy and I appreciate your fairness."

"The law doesn't take sides," said Baker. "I'm just trying to maintain law and order."

"Sometimes the law has to take sides," Leslie pressed again. "No decent adult could think it's a good idea to scare children with weapons. I appreciate how you're handling your lawmen and this crisis. Some of these children are very young for goodness sake. So thank you." And, as an after thought she added, "And God bless you."

Baker saw how earnest she was and replied graciously. "You're welcome."

It was late that afternoon that Elverse pulled up to the Good Samaritan Hospital to pick up a very tired Mandy who stood waiting for him on the sidewalk, as there were no benches. Mandy slid into the passenger's side of the car and gave Elverse a quick kiss before turning to greet the children sitting in back. Elverse carefully pulled out into the street and headed for Carla Grace's house.

"Evening, Carlton," Mandy said cheerfully. "Is that you back there, Carla Grace?"

"Yes ma'am," Carla Grace replied. "Evening."

"Hi, Mom," Carlton answered.

"We're taking Carla Grace home. There was bad trouble today," Elverse informed her. Mandy shot Elverse an alarmed look. He gripped the steering wheel tighter.

"Like what?" Mandy asked slowly. There was a long, strained silence. Mandy looked at her husband whose temples were working overtime as he clenched and unclenched his teeth. Carlton filled in the silence.

"Moses said nobody would get arrested today. We drilled and practiced and all. We were all agreed to march respectfully and not look for trouble. Moses said Mr. Baker said we could march and everything would be fine. Seems Sheriff Clark had a different notion."

Mandy listened quietly and closed her eyes to steel herself against what might be coming next, not sure she could bear to know. "So you tried to march today. Were you arrested my sweet boy?"

"No, Mama. I was cattle prodded."

Mandy's eyelids flew open. She jerked her head around to stare at her son in horror. She studied his face, trying to read him. "Where, Carlton? Where did they cattle prod you? What happened? And why?"

"On my back," Carlton explained. "It stung but I was wearing my jacket so it wasn't too bad. My jacket does have a little burnt spot now, though."

"Sweet lord of mercy, my baby," cried Mandy. She reached for his hand and clasped it. Carlton looked at his mother, his eyes full of pain. Carla Grace began to cry all over again.

"He was trying to help me," Carla Grace wailed, gulping back her unfounded guilt. "This man came up on his horse and wouldn't let him and zapped him with a long stick."

"It wasn't your fault, Carla Grace," said Mandy gently. "Those men were doing things they had no right to do." Mandy turned from Carla Grace and locked eyes with her son. She set her jaw. A grim silence settled over the car as a tightlipped Elverse drove on.

The town was abuzz about Clark's ill-advised stunt with the children. Most felt he had stepped over some invisible line to which even many separatists objected. Joe Smitherman called Sheriff Clark to his office to account for his actions. Clark leaned back in a swivel oak chair, cleaning his nails as Smitherman paced back and forth in front of him. The mayor kept running his fingers through his hair, hoping his mind would come up with some answer to what he knew invariably would become a very problematic, public issue.

"Where the hell were you marching those kids to, anyway?" Joe demanded.

Clark answered without looking away from his fingernails. "The jail's already full of these hard asses. We was headed for the Fraternal Lodge."

Smitherman stopped in his tracks and looked at Clark incredulously. "The Fraternal Lodge? That's six miles out! You were gonna run those kids six miles?"

"They were jus' walking fast. What was I supposed to do with 'um?" Clark demanded.

"Hell if I know," Joe answered. "But they were kids."

"They weren't goin' to no picnic, Joe," Clark said. "They were going to demonstrate through town. Cause a traffic jam. Cause trouble."

"Jesus." The mayor was sweating. "And you didn't cause a traffic jam? I heard some kids almost got run over. The press will crucify us. Even the Times-Journal said they'd run a denunciation, for Christ's sake."

Clark adjusted his shirt cuff links and ran his fingers along the sharp crease of his pant leg. "Those darkies broke the law and I get busted for doing my job," Clark complained.

"Listen, Jim," Joe said, exasperation rising in his voice. "King is here because of you. Don't you understand that? Don't you know you're the fuse they need to get sympathy from the damn press? Don't you get how this works?"

There was a quick knock at the door and Wilson Baker strode into the room. He stopped short when he saw Clark. The two men glowered at each other. Clark rocked back even further in his chair and returned to cleaning his nails.

Baker turned to the mayor. "Sorry, Joe. Didn't know you were busy. Wanted to let you know that the kid shot by the trooper over in Marion last week just died in our hospital here. We could have a riot on our hands."

Smitherman whistled and turned pale. Clark shrugged as Baker continued.

"We've got to be real careful now. Real controlled. If anybody breaks the law, we arrest them peacefully. No violence. No headlines."

The mayor nodded his head vigorously while the sheriff snorted contemptuously.

"And where you gonna put 'um?" Clark snarled. "We've arrested over three thousand since this damn thing started. The jail's overflowing. You gonna to put 'um up at the Prince Albert? Give 'um room service?"

Baker glared at Clark. "Look here, you imbecile. A trooper murdered a man. That ratchets the stakes up and makes our job harder."

"Bring them on," Clark snapped. "I can handle 'um. Some of us aren't pansies. Besides. Weren't no murder. You calling it that doesn't make it so. That's a big nigger lie. That trooper acted in self-defense. He was surrounded by an unruly mob in that there restaurant. He was just trying to protect hisself."

✤

FIVE

I t rained the day they buried Jimmie Lee Jackson. The service was held in Marion where the demonstration had taken place. Mourners gathered by the hundreds at Zion Chapel Methodist Church to pay their last respects and hear Martin Luther King, Jr. deliver the eulogy. Realizing how things had heated up, King concluded he had to return and be present for the funeral in order to focus the media light on Southern violence. The church was packed to overflowing and many had to stand in the wet outdoors beyond the chapel entrance.

Moses and Carlton played hooky from school; hearing Dr. King speak at the funeral felt more educational. Mandy had gotten off her shift late so the steps were the only place left when Elverse, Mandy, Carlton, Moses, and Elmira, arrived. Leslie had driven Annie Lee and Jackson yet they, too, were too late for a pew and stood in the narthex. Speakers had been set up on stands so the overflow crowd could still hear King even if they weren't inside the sanctuary.

A rain soaked banner hung over the church door that read:

"RACISM KILLED OUR BROTHER"

King's voice rang out as his confrontational words rolled from the podium.

"Who killed Jimmie Lee Jackson?" he queried. He answered his own question by calling out brutal sheriffs who themselves become lawless and politicians from governors on

down who accept and practice racism. And he blamed Negroes that accepted segregation and stood on the sidelines of their struggle. Mosses readily agreed with that.

Leslie hung on his every word and shook her head in agreement when he stated the federal government was spending millions of dollars to defend Vietnam but did not see fit to protect the rights of American citizens at home.

Annie Lee glanced over at Leslie's intense concentration and frowned a bit. If Leslie got drawn in to the movement Annie Lee feared Leslie's husband would be certain to blame her. Leslie needed to return home to take her place as the mother of her children and leave the movement to her, the Committee, and the citizens of Selma.

Annie Lee loved Leslie dearly—more than her own self—but she was going to have to find a way to break off Leslie's visit. She had to admit deep down that she didn't want Leslie watching her every move. She was sure Leslie would not support her involvement in demonstrations and Annie Lee had no intention of stopping her protests. She was wholeheartedly behind King's words that they must work relentlessly to make the American dream a reality for all. Even worse, Annie Lee feared Leslie would express negative opinions about their tactics that would surely lead to more arguments and they would have a falling out. That would break her heart.

Dr. King solemnly concluded with his most challenging statement of all. He asked the assembled not to be bitter or retaliate with violence. He appealed to them not to lose faith in their white brothers. Leslie whispered, "Amen."

The hearse carrying Jackson's body crept down Highway 14. It was followed by a sea of bobbing black umbrellas that hovered over the walking mourners as they made their way to Heard Cemetery, an old slave burial ground three miles away. Jimmie Lee's father was buried there so the family decided Jimmie Lee's final resting place should be next to him. Once the procession reached the site of the freshly dug hole, the casket was rolled from the hearse and lowered into the ground. Floral wreaths formed a virtual wall around the grave.

James Bevel, the Director of Direct Action and Nonviolent Education for King's organization, delivered the final eulogy at the gravesite. It was at this site next to the martyr's casket that the idea to march from Selma to Montgomery was born.

"We shall march every day," Bevel thundered. "We shall not let up until the power of the vote is in our hands. We will march to Montgomery and deliver a petition to Governor Wallace to demand our right to vote."

Was it Bevel's idea alone, an inspiration of the moment, or was his oratory a planned prelude to a march that would take them to the seat of power in Alabama? No one on the Committee knew for certain but it was an idea that immediately caught fire.

The rain turned to drizzle as the mourners retraced their steps over the wet miles back to Marion and their cars. Committee members, along with Leslie who silently listened, reflected on the movement's next step.

"It's right smart to march to the State Capitol with a petition in hand to present to Wallace," offered Annie Lee who was walking slowly, her swollen ankles aching with every step. "Put the vote issue right at his feet. And hold those big feet of his to the fire."

"Should make for some mighty fine press," Moses agreed.

"I like the idea of a petition. It sounds more legal. Demonstrations are becoming too dangerous," Elverse mused. "It's a much safer strategy than challenging all the restrictive laws they've slapped on us."

"So they can arrest us," agreed Annie Lee.

"I don't know," ventured Elmira. "Seems like we'll keep the demonstrations up, too? Otherwise, what did Bevel mean about marching every day? We demonstrate every day as it is with our lines down at the courthouse. But marching across half the state of Alabama to Montgomery? That's plum-nelly!"

"Especially because we'll have to march through Lowndes County," Jackson added.

"That's right. That would be suicide for certain," Mandy said as they passed through a stonewall clearing that delineated the cemetery.

While it was barely raining, the road was muddy and the entire ensemble felt their feet grow heavier with each step as mud caked thicker and thicker on their shoes. Mandy was particularly bothered that her one pair of pumps were being ruined.

"Not only that," Mandy continued, "How could we march that far with so many people?" She looked down at her filthy shoes and wished she had worn boots. "It could be weather like today and then where would we be? If we had to stay off the pavement on the side of the highway in the mud we would all end up looking like Bre'r Rabbit."

"At least he could run fast," said Carlton.

"Not in this mud," quipped Elverse.

"The bigger question is the effort we'd have to mount to feed that many people. And where would we sleep?" Elmira asked. "Folks can't just fall asleep along side of the road. We need some kind of lodging. I don't know of one place that would take Negroes in along the highway. No, not one between Selma and Montgomery and that's almost sixty miles away."

Annie Lee considered this problem. "Well, I'm sure Sister Boynton, the good doctor, and John Lewis and the rest have something in mind," she said. "We'll just keep marching 'round Selma to keep the pressure on. Once it's got all figured out we'll march to Montgomery all right."

Leslie bit her tongue, forcing herself to remain quiet as the discussion progressed. She was chilled-to-the-bone from the rain but shuttered from sensing Annie Lee was slipping out of reach to ever agreeing to leave. They trudged on in silence; Annie Lee glanced at Leslie to gauge her reaction to their talk of a Montgomery march and saw her doubts had been correct. Leslie was frowning, disapproval written all over her face. Leslie's idea of the future was definitely not in sync with her own.

Heard cemetery was far enough out in the countryside to feel separate from Marion. On a distant rise overlooking the uninhabited hills and forests, Sparky and Choice were hun-

kered down watching the mourners pass. Sparky raised himself up slightly from his crouched position and extended his
arm and aimed an imaginary gun at the somber processional.

"Pow. Pow. Pow. Pow." He spit. "Bet I could pick off a hundred of 'um with a semi-automatic."

Choice could no longer maintain his squat position and let
his body rock back until he bumped down on the wet grass. He
removed one of his shoes and pulled at his white sock.

Sparky looked down at him with amusement. "Whatcha'
doin', big brother? You're gonna get a real wet butt."

"My toes hurt," complained Choice.

"Hey, you ain't got all your toes, remember? Froze those
suckers right off at the meatpacking plant. You better get in
shape, Choice, or we'll have to change your name to ham-
burger." Sparky laughed at his own little joke. "There's gonna
be a lot of action coming up."

"Yah, yah," mumbled Choice and kept rubbing his foot.

The funeral over, the mourners returned to their homes to
get warm, change their wet clothes and muddied shoes, and
fix dinner before the Committee met again. Leslie cooked up
some Southern fried steak with mashed potatoes and gravy
while Annie Lee took a hot bath to soothe her aching, swollen
ankles. After dinner, Annie Lee left for the Committee meeting
at Amelia Boynton's house.

Leslie decided to spend her evening writing letters home
to her family. She sat at the kitchen table and stared at the
paper. Annie Lee's quiet apartment made her restless; she
longed to hear the hustle and bustle of her children in her
own house. Finally, she settled down to write each one an
individual note to let them know how much she missed them.
And David. The last time they had spoken he tried to be so
positive, so accommodating even though she couldn't say
when she might return with Annie Lee. His loyalty immediately triggered her guilt. But her guilt lost out to her overriding
panic about Annie Lee, whom she loved so very dearly. The
plan she overheard discussed as they walked away from the
cemetery had Southern danger written all over it. She couldn't

share that concern in David's letter. She would keep the letter light, as was her way when thorny issues became more real and choices more complicated. She definitely would not mention Montgomery.

Annie Lee arrived at the Steering Committee meeting and immediately brought up how they should consider James Bevel's call to march on Montgomery. Emboldened by this challenge, the Committee fantasized making the idea real and keeping the momentum going before the affect of Jimmie Lee's death dissipated.

In reality, to accomplish such an ambitious march, the Committee would need considerable preparation time—and money. They had neither. It was an idea without form. It had not even been an idea before that afternoon. Yet, ever flexible, dedicated, and capable of sacrifice, the Committee set about determining how to flush out just such a march. They would will it to happen.

Discussion was again brisk and pointed. Someone suggested they march the very next Sunday.

Mandy was in attendance and had been trying to make every meeting ever since Carlton had been cattle prodded.

"Let's be realistic," she admonished. "We can't march that far with so many people. It will take a lot of planning, and organization, and money." She emphasized the latter. "A lot of money. The Committee doesn't have that kind of money and even if we did, we don't have enough time to plan it properly," she reasoned.

"But Dr. King's SCLC has money," countered Annie Lee, studiously ignoring the former part of Mandy's argument. "Good thing Sister Boynton here asked them to join us. Between the Doctor's flush organization and Lewis' SNCC money, it could happen. It should happen. It *will* happen, mark my words."

"Maybe sometime soon, but certainly not by this Sunday," countered Mandy.

Amelia Boynton already envisioned herself standing on the Alabama Capitol steps and could taste victory. Why should they wait? She spoke with fervor.

"We have to believe. All things are possible with God. Brother Bevel most likely was instructed to be spokesman about such a march or he wouldn't have announced it at the cemetery. This isn't an empty words movement. If he said it, they must have a plan to back it up, you can be sure. They'll be sharing the plan with us any time now. We're always consulted when decisions are made so they'll tell us what we need to do. We must trust our faith and believe in miracles that all will fall into place. Yes! With God all things are possible. I say we all go out and buy ourselves some new marching shoes with real cushy soles and be ready."

The room took on a glow of inspiration, casting doubt aside. It just took faith. Lord I believe. Help thou mine unbelief. Annie Lee nodded her approval so hard her head looked like a bobble doll. Mandy, ever practical, just shook her head at such wishful, pipe-dream thinking. She exchanged a frustrated glance with Elmira who also shook her head. But neither tried to dampen the Committee's enthusiasm. As the Committee moved forward, they would simply try to be the voice of reason and push for sensible steps as the idea took form.

Elverse also was less sure but got caught up in the moment and wanted to believe it was possible that even a limited plan could work if everyone pitched in and made it so. The meeting broke up with the majority of members agreeing they should move ahead with all deliberate speed and pursue the possibility of a march by meeting with SCLC's representative still in town, James Bevel. Moving forward would rest with him. As bad as they wanted to make the march happen immediately, they realized it would only be possible if King's well-heeled organization agreed.

By nightfall the drizzle had turned to fog. The same black Cadillac that cruised the Selma streets turned off a main road and drove around to the back door of an abandoned stone gristmill. Four men got out. Uncle walked to his trunk and popped it open; the dim trunk light illuminated a small ineffectual glow into the night. He unlocked a wooden box buried under rags and removed folded white sheet robes, checking the labels in the back of each neck opening. He handed the top one to Rusty Denton, his simple young nephew in his early twenties who could have been a Woody Allen double except for his pimples and growing beer belly.

Sparky noticed the hand off. "Finally got your very own now, eh Rusty?" asked Sparky.

Rusty grinned shyly. "It was my Christmas present, right Uncle?"

"Damn straight," Uncle boomed. "Looks damn good on you, too, little nephew. Covers up your baby fat."

The men laughed at Rusty who blushed. Choice gave him a noogie on his head. Uncle then handed robes to Sparky and Choice. He took the last sheet for himself and locked up his trunk. Together they walked to the wooden door of the mill, still carrying the sheets they would put on once inside. Uncle knocked a pass code on the weathered panel. A voice came through from the other side.

"Go away!"

"Hell, no!" declared Uncle. "God bless America, damn it!"

The door creaked open and the four men slipped inside.

Later that night when most people were in bed asleep, two cars approached each other on County Road 41, just past Craig Air Force Base. One car flashed its headlights twice. The other car responded with three flashes. The two cars passed each other, then made quick u-turns and turned off onto a small dirt road that stopped at a small clearing. They shut off their motors. The drivers got out of their cars and walked over to each other. The FBI agent from Selma nodded to Choice. The agent lit two cigarettes and handed one to his informant. They stood for a moment, dragging on their cigarettes and taking in the night air that smelled of fresh rain.

"Well?" The FBI guy blew a smoke ring.

"They want to pick off the top. They think they can kill King and then as many others as possible before they have to make a run for it."

"A lot of people talk about killing King," the agent shrugged. "What makes them think they can do it?"

"High powered assault rifles. Wait in ambush when the niggers march to Montgomery. One guy owns property along Route 80, the route they're most likely to take. They figure to use the swamp for their getaway."

The agent nodded. "They possess these rifles?"

"I done told you they do the last time I reported," Choice said testily. "They're serious. They mean to do this!"

"All right, all right," said the agent.

A moment of silence passed between them.

"How you holding up?" asked the agent.

"I need more cash," said Choice.

"Figured as much," said the agent. "Got a new system." The agent pulled a business card from his pocket and flicked open his lighter to shed light on the number written on the back of it.

"This here's a new number. Call it when something is up but you can't talk. Dial the number and let the receiver hang down so it will keep ringing. We'll trace it."

"What about the old number?" Choice asked.

"Still use it to get to me directly. My office will know where I am and I'll call you back."

"OK," said Choice. "Old number to talk to you. New number to dial on the run and your guys will trace it."

The agent smiled. "You'd make a good agent."

"Thanks," said Choice with a tinge on pride in his voice. "You got any openings?"

"Maybe," the agent responded coyly. "Let's see how you work out on this assignment first."

The agent took out an envelope from his coat pocket and stuffed it into Choice's corduroy jacket pocket. Choice padded the bulge.

"God bless the American taxpayer," Choice said with a grin.

"You'll be working overtime till these Commie agitators leave town so there's a bonus in there for you" said the FBI man. "So long."

Choice gave him a self-satisfied smile. "So long."

The next morning after the funeral Leslie drove Annie Lee to one of the houses she cleaned. The day was overcast and grey, much like Leslie's pensive mood. The radio was turned off.

"You sure are quiet this morning," commented Annie Lee. "You missing home?"

"Oh, sure. Writing to them last night always makes me miss them. But it's not that, Annie Lee. I've just been thinking."

They turned onto a lovely street. Had Spring been in season, the lane would have displayed a cool, green Southern graciousness with its trees forming an arched canopy over the street and a landscape blooming and bursting with color. The houses were set back on expansive lawns that gently curved down to spotless sidewalks, even after the rain. Leslie slowed in front of a two story Southern Antebellum with sturdy columns lining its porch. Annie Lee looked up at the house.

"These good white folk here?" She motioned to the stately home. "They got me out of jail. Wouldn't even let me pay them back, neither. Said they couldn't believe I was arrested when it was the Sheriff who accosted me. Said they were embarrassed to pay the salary for such a supposed lawman who would actually sit on a woman."

"I'm glad to know such people exist like that down here," said Leslie. Annie Lee agreed. "Yes sir, they're real good folk." Annie Lee gathered up her purse and work gloves. "What are you gonna do today, sugar?" she asked.

"Nothing much," said Leslie. "That's just it. Maybe there's something I could do that would help make this march you're talking about happen faster?"

"Honey, nothing ever fast happens down here. That's why I think you need to strongly consider returning home to your children."

"But If I did stay until the march, would you go back to Flint with me then?"

"Leslie May, as God is my witness, I'm not making any promises and I don't intend to, neither. I just don't know how long it's going to be before we get to march to Montgomery. It could be this Sunday. It could be next month. It could be a real long time from now. But one thing's for sure. No matter when it happens, I'll be marching. And you can't just hang around forever. Much as I love your company, I know you got responsibilities in Michigan and it makes me mighty uncomfortable to know you're staying on account of my account and that's the truth."

Leslie sighed. Annie Lee patted Leslie's knee then opened the car door.

"Don't you think you need to take a break from all this, Annie Lee?" Leslie pleaded one more time. "Give yourself a little rest?"

Annie Lee laughed as she climbed out. "Oh, wee! You are one Johnny one note. I ain't tired. Bye, honey. Thanks for the ride. See you later."

Annie Lee closed the door and Leslie watched her walk up the path to the house. Leslie sighed again and sat there thinking about Annie Lee's admonition. She must be wearing out her welcome. That thought filled her with melancholy. She loved Annie Lee so much, not more than her own family, of course, but as much. Leslie studied her hands and tried to remember what the lines meant on her palms. Could one of the lines represent Annie Lee? And if so, would it ever cross her lifeline, or better yet, intertwine? She rubbed her palms together as if to rub away her sad thoughts and drove off to spend her day doing nothing in particular. In the end she went to the grocery store and bought ingredients to bake a carrot cake for Annie Lee to take to the Committee meeting being held that night at Moses and Elmira's home. Planning for a march had taken over their lives.

Amelia, Elmira, and Elverse conferred with James Bevel that same afternoon. They made a strategic argument that the march from Selma to Montgomery should happen sooner rather than later because the energized anger after the funeral had to be seized upon and funneled into action. Anger creates motivation. Bevel gave his excited approval, an endorsement the threesome assumed meant that SCLC was on board.

The Committee was ecstatic when they heard and boldly set the date for the very next Sunday: March 7, 1965. Obviously they had no time to plan the many details but they put their faith into practice, confident the logistics would be worked out as the march went along. Somehow.

When they spoke with John Lewis, however, the news was not positive. He was sorry to have to tell them that SNCC had determined not to participate, claiming it was too dangerous. Lewis disagreed but had been voted down. As Chairman, he had to sign the SNCC letter formally informing King's SCLC organization and the Committee that SNCC would be only minimally involved.

Yet, being John Lewis, he knew in his heart he had to be with the marchers, ill prepared as they were. Representing himself only, he said he would be there. He would march.

News traveled fast to the office of the governor, Mr. George Wallace. Once the governor got wind a march was being planned on state highways between Selma and Montgomery, he set about making certain it would not happen. Bill Jones was his silver-tongued press secretary and it fell to him to announce Wallace's resolute opposition.

During such turbulent times, Jones attempted to put the best spin possible on the state's racism. The possibility of such a march had become national news so Jones was obligated to call a press conference to explain why Alabama would not tolerate such a demonstration. He needed to choose his words carefully.

Mr. Jones stood at a podium laden with microphones in front of a large portrait of Governor Wallace. All of the three main news networks and newspaper reporters were there, eager to know what the state's response was going to be to this latest development. Jones cleared his throat and proceeded to read his prepared statement.

"Governor Wallace of the great state of Alabama has concluded the Southern Christian Leadership Conference's march from Selma to Montgomery is not in the interest of public safety. He will therefore stop the march at all costs."

Jones did not take any questions and was whisked out of the room, even though eager newsmen fired questions at his retreating back.

"How does Governor Wallace intend to stop the march?"

"What are the Governor's plans if they march anyway?"

"Did Governor Wallace confer with Dr. King? Did they make a deal?"

One reactionary reporter even shouted, "Did the Governor discover a Communist plot?"

Such a political pronouncement from Wallace's office did not sit well with Selma's Director of Public Safety. Baker barged into the Mayor's office without knocking and found Smitherman sitting behind his desk. Baker charged right up to it.

"OK, Joe. How do they plan to stop it?"

Smitherman blanched. "Don't worry, Wilson. Everything's under control," he said.

"Right. Like it was in Marion? Or the kid's march? Look, Joe. You hired me to keep a lid on this thing. If Clark and Lingo get their heads together—"

"—Wallace's staff assured me it'll be a peaceful stop," Smitherman entreated.

"Oh, right," Baker jeered. "There's no such thing with them. How will they get their rocks off this time? Bayonets? Tear gas? More cattle prods? Pistols? What?"

"You got it all wrong, Wilson."

"Yeah? Well, if I don't, you can pack up this job and stuff it," Baker snapped. He stomped over to the door and yanked it open. "You can piss on it! These ignoramuses are just making my job harder."

Baker left, letting the door bang behind him. Smitherman, shaken, his blood pressure shooting up to a dangerous degree, buzzed his intercom.

"Yes?"

"Get me Wallace's office," he said. What a time to be mayor, he thought regretfully. What lousy timing to start a political career.

Originally Bevel told the Committee that of course King would lead the march to Montgomery. Then word came from SCLC that King would *not* appear on the Sunday they had selected and requested they change the march to a later date. King's message to the Selma Committee said he felt he needed to remain at his church that Sunday to preach the sermon. He had already missed too many Sundays. Committee members didn't know what to make of this postponement. They had momentum. Why wouldn't he come? They suspected they were not being told the true reasons. Had he been threatened? How could he postpone their march when it was building on the increased publicity they were now receiving? And how would it look, caving in to Wallace's threats?

During the Committee discussions of this most dire setback, most members strongly urged going ahead anyway with the march. Moses explained his position clearly.

"No disrespect to Dr. King and his Conference, but we've been demonstrating down here for a long time without national leadership. I see no reason why we should wait now."

Elverse wasn't so sure. Mandy was not present but he had understood her objections and realized it wasn't wise to rush such a move.

"Mandy had a good point at our last meeting. We really don't have enough time to mount an effective march. We don't want to look like we don't know what we're doing and we don't want to appear to be blundering fools. Maybe this is a blessing that King is asking us to postpone it another week or two."

But Amelia Boynton strongly concurred with Moses.

"Even though we don't have it all planned out, we know the longest journey begins with the first step. Let us take those first steps and figure out what we need as we go along. Those who aren't marching will support those of us who are. We'll march this Sunday and show them a thing or two."

"That's right," agreed Annie Lee. "It would send the wrong message to be seen as backing down."

"It would look like Wallace has won," agreed Moses.

"And we ain't gonna let that happen no way. We may be nobodies but we're determined nobodies," Annie Lee boomed.

That evening Elverse picked up an exhausted Mandy after a long shift, so he swung by the local pizza shop where they picked up dinner. As the family sat around their kitchen table and after they had said grace, Elverse told his wife and son that King wouldn't be coming to town after all.

"Really? And I thought I was finally going to get to shake his hand," lamented Carlton.

"So the march is postponed then, right?" said Mandy.

"No," said Elverse with a resigned shrug. "The Committee decided that while it suits SCLC to change the date for whatever reason—and we don't really know why—it doesn't suit the people of Selma. The Committee thinks it's more important to channel the folks who are getting frustrated with the movement. That they need to be given some kind of positive action. That we can't just sit around and wait for King. And beginning to march, even if Wallace stops us, will signal to the world we mean to become voters."

"But Elverse," Mandy demurred, "there's been almost no planning. You can't just start off with no plan. That's ridiculous! Especially since Wallace said he'll stop such a march at any cost. That's a big threat and you know he'll carry it out."

Elverse sighed and laid down his piece of pizza. How to explain why the Committee is going ahead against all odds?

"I know," he said. "I have my doubts, too, and said so. But Amelia believes we just need to do it. Many people think the publicity will keep us safe. And those who aren't marching will bring supplies to those who are. They think we can create a buddy system where one person in town sponsors one marcher and every day that sponsor brings whatever the marcher needs."

"Heavens," said Mandy. "It can't work like that. That's like saying a doctor can go into an operating room without any supplies and expect nurses to bring him what he needs once the patient has been cut open."

"I'd hate to be the patient," cracked Carlton.

"Exactly," agreed Mandy. "And another very basic thing. What will the marchers do when they have to go to the bathroom?"

"Pee in the bushes!" said Carlton enthusiastically. Elverse cuffed his son's cheek in playful admonition.

Mandy shook her head and rolled her eyes as she said, "You can't have hundreds of people peeing by the side of the road. That's not hygienic."

"Hygienic? Shoot, we'd be arrested as soon as anyone unzipped," alleged Elverse. "And someone would be sure to take a picture. What a publicity shot that would be."

Carlton cracked up.

"Elverse! Stop," Mandy scolded.

But Carlton enjoyed the image and had to add, "Just think? We could all moon the troopers."

They laughed at that mental image despite themselves.

"To tell you the truth," Elverse continued more seriously, "I don't think anyone really expects us to march beyond the city limits? Once we leave Selma and cross into county territory where Clark is in charge, we'll probably all be arrested. But at least it will be a symbolic show of our determination if nothing else."

"Sweetheart," Mandy said in a tone intended to end the conversation, "it's a half baked idea."

"And that's how the Jews invented matzos," Elverse retorted.

"What's matzos?" asked Carlton. His parents laughed.

"Son, I need to take you North more often to broaden your education," said Elverse.

When Annie Lee told the exciting news about a Sunday march to Leslie, her reaction was joyous. Leslie was thrilled it would be happening that very weekend, so soon after the funeral. To her mind it meant she could then go home with Annie Lee in tow. She actually had wrangled a promise from Annie Lee to consider leaving Selma to visit Flint after the march was over, which, to Leslie's optimistic way of thinking was as good as both of them driving back together.

"Now, Leslie May," Annie Lee had cautioned. "Remember. I said I might consider a visit after the march is over."

"I know, I know," said Leslie feigning agreement. Secretly, she was sure she'd be able to convince Annie Lee to make the trip.

⁓

SIX

While the Committee tried to put together some essentials, at least have a couple of portable toilets trailing along on a truck for starters, their efforts were not even close to a full-scale plan. Hosea Williams from SCLC was assigned to help as much as possible within the short time left before Sunday, yet progress faltered without the credibility of Martin Luther King himself leading the march. No one seemed certain whether there even would be any kind of a march without him; many would-be marchers might not show up.

Those trying to bring about this vision were also handicapped by the realistic fear that Wallace would have all the marchers arrested. Steering Committee members might be willing to go to jail for the cause but not all demonstrators were of that same persuasion. A few days in a crowded jail cell was an incredible economic hardship, not to mention the potential for physical and emotional harm to one's body.

Every citizen in the state of Alabama seemed to learn of the Selma march. Saturday, the day before the march was to commence, Reverend Joseph Ellwanger, a white minister of the St. Paul Lutheran church in Birmingham, gathered together seventy-two very daring white citizens who openly supported voting rights for all. To show their concern and solidarity for equality, they planned to march on the Selma streets just as Negro marchers did. Such acts, however, simply were not done in the South by whites. It was one thing for religious and professional white leaders to speak out in favor of change generally and preach from their pulpits, but to take public action was unthinkable. The White Citizens Council and KKK types considered such a public stand to be treasonous to the white race.

Leslie had dropped off Annie Lee at one of her cleaning houses and drove downtown to finally buy Annie Lee a new coat. As she was about to pass the Courthouse, she saw about fifty hostile Southerners lined up along one side of the street shouting slurs at Reverend Ellwanger's group that stood in front of the courthouse and sang "My Country 'Tis of Thee." On the opposite side of the street approximately one hundred blacks quietly stood in silent support of Ellwanger's demonstrators. On the steps themselves appeared to be Sheriff Clark and a few of his deputy sheriffs.

Leslie parked her car and edged toward the demonstration. On the confrontational side of the street, whites started revving their car engines. They had put Limburger cheese on top of their manifolds and created a lot of billowing smoke that blew toward Ellwanger's group and burned their eyes. When the revving stopped, the Reverend attempted to deliver his "Statement of Concern," but Leslie could catch only a few words as the hostile side began to sing "Dixie." The blacks on the other side of the street responded by singing, "We Shall Overcome." Leslie marveled at the white demonstrators literally caught in the middle who stood their ground with their heads bowed. She wondered if she could be that brave? Their bravery was inspiring but also frightening. Leslie teared up not from the stinking smoke but from witnessing such crude intolerance. It was no longer the good ole boys being boys, it was moronic and she felt ashamed of her race.

Wilson Baker arrived and spoke to Reverend Ellwanger. Leslie didn't wait to see if the confrontation would escalate. She returned to her car and drove away. Buying a new coat for Annie Lee took on greater significance than passively witnessing a clash of beliefs.

But a confrontation didn't erupt. Baker led Ellwanger's shaken demonstrators away from the courthouse by an alternate route even as the hostile crowd began to jostle them. Fortunately, no one was knocked down, and there was no violence beyond the hateful words hurled at the group. Baker made sure of that.

Even without anything resembling a clear plan, marchers began to gather at the Brown Chapel churchyard on Sunday afternoon of March 7, 1965, just in case. The need to challenge Wallace ran deep. Most of those assembled, having attended religious services all morning, still wore their Sunday best, accessorized with a willing spirit to walk until they assumed troopers would stop them. Many women wore high-heeled shoes and many men wore their ties and suit jackets, hardly appropriate apparel if they truly believed they could walk all the way to Montgomery. They didn't care. It was a show of their resolve. If by some miracle they wouldn't be thwarted by state troopers, then others from the movement would bring them necessary supplies and food, and they would sleep along the side of the road if their determination required it. They were climbing a mountain. It just wasn't vertical.

After attending church Leslie and Annie Lee returned home to grab a bite before the march. Annie Lee recognized she would need to change her shoes; her swollen ankles barely made it through the morning service in her Sunday shoes; her feet were complaining bitterly. Sunday best or no, if Annie Lee were to march, she would need to don her white work shoes with lace up support.

Leslie called home to hear her family's voices before she ventured into the unknown territory of the afternoon march. She sat on a small wooden chair next to the telephone table in the kitchen alcove and looked out at the barren tree branches as she spoke. Her husband David wanted reassurance yet again that she would not be among the marchers, even though she had promised him several times in former conversations that she would not march.

Annie Lee strained to overhear the exchange as she washed up the lunch dishes at the kitchen sink and kept the water to a mere drizzle so she could hear better.

"They tried to get an injunction this past week so Wallace couldn't stop the march but it was denied," Leslie said.

There was a pause.

"Right," she said grimly, "It is the South."

Annie Lee grimaced.

"Darling, I promised you I'm not marching and I'm not. I'll just be at the church helping to send them off. Most likely they'll return sometime before nightfall so we'll have hot coffee and biscuits ready."

Annie Lee imagined how worried David must be, thinking Leslie would march despite her promise. She wished she could grab the phone and shout into it, "No way will I let her march, don't you worry."

The conversation moved on and Annie Lee heard Leslie say, "Well, they're marching anyway because...." David must have cut her off with his own theory. Leslie countered with, "No, they're angry about the murder and need to march. It was decided they would get as far as they could today before they get stopped."

Annie Lee's ears began to burn as she listened further.

"She won't consider leaving until she's marched. She might come with me after that. She's considering." There was a long pause. Then, "I know."

Annie Lee wondered *what* did she know? One thing Annie Lee knew for sure was how much she deemed Alabama her home and could never leave her beloved people for good. How long would she ever consider leaving all she'd ever known? A week? A month? A year? Maybe two, three years? She shuddered at the thought. Her whole life had been spent in Selma and she never imagined being anywhere else.

Leslie finished her conversation by saying, "Yes, darling. I miss you, too. Thanks for holding down the fort. It won't be long now. OK, Bye. I love you, too."

Annie Lee ran the water harder as if she'd been preoccupied at the sink the whole time. She didn't hear Leslie say after a brief pause,

"Yes, Justin?" Leslie shut her eyes as she held back the rush of emotion when her oldest son's voice praised her. "Thank you, sweetie. I'm very proud of you, too. Thank you for helping Grandma and your Dad. I'll call back tomorrow to tell you all about the march. I love you. Bye, bye."

Leslie hung up the phone reluctantly and sat a moment longer gazing out the window. A Yellowhammer, the only U.S. state bird that is a woodpecker, landed on the tree branch and all the frightened little Carolina wrens flew away. Annie Lee wiped her hands and went to find her new warm coat Leslie had bought that replaced her old torn one. That old coat was so shabby she was happy to be rid of it, the torn collar being the least of it.

The Turner family also had returned home from church for a quick meal before heading to the church grounds. Carlton found his father combing his hair in front of the bureau mirror and pulled up his new polyester pant legs to display his sneakers.

"Dad, do you think it's OK to march in my sneakers or do you think I should have kept my dress shoes on?"

Elverse looked over at his earnest son and grinned. "Well, now," he said solemnly, as if seriously considering the question. "Guess that depends on whether you plan to strut your stuff or not?"

"Dad," Carlton pleaded. "Really. Which ones do you think?"

Mandy came to the door and gave them a stern look. "There won't be any marching unless you two get yourselves out to the table. Dinner's ready."

"Wear what you've got on, Carlton," Elverse advised. "They're more practical."

Carlton took his mother's arm and steered her toward the kitchen. "Lighten up, Mom. This afternoon is going to be fun."

"Right," agreed Elverse. "Think of it as a parade. More than likely they're going to turn us right around anyway when we reach the outskirts of town."

"Which would be doing us all a favor," Mandy shot back. "Marching through this racist state is no Mardi Gras. The only reason I agreed that both of you could march is because they've gotten so much bad publicity lately, they won't dare do anything today in broad daylight."

Hundreds of marchers gathered under a brisk sky at Brown Chapel grounds. They filled the churchyard, the ball field, and the basketball courts across the street. King had sent Andrew Young to Selma in a last ditch effort to persuade the Committee to postpone the march but to no avail. The town was marching. Without Dr. King, all waited to see who would lead the march.

Annie Lee spotted John Lewis and caught up with him.

"Heard there was a coin toss to replace the good doctor," she greeted him. "So who won?"

"Hi, Annie Lee. Hosea. He'll be representing Martin and he and I will march together up front."

"Great! Double our pleasure, double our fun and better than gum," Annie Lee said, smiling broadly.

"We'll be lucky if we reach the city limits before they turn us back," John replied with an equally broad smile. Neither could contain their excitement for what was about to happen, regardless of Wallace's promise to stop them. Lewis looked up from Annie Lee and noticed Hosea Williams conferring with Police Chief Baker and a man unknown to him.

"Better see what the powwow is about. Please excuse me, Annie Lee."

On the ball field, Elverse and Carlton greeted Moses and Elmira who both carried bedrolls and a snack bag.

Elverse eyed the bedrolls. "I'd say that's wishful thinking. We'll never get that far."

"Maybe so," Moses allowed. "Then again, Wallace may be saying we can't march so we won't be ready and then he'll let us through so we'll look like idiots. I figured there was no harm in carrying it whichever way it goes."

"I think it's smart," said Carlton shyly. "You're ready no matter what."

"That fox always has a trick up his sleeve," Elmira interjected. "So Where's Mandy?"

"Over at first-aid," Elverse said. He pointed to a huge red cross that hung on the exterior church wall above tables holding medical supplies. "She's staying back with the medical team in case there's any trouble. But we won't be another Marion. The press is here today. Hope not, anyway," he added as he tousled Carlton's hair, trying to convince himself his son would be safe.

Together they crossed the field and moved with the others into the packed churchyard. Hosea Williams stepped onto a long wooden crate to address those assembled.

"Welcome," he boomed through a bullhorn. "I commend you all for coming in the face of danger. We have just learned the state troopers have tear gas."

A murmur raced through the crowd. Such a tactic was not expected. Was it just to scare them? Williams continued.

"They may use it, they may not. But we should be prepared. Dr. Moldovan is here from New York. He will advise us."

Williams stepped down and exchanged places with the physician. Mandy who was wearing her nurse's uniform wove her way to Carlton and Elverse as Dr. Moldovan began his instructions.

"In the event of an emergency, there are three doctors to assist you. If they do use tear gas, keep low to the ground as gas rises," instructed Dr. Moldovan.

Mandy put her arms about her son protectively. She exchanged a fearful look with Elverse.

Dr. Moldovan continued. "Don't rub your eyes. Flush them with water as soon as you're able. We'll be right behind your march in three ambulances. Bless you." Moldovan stepped down. More murmurs.

Elverse turned to Carlton. "Son, in light of this news, I don't want you to march today."

Carlton stepped away and looked squarely at his father. "Dad, if every Negro backed down in the face of danger, we'd–"

"–You're still a boy, son," Elverse stated evenly. "It sounds like it could get very dangerous. You'll have plenty of time to right all the Alabama wrongs when you're older."

"No, sir," Carlton said. "Today I'm a man."

Elverse implored Mandy to intervene. "Mandy. Talk sense into our boy."

Mandy regarded her husband and the almost six hundred marchers who were present. She hadn't believed in this march but today felt different. With the press and the whole world watching, perhaps it would be the attention they needed to create the change they'd worked so long to achieve. She studied her son, a teenager, no longer a boy, not yet a man, who stood before her with such fierce determination. What kind of message would they as parents be sending to their child if they discouraged him from being involved? She turned back to Elverse and answered with words that surprised even her.

"You heard what our little man said."

Carlton jumped forward and gave his mother a big hug. Leslie immediately regretted her words but knew she couldn't take them back. She kissed the top of his head and offered a prayer up to heaven to keep him safe.

John Lewis and Hosea Williams stepped up to the church-yard gate where Leslie stood with another volunteer, one on each side of the exit. Williams instructed them how to cross their outstretched arms to form a barrier so they could control the flow of marchers as they left the yard in twos.

Lewis beamed at them as he adjusted the straps on the small knapsack he wore on his back. "Now remember, this is not a parade. It's just a little stroll. Make sure everyone keeps the distance needed between each pair."

"We'll do our best," said the other gatekeeper. "Good Luck!"

"Thank you," Lewis said. "We'll probably need it. Well, here goes."

Lewis and Williams passed through the gate and thus began the march. When they were about ten feet away, Annie Lee and Mrs. Boynton stepped up. Leslie studied Annie Lee's face so full of purpose. She gave her a quick kiss on the cheek.

"You look like a real professional marcher," Leslie said lightly, hoping to keep her dread in check. Annie Lee grinned.

"If we *do* get through by God's good grace, you'll bring me the blankets I set out?"

"Of course," Leslie agreed. "You two take good care of each other," she added.

"Will do," Amelia Boynton answered gaily. "It's an amazing day for us today and a long time coming."

Two more marchers passed through the exit, then Carlton and Elverse stepped up and pressed against the women's arms, eager to get going.

"Hold on," the volunteer advised. "We don't want any arrests for parading without a permit."

Elverse and Carlton held back. Leslie addressed Carlton.

"My boy wishes he could be here marching with you, Carlton."

Carlton beamed. "Thank you, ma'am. That would've been real fine."

"We know he's here in spirit, Leslie. We know he's rooting for us," Elverse said kindly. They passed through the gate and Moses and Elmira stepped up.

"The whole country's here is spirit," Moses claimed.

"I wish my feet were here in spirit," complained Elmira. "My corns are already giving me grief and I know I'm going to pay for this little stroll tonight."

The disciplined marchers, still two abreast and separated by yards of space, walked past state troopers lounging on the lawn of the Selma Times-Journal newspaper building. The marchers eyed them warily, almost expecting them to spring into action and block their path. But the men appeared to ignore the procession passing them by as if it were an everyday occurrence.

It was a somber pageant with only the sound of their feet shuffling along the sidewalk. They did not sing or talk among themselves as often happened when they marched around the courthouse. Breaking the law and knowing troopers could be ready to stop you at any moment induced a reflective quiet. Disobeying the Governor's orders was tempting devilish gods.

They reached the base of Pettus Bridge that spanned the Alabama River, a mere six blocks from the church. Hosea Williams and John Lewis stepped onto the high arched steel and concrete structure and proceeded to cross. The river moved rapidly below them. When they reached the crest of the bridge they could see sunlight playing off helmets of troopers gathered on the opposite side.

"I guess we won't even be marching to the city limits," surmised John.

"Looks like we could see the underside of the Alabama River," Hosea agreed. "Can you swim?"

"No," said Lewis. "Can you?"

"No," Williams said, "But it looks like we might have to learn real fast."

Lewis plunged his hands deeper into the pockets of his tan trench coat and continued walking toward the troopers with Williams. Standing shoulder to shoulder were well over sixty state troopers in full riot gear, confederate flag decals slapped on their helmets. The troopers stretched across the entire four-lane highway and center divider. Behind this flank of troopers was another large flank of sheriff deputies and volunteer deputies. About fifteen troopers on horseback in the very back had an elevated view of the entire confrontation.

Annie Lee and Mrs. Boynton reached the crest and briefly stopped as they took in the sight.

"Well, go to war Miss Mitchell!" Annie Lee exclaimed. "Look what they brought out to greet us."

When Elverse and Carlton reached the rise, Elverse instinctively put his arm around his son. Moses and Elmira stepped up to them and Moses let out a low whistle. He surveyed the wall of force and commented, "Guess you were right. I won't need my bedroll."

The spacing between the pairs collapsed as the marchers picked up speed and sought safety in their numbers. Their pace quickened as they crossed the midpoint of the bridge. The three ambulances trailing the tail end of the marchers were stopped as they began to descend the bridge.

A trooper strode over to the window of the first ambulance and spoke to the driver. "You can't take these vehicles over the bridge," he announced with a malevolent grin. "It's closed to traffic on account of this here march."

There were more malevolent grins on the faces of over a hundred jeering whites who came to see a showdown. They jostled for position in front of the Chick-N-Treat Café to the right of the troopers' line and a Pontiac dealership on the left. Sparky, Choice, and Uncle Parker passed a bottle of whiskey back and forth as they held their ground near the front.

John Lewis and Hosea Williams stopped about twenty feet from the troopers. They observed a couple of troopers placing gas masks over their faces. The rest stood at the ready. A Major stepped forward with a bullhorn. The bullhorn crackled, followed by his piercing voice.

"Stop! This is Major John Cloud speaking. This is an unlawful assembly. Your march is not conducive to the public safety. You are ordered to disperse and go back to your church and your homes."

All eyes were glued on Williams and Lewis as they inched into the "no man's zone" between their front line and the troopers' line. Horses snorted and the wind whistled, filling the suddenly silent air with a chill.

Williams stepped forward. "May we have a word with you, Major?"

Jim Clark and the State Trooper Chief sat in Clark's car, the doors open, and watched impassively. The amplifier squawked.

"There is no word to be had," Cloud's voice rang out.

Williams took another step. "Major, may we please have a word?" Lewis joined him and both looked at Cloud, who continued to use the bullhorn even though the three men were practically facing each other.

"I said there is no word to be had," Cloud's deafening voice echoed. "You have two minutes to disperse."

John checked his watch. They continued to stand their ground. Reporters restrained behind barricades began to snap pictures, and roll film, and take notes under the disapproving eyes of the troops. Television cameras began to roll, beaming their live coverage to the entire United States.

John whispered to Hosea. "We should kneel and pray." Williams nodded and the two men turned to spread the word back to the assembled that they would bow in prayer. The amplifier squawked again and Lewis glanced at his watch a second time. They had one minute to go.

"Troopers advance!" Cloud shouted forcefully.

Lewis jerked his eyes up from his watch, stunned at the order. With the marchers tightly behind them, Lewis and Williams had nowhere to move. Troopers were on them immediately. Without a word a husky trooper swung his billy club against Lewis' cranium. Lewis' legs buckled and he started to go down as the trooper swung again, hitting him squarely up the side of his head. More troopers surrounded Hosea and he, too, began to be beaten fiercely. Then they were on to Amelia Boynton and Annie Lee. It made no difference that they were women. Terrified screams pierced the air.

Troopers formed a human wedge and swept into the marchers. Holding their nightsticks with their arms crossed over their chests, the line was tight and swift, an impenetrable moving wall ready to trample anything in its way. The marchers desperately tried to scatter in all directions but there was no place to go. The wedge rolled over them like a war tank.

As the human wedge shoved past Elverse and Carlton, they both fell. The trooper wedge was now behind them and posse men on horseback were rushing toward them from the front. Scrambling to their feet, they bolted to cross the divider. One posse on horseback chased them and caught Elverse on the back of his neck with a bullwhip. Elverse went down and his head hit the curb with a soft thud. He didn't move. Carlton was frantic.

"DAD! DAD! DAAAAD!" He shouted. Carlton dropped down to his father's side and rolled him over. Elverse's eyes fluttered open.

"Dad! Get Up," Carlton insisted. "You got to get up."

Someone yelled, "Tear Gas!" More posse men donned their gas masks and began shooting canisters into the panicked knot of marchers who pushed and shoved as they tried to escape back across the bridge. Sheriff Clark jumped from his car and swung into action, protected from sight by the forming thick gas cloud.

"Get those goddamned niggers," he shouted. "And get those goddamned white niggers with 'um!"

Shrieks, screams, and cries of pain could be heard clear across the span of the bridge where the doctors were standing helplessly outside their halted ambulances. Then they saw the cloud of the tear gas rising.

"For God's sake," Dr. Moldovan pleaded. "Let us through!"

Marchers were coughing and choking. Some were vomiting. The tear gas the state had selected was the most toxic form of all: C-4. The tear gas cloud settled over the violence and what people at home watching TV witnessed was a posse's helmet and gas mask rising up above the white cloud, followed by a swinging baton that then disappeared again into the cloud to allow another helmet to rise and swing like a choreographed dance of death.

Carlton managed to get his dazed father to his feet. Blood was oozing from Elverse's head. The smoke billowed around them and they could barely see. Nor could they stop coughing. Through the smoke they heard Elmira scream; Moses was under attack. Elmira leapt to Moses being pummeled by a man double his size. She drummed her fists on the perpetrator's broad back and wailed, "Let him go! Let him go! Let him go!"

The trooper turned and jabbed Elmira hard into her stomach with his nightstick. She fell backwards to the pavement just as a skittish, frantic horse stepped on her arm. A cracking sound pierced the smoke. The attacking trooper ran off and the rider kept forcing his horse forward; both left Elmira lying there. Moses rushed to her side to help her up. A stab of pain ran up her arm; she cradled it against her breast as she rose and tried to walk.

Annie Lee and Amelia were nowhere to be seen.

Through the stinging maze Elverse leaned heavily on his son. Carlton struggled to keep his father moving; his thighs smarted from the strain of trying to walk while in a crouched position. They stayed low but the burning was so intense, it didn't seem to matter.

The smoke cleared ever so slightly and they spotted John Lewis who was a mere three feet ahead of them. He had managed to rise to his feet after his attack. Elverse and Carlton joined him and together they staggered back across the bridge. Elmira and Moses came into view and joined them. This ragged five-some headed for the church while an ambulance drove slowly past, heading toward the worst of the riot scene at the bridge's end.

Annie Lee was left on the ground, unconscious. A trooper almost tripped over her and regarded her through his mask. He spied a gas canister nearby and kicked it under her face so its billowing smoke would waft directly into her nose and eyes. Nearby, Mrs. Amelia Boynton had been so savagely beaten, she, too, was unconscious and appeared to be dead. Another marcher cradled her in her arms and kept screaming for someone to come and help.

Troopers with gas masks who attacked the marchers didn't bother to chase after them back across Pettus Bridge. Still, the marchers were not out of harm's way once they reached their own side. They needed to cross in front of the Selma Times-Journal building where men had nonchalantly lounged when they began their march out of town. Now these troopers were very much active and waded into the street, indiscriminately thumping demonstrators with their clubs as the marchers tore by, like cowboys driving cattle through a chute.

Wilson Baker stood next to his car, observing the demonstrators being chased. He caught sight of Clark on his horse and held up his hand, motioning him to come over. Clark rode up to him.

"All right," said Baker. "They're back in city limits. I'll take over now."

"Like hell you will," exclaimed Clark and spurred his horse to rejoin his men and the posse charge.

Brown Chapel churchyard became an outdoor makeshift emergency response ward with nurses scurrying from victim to victim. Leslie carried a dish of solution and a roll of cotton to help marchers rinse out their eyes as they leaned up against the fence. As she administered the solution, she repeated the same questions over and over again.

"Did you see Annie Lee Jones? Do you know what might have happened to Annie Lee Jones?"

Near the medical table Mandy pressed a cloth to what turned out to be a superficial wound on Elverse's forehead. He opened his eyes and looked despondently at his wife.

"Where's Carlton?" he asked.

"Inside, lying down on one of the pews. Shh."

"I couldn't protect him," Elverse lamented. "We both fell but I guess I hit my head."

"Maybe you should be checked out by a doctor? Ambulances are relaying people to Good Samaritan," said Mandy.

"No. I'll be OK. There are a lot more hurt than I am. Where are John Lewis and Hosea? They got clubbed pretty bad."

"They're inside meeting with Andy Young. They're deciding how to respond. Everyone is outraged. I can't believe they actually attacked a peaceful march in broad daylight for all the world to see. They are evil to the core thinking they can continue to beat people up and assume there won't be consequences." Mandy shook with indignation. "How dare they. How dare they!"

On Pettus Bridge, help finally came to assist Amelia Boynton and rushed her to the hospital. Another doctor and driver discovered Annie Lee.

"Hello," said the doctor gently as he bent down next to her. "We've come to take you across. Are you able to stand?"

"Are you taking me across to the promised land? I just been lying here. I can't see a thing and thought maybe I was already dead."

The doctor and driver chuckled.

"No, you're not dead. And you're not going to die, either, dear," said the doctor kindly.

"Oh, good. Then can you see if there's a black pocket book lying anywhere around?" The doctor stood and looked over the grass and street.

"There are lots of things strewn about but I don't see a pocket book nearby. I'm sorry to say you're also missing a shoe."

The men carefully helped Annie Lee up and placed her in their ambulance. As they drove back over the bridge, the driver zigzagged to avoid the many personal items now littering the street: shoes, lunch bags, bedrolls, hats, and tear gas canisters still smoldering. It looked like the aftermath in a war zone.

As the sun began to set, the troopers continued to occupy the Negro neighborhood. The George Washington Carver Housing Project was particularly vulnerable. Clark led half a dozen men through the area. Troopers strolled on foot, yelling at any Negro who dared to be on the street. One Negro was actually beaten on his own porch.

Clark saw a woman walking and shouted from his horse.

"Off the street. Git! Back into your homes. Nobody on the streets!"

Petrified, the woman dropped a bag of apples she'd been given by a neighbor and ran in terror. An apple rolled from her bag and was picked up by a roving trooper on foot. He nonchalantly rubbed it on his jacket, preparing to take a bite. His action incensed Clark.

"Drop that apple," Clark commanded. "We don't steal!"

In front of the Brown Chapel African Methodist Episcopal Church, four more roving posse caught up with a black boy and each grabbed an arm or a leg. "We said get back to your churches," one of them roared. The men then swung the boy through one of the stained glass windows that depicted Jesus as the Good Shepherd. The boy landed shrieking inside amid the shattered shards.

From a shadowy alley, rocks began to pelt the posse men so they fled. A brick flew through the air and found its mark on the last trooper bringing up the rear.

That evening over six hundred people crammed into Brown Chapel sanctuary. There would have been more but for the many who marched and were recovering in the hospital or were forced to take to their bed after becoming dehydrated from their retching. Of those present, many were bandaged and bruised from the day's assault. One marcher kept running her tongue over a gaping hole where her front teeth had been.

Elverse was grateful he was there to hear his leader and he squeezed Carlton's arm sitting next to him. Carlton had insisted on remaining for the rally but his eyes were heavy. Elverse drew him close so his son could lean against his shoulder.

John Lewis had put off going to the hospital as he continued to confer about how to react to this latest calamity. After such an attack, how could he convince the people nonviolence was still the way to protest? He understood well the anger they felt. He himself was seething and his head was pounding. Lewis took to the podium, his hair matted with blood and his trench coat covered in dirt and dried blood. He was running on pure adrenalin. His heartfelt words poured out of him spontaneously.

"I don't know how President Johnson can send troops to Vietnam. I don't see how he can send troops to the Congo. I don't see how he can send troops to Africa, and he can't send troops to Selma, Alabama."

The congregation agreed with Amens. He looked upon the assembled, turning his head from left to right despite his throbbing brain.

"Next time we march we may have to keep going when we get to Montgomery. We may have to go on to Washington!"

People shouted out and clapped in agreement. Completely spent, John left the podium and finally agreed to be taken to the hospital. How he was even coherent was a miracle.

It fell to the inexperienced new Mayor, Joe Smitherman, to try and justify the violence, and he called a hasty press conference. In no time, the camera lights heated up his cramped office mercilessly and he began to sweat profusely.

"It should be obvious to the Negro people by now that King and the other leaders who ask them to break the law are always absent. In the name of nonviolence, they expect there to be no reaction. No one talks about how long we've endured these marches. Do you know how long marches would be allowed to disrupt New York City? Zip!"

Smitherman wiped beads of perspiration from his worked up brow. Reporters duly recorded his words. News cameras cranked away.

"Our men are conducting themselves admirably, considering," he alleged. "These marches are a total disruption of our way of life."

Good Samaritan Hospital was filled to capacity and ablaze as people came and went to visit those injured. Annie Lee had been placed in a tiny room near the nurse's station. She had bandages everywhere covering multiple cuts and her face was terribly swollen. Her skin looked like an overripe concord grape, a taunt, deep dark blue. Giant bruises peeked out beyond her bandages from the attack she endured. Jackson had pulled up a chair and was sitting next to her, holding her hand when Leslie slipped into the room. The door made a soft whooshing sound and Annie Lee turned her head expectantly, even though her eyes were bandaged and she could not see. Leslie tiptoed over to the bed as Jackson rose and gave her a hug.

"Hi Annie Lee," whispered Leslie. "It's me, Leslie." She bent over and gently kissed Annie Lee's puffy cheek.

"No need to whisper," said Annie Lee. "The devil's gone." Annie Lee reached out with her hand and Leslie clasped it tightly.

"How do you feel?" Leslie asked absurdly but didn't know what else to say.

"Like the devil got his due," replied Annie Lee. "Actually, like I was the sparing partner for Cassius Clay."

"Muhammad Ali," corrected Jackson.

"Whatever his name is now. I lost." She giggled in spite of herself. Leslie and Jackson exchanged looks.

Jackson, hoping to keep it light, joked, "Imagine what you could have done if you'd had boxing gloves on?"

"I wonder if they would count as non-violent?" Annie Lee chuckled again in a foggy, distant way.

"Probably not," said Jackson, "They're not exactly Sunday church gloves."

Leslie kept studying Annie Lee's condition and fought back tears.

"Come," said Jackson kindly to Leslie. "Sit in my chair. I have to leave now anyway. It's back to work or I won't have a job." Leslie sat down, all the while still holding on to Annie Lee's hand. Jackson rounded the iron bed to the other side.

"I'll be back tomorrow, Sugar," he said and leaned down to kiss Annie Lee's forehead. As Jackson left he gave Leslie a little peck on her head, too, and whispered in her ear, "Go easy on her."

The two women sat in silence, alternating big sighs and refraining from speaking what was really on their minds.

"What do you hear of Amelia?" Annie Lee broke the silence.

"I heard the troopers almost beat her to death. She's in intensive care right now. She was wearing a heavy coat that probably saved her."

Annie Lee shook her head. "Unbelievable," she said. "We all underestimated them. How much sadistic hate must exist in our law enforcement."

"And entitlement," said Leslie. "They did it in broad daylight. They don't even have any shame. Don't seem to care what the rest of the world thinks of their crimes."

"No shame and no blame," Annie Lee concurred.

More silence.

"So? What's the word? What next?" Annie Lee asked.

Leslie answered, "The Committee and leadership are going to ask a Judge Johnson to issue an injunction against Wallace so he can't stop us from doing a repeat march. Dr. King is coming tomorrow to lead another march himself on Tuesday. He's asking clergy from all over the country to join him."

Annie Lee nodded approvingly.

"That sounds good. Johnson is a good judge. He's fair. He'll issue the injunction. And having King here with lots of other folks will bring us the publicity we need. King's presence will definitely raise the ante."

"Oh, there's plenty of publicity," said Leslie. It already was on TV tonight."

"That so?" Annie Lee said, surprised.

"Yes," confirmed Leslie. "On national stations. ABC cut into "Judgment At Nuremberg" and showed live footage of the bridge. David called and told me they were watching this movie when it was interrupted. At first Justin thought the footage was part of the story."

"That's understandable," said Annie Lee. "There are remarkable similarities."

"I guess the footage was on all the prime time news stations. And I just heard there are demonstrations across the country."

"Amazing! Our march finally woke this country up," said Annie Lee.

"But if the injunction doesn't come, nobody seems to know what will happen next," admitted Leslie.

"It'll come through."

"I was hoping we'd pack you up and leave this week."

"I told you I'm marching."

"Annie Lee, you've been hurt three times now. What do they have to do before you let somebody else take your place?"

"They have to kill me," Annie Lee said quietly.

"Oh, Annie Lee." Leslie was exasperated. "Don't talk such nonsense."

"Leave it be, Leslie May. It's not your fight."

"Of course it is. If it affects you, it affects me. There's a time to fight and a time to be safe. You need to take leave of this movement, at least for a little while."

"What I need," Annie Lee emphasized, her voice becoming agitated, "is to walk into a voting booth, here, in Selma, just like you do in Michigan."

Both women were now hooked by frustrated anger.

"Why must it be here, Annie Lee? Why won't you listen to me?"

"Stop, Leslie May. Just because you're white don't think you can pull rank on me."

"What?" Leslie asked incredulously. "What are you saying?"

"You heard what I said. You thought you'd come down here and I'd do what you asked. A child telling her elder what to do. What made you think that, Leslie May? What made you think your want trumps my want? You don't even realize how deep this goes inside you; it's the Southern way of life for whites to feel superior since the day you were born. You assume you can have it your way because I was hired help for your family. But you can't, honey, you can't. I decide what Annie Lee Jones is gonna do and Annie Lee Jones is gonna see this thing through, here, in Selma, in the state of Alabama."

Leslie was stunned and deeply hurt. Tears sprang to her eyes and she could hardly breathe.

"Annie Lee," she said, her voice trembling. "How could you say such things? To me?"

A pang of remorse shot through the drugs that eased Annie Lee's physical pain.

"Maybe my words ain't quite right but it's the truth. You feel entitled. All white folk do, sometimes without them even knowing it, and we black folk let 'um. Anyway," Annie Lee said after a pause, "I'm gonna be in here for a few days."

Leslie raised her head and searched Annie Lee's face that didn't look anything like the Annie Lee she knew. She wished she could see Annie Lee's eyes that had always expressed so much love.

"You mean you won't be able to march on Tuesday?" Leslie asked.

"Most likely not," Annie Lee allowed. Leslie considered this news. A plan formed in her head.

"Then…" said Leslie, as she visualized her plan, "…I'll march in your place." Leslie rose from the chair.

"Now Leslie—"

"—And you'll come home with me as soon as they let you go. You marched today even if it didn't go well and you will have marched via me on Tuesday. So you will have marched. And I say this without pulling any "white" rank."

"Your family is waiting for you to return," Annie Lee reminded her.

"You're my family, too. I can't bear to see you risking your life over and over again. You're tempting fate. You're just... you're just not using good judgment. These guys *will* kill you and they couldn't care less. But I care."

Annie Lee was now worried. She heard Leslie pacing the floor. She heard her start to cry.

"I don't want you marching for me, Leslie. It's too dangerous."

"That's what I've been trying to tell you!" Leslie shouted as her tears flowed. "It *is* too dangerous. Maybe you'll see how dangerous it is if I march in your place. Maybe then you won't be so stubborn."

"Leslie May—"

"—Yes. I'll march and march and march until Alabama freezes over. Hired help. You *were* my mother to me and segregation didn't change that, Southern rules be damned."

"Don't."

Leslie was now sobbing; hurt oozed from her as she circled the room. She became a motherless little girl.

"When you tucked me in at night and left the room, I would whisper, 'Good night, Mommy.' I did! Maybe you forbid me to say it, but I said it to God and to all my dollies and stuffed animals every night once you left the room. I said it for my own ears to hear. I'm saying it now. Please. Mama! Come home with me."

Annie Lee clasped her hands in prayer, too exhausted and remorseful to argue. Leslie continued to circle the room until her sobs subsided but she could not compose herself. She stopped and gazed at the bandaged woman she cherished and detected tears trickling down from underneath the bandages.

"I'm sorry, Annie Lee. I don't understand anything right now. I need to leave. I'll see you tomorrow."

Leslie's words were barely audible. She exited the room without a good-bye. Or a kiss.

A stifled sob escaped from Annie Lee. "Laud, Laud, Laud," she moaned. "What made me say such things?"

Leslie found her way to the canteen and sat down at a small table in a dark corner having made herself a dish of ice cream. The lack of light matched her mood. But even ice cream couldn't comfort her. She simply played with the spoon as she considered how she had grown up in the South. Her parents weren't racists. Nobody in her family was. Her mother and father always treated everyone, both black and white, with respect. They were kind, caring people. And yet… and yet what? And yet they never challenged their assigned stations. They accepted the status quo. Why had she never realized this before?

Mandy Turner entered and walked with purpose to the coffee urns and began pouring herself a cup of coffee. Leslie looked up as she heard coffee being poured.

"Mrs. Turner?" Leslie said. "Hello."

Mandy hadn't noticed anyone in the room and almost spilled her coffee when she heard her name. She spun around and peered into the darkness.

"It's me. Leslie Cole. I'm here in the corner."

"Oh, hello." Mandy answered. She set down the pot. "Were you visiting Aunty Jones?"

"Aunty?" Leslie asked, taken aback. "Annie Lee Jones is your Aunt?"

Mandy took a sip of coffee and remained on the other side of the room.

"Her mother was my mother's older half sister by marriage. But there was such an age difference we just always called her 'Aunt.'"

"I never knew that," said Leslie, amazed.

"I suppose there are lots of things folks don't know," said Mandy, not unkindly.

"Yes. I'm discovering that this trip," said Leslie. "You're certainly working late. You must be exhausted after everything that happened today."

"Elverse has to close his store a lot in order to march. We're grateful for the overtime if not for the reason."

"How is Elverse?" Leslie inquired as she took a small bite of ice cream. It had no taste.

"What do you mean?" Mandy asked suspiciously. Too lost in her own thoughts, Leslie didn't catch Mandy's tone. She answered innocently, "I heard he'd been hurt, too. Is he here at the hospital?"

"No," Mandy said. "He didn't want to take up space. His wound wasn't as bad as we first thought. Turned out to be superficial once we got it cleaned out."

"Oh, that's good. Please give him a special hello from me?"

Mandy stiffened and changed the subject.

"We've treated over sixty people," she said, her voice taking on a formal tone. "John Lewis has a fractured skull."

"Oh, no!" exclaimed Leslie. "And he was walking around worrying about everyone else? My goodness, will he be all right?"

Mandy turned around and placed her cup on the counter as she added a little cream and sugar.

"You can't keep such a leader down," she said as she stirred her coffee.

"And what about Carlton?" asked Leslie.

Mandy turned and faced Leslie.

"He had to grow up fast today."

"What a nightmare he had to witness," Leslie sympathized.

"Yes," said Mandy softly. "It was a nightmare, only we were all awake."

An awkward moment passed between them. Then Mandy shook her shoulders and said, "I must get back to my station. Good night, Mrs. Cole."

Mandy headed for the door without her coffee so Leslie sprang up to pick up the cup and sprinted after her.

"Mrs. Turner! Wait! Your coffee." Mandy stopped and accepted the cup a little sheepishly.

"I guess I'm more tired than I realized. Thank you. Good night."

"Good night," said Leslie. "I think we're all a little more tired than we realize. Say hello to that brave boy of yours."

༄

PART THREE

ALL THE WORLD SEES

SEVEN

B etween the offending images that flashed across American
television screens and Dr. King's urgent plea, clergy and
people of conscience who were able boarded planes and trains
or drove to Alabama. The outpouring was astonishing. Thousands headed for Selma. Unfortunately, that was not true of
Selma itself. Selma's local white ministers ignored the call and
continued their separate business-as-usual duties. Reverend Ellwanger, the Birmingham Lutheran minister, was the lone
Alabama exception. Despite his near brush with violence he
endured during the Saturday white march, he showed up.

The nursing staff at the Good Samaritan Hospital where
Mandy worked was being addressed by the hospital Administrator, a black priest.

"We must be ready for tomorrow and anticipate the
worst," he admonished.

One of the Catholic nurses spoke up. "It's not just the
march. There's also great danger if our newcomers stray out of
the neighborhood."

"True," agreed the administrator, "but I think that's being
covered in orientation when folks arrive? How is housing
coming along?"

"Slow," answered the head nurse who wore a habit.
"They'll never place everyone by tomorrow. It's truly amazing
how many people across the country answered Doctor King's
call. And they're still coming. It's God at work."

Mandy stood on the edge of the ring of staff. While she was exhausted from back to back shifts, she had followed the discussion when an idea formed in her head.

In a barely audible voice she asked, "What if we turn a wing here into a dormitory?"

"I beg your pardon?" The administrator tried to discern who had spoken. Everyone turned and looked expectantly at Mandy.

"Well, we're low in OB. We could combine with surgery and open the west wing rooms to the ministers. In addition to the beds in the rooms, there are extra mattresses in east wing storage. We could line them up on the floor against the walls in the hallways. It wouldn't be hotel accommodations but at least they would have a safe roof over their heads and we could accommodate a lot of visitors."

"Hmmm," mused the administrator. "What an interesting idea." Addressing the entire staff, he asked, "Could we combine departments and carry on around them?"

The staff nodded their heads enthusiastically. Mandy smiled, pleased they hadn't scoffed at her unorthodox contribution.

It was unusually hectic at the Birmingham Airport. People from all over the country arrived from morning till night. Nuns in their habits walked purposefully off the tarmac and Red Cap porters scurried to and fro. A lone table was set up by the exit with a sign that read:

NCC TRANSPORTATION

Volunteers stood behind it, trying to assist the overwhelming numbers of people who spotted their table.

Reverend James Frey, a white, amiable minister in a suit and bow tie walked up to the busy table with his friend, Reverend Anton Engel, also wearing a suit.

"Good afternoon," Frey said pleasantly. "Are you offering to help those of us coming to march with Dr. King tomorrow?"

"We certainly are," beamed the volunteer.

"Great," said Anton. "I'm Reverend Engel and this is my friend here, Reverend Frey. We're both from Boston."

The volunteer laughed. "Well I could have detected that from the accent y'all have."

"What do you mean?" Frey teased, whose accent wasn't that distinct, not having lived in Boston that long. "You're all the ones with the accent."

Reverends Frey and Engel were instructed to wait outside by the curb and if there weren't a car waiting marked "National Council of Churches," there soon would be. Two nuns joined them and they exchanged greetings as a marked station wagon drove up. The driver jumped out and everyone shook hands. With such a sense of purpose, the assembled felt an immediate simpatico camaraderie. The driver opened the doors and Frey and Engel helped the nuns into the back seat.

A tall man in a blue pullover sweater, looking more like a college professor than a minister, trotted up to the car.

"Hi there," he said, smiling a Jimmy Stewart grin. "Got room for one more to Selma?"

"Sure do," answered the friendly driver. Frey turned and beamed at the new traveler and offered his hand.

"Hello. Jim Frey from Boston," he said as he pushed his glasses back up the bridge of his nose.

"Winston Phillips—Winnie—from California. Pleasure."

Anton also extended his hand. "Welcome! Anton Engel, also from Boston. Boy, you came a long way."

"Had to. I couldn't believe the images on TV."

"I know the feeling," agreed Frey.

The men squeezed themselves into the car and the driver took off. As the passengers settled in, so did a fatigue for having interrupted their lives on such short notice. Except for Frey. He seemed wound up and energized by the whole event. He introduced the nuns to Winnie.

"I'd like you to meet Sisters Stella and Mary, both from Chicago."

"Very nice to meet you," said Winnie earnestly. "Gee, I guess all parts of the country are represented."

Sister Stella asked, "Does anyone have a copy of King's actual request? We didn't hear it directly. Our Mother Superior told us of his announcement."

"I have a copy," offered Frey. He removed a folded telegram from his breast pocket and handed it to Sister. She began to read it silently as the conversation continued.

"I didn't get a telegram but heard the appeal over the radio. I also heard the entire New Jersey State Assembly denounced the violence," ventured Winnie.

"I heard both Houses of Congress condemned the attack," Engel said, and then added, "and I kept hearing about demonstrations going on in cities all across the country."

"Our church denounced the violence," Frey added. "And a lot of other churches from what I heard. The American Friends Service Committee where I work immediately began to plan a protest training."

Sister Mary glowed. "This has changed the role of the Church. Christians are taking a stand. The turnout is thrilling."

The car fell silent as Sister Stella asked to read King's request aloud.

"*In the vicious maltreatment of defenseless citizens of Selma, where old women and young children were gassed and clubbed at random, we have witnessed an eruption of the disease of racism which seeks to destroy all America. No American is without responsibility. The people of Selma will struggle on for the soul of the nation, but it is fitting that all Americans help to bear the burden. I call, therefore, on clergy of all faiths to join me in Selma for a ministers march to Montgomery on Tuesday morning, March ninth.*"

"Amen," said Sister Mary softly.

Sister Stella carefully refolded the telegram and handed it back to Frey.

"He's so eloquent," Anton noted.

"It will be fantastic to meet him," agreed Winnie.

"It's an incredible privilege to be here," Frey said.

"It's a thrill," concurred Sister Mary.

"It's scary as hell!" admonished Sister Stella and everybody laughed.

By the time they arrived at the church in Selma, this little group felt like old friends. They tumbled out of the car, each carrying a small suitcase or valise and thanked the driver profusely who would return to the airport for one last run.

They entered the church and saw a huge poster indicating to head for the basement. As they descended the stairs, chaotic noise greeted them. It was not obvious what they were supposed to do; they took in the many dozens of people milling around or standing in front of tables. The room looked like a campaign office the day before an election. Frey found it invigorating.

"Look what we're achieving," he said, grinning.

"Bedlam!" said Sister Stella. She spied a check-in table and strode over to it; the others followed her lead. Two kindly elderly women stood behind the table, one white, and one black. Both greeted the group warmly.

"Welcome to Selma," the smaller woman hollered above the din. "Please sign in with your name, address, and emergency telephone number of someone who knows you're here."

The other woman continued. "Then, do pick up a map of the neighborhood and we'll try to find you lodging. I'm afraid the Prince Albert Hotel is already full. Oh. And be sure to remain in the neighborhood indicated on the map for your own safety. Once you all are signed in here, please move to the next table where they're finding homes willing to take you in. You also will need to attend a quick course in nonviolent action that includes how to defend yourself if you're attacked. Those classes are in the Sunday school wing."

Those words immediately sobered the group.

"Yes," added the first lady sweetly. "And at the third table there are some sandwiches and coffee in case you're hungry. Thank you so much for answering Dr. King's call."

The two women smiled at each other, pleased they had remembered all their points. After saying the same thing over and over, sometimes their minds played tricks and they thought they'd mentioned something when they hadn't. In this case, two heads were definitely better than one.

The grateful five-some signed in, Winnie signing in last. He surveyed the room and noticed the busy next table. Leslie sat behind it, feverishly bent over some cards she seemed to be filling out. Jackson sat next to her. Some people moved away and Winnie was able to read a big, hand printed "LODGING" sign taped to the front of the table.

Jackson was speaking to a couple standing before him who hoped to be assigned to a house. He sifted through the list he had created on a thick legal sized pad, trying to pair the new arrivals' needs with one of the volunteer homes.

Elverse, a band-aid covering his forehead gash, sat on a high stool to better reach the wall phone he was yelling into. He waved the thick church directory as he shouted into the receiver.

"Yes, Myra, right. You can manage five? Oh, that's great, just great. Bless you, sister." He hung up and shouted to Jackson and Leslie, "Myra Penick down for five, plus meals!"

"Got it!" Jackson and Leslie shouted back in unison. Jackson added the name and number of guests to his list and made a check mark in the food column. Leslie looked up the name in her church directory to make out an address card that would then be given to the visitors. It was a tedious method without a typewriter but it worked. Frey and Engel were assigned to a home almost out of town and Winnie was assigned to the hospital; the two nuns were given hospitality in the Carver Projects.

Even though it was late, the Turner family finally sat down to dinner all together. Mandy dished up a bean stew over rice on their plates and they offered thanks. Elverse vigorously buttered a slice of bread that matched his animated description of the day.

"We placed eight hundred and sixty people today. Eight hundred and sixty! It's heartwarming to see how many folks came to help us march. What a showing we're going to have."

Mandy picked up her fork and took a bite. Carlton listened, mesmerized.

"Leslie Cole came up with this great system to keep track of all the home stays. She's incredible!" Elverse continued. "And then, when she realized we missed lunch? She pops up and got sandwiches for us all."

"Leslie, Leslie, Leslie," Mandy said. "You'd think she was running the whole show."

"Just giving credit where credit's due. And then we heard your hospital would take in whoever still needed lodging so we started sending men there. Isn't that great?"

"Yes, I did hear about that. Other people can come up with good ideas, too," said Mandy coyly. "As for Leslie, her white self should be home with her family." There was an edge in her voice. Carlton was stunned.

"Mama! Why you separating her out by color? You always said we're the same underneath, that we all bleed the same red blood. What have you got against Leslie?"

"We're talking freedom here," his mother answered testily. "She's got hers."

"Well, now," reasoned Elverse. "We weren't doing so good by ourselves. If it takes some white folks to help us achieve our goals then so be it. I welcome them. In fact, I'm glad. All the better if our movement looks like a melting pot."

"We were managing OK," said Mandy.

"The people arriving are good people, Mandy. You can't lump all whites together," Elverse said sternly. "And for that, I think we should open our house to a Northerner, too. There's a great shortage of—"

"—I'm aware of the shortage, Elverse, but we don't have room. Not only that, we live too far from Sylvan Street. It—"

"—Excuses," Elverse said. "They could come and go with me."

"Who? Like Leslie Cole?" Mandy demanded.

"My, my—whoa! Are you jealous woman?" Elverse looked sharply at his wife. Mandy rose from the table, her whole body was shaking.

"Any reason I should be?"

"No. Of course not. What's gotten into you, Mandy?"

"No white person has ever stepped into this house and no white person is welcome!"

With that, Mandy ran to their bedroom and slammed the door. Elverse avoided Carlton's eyes and tried to eat but the food stuck in his throat. It was the moment Elverse had dreaded ever since his son was old enough to think independently. Carlton, too, was only playing with his food and not actually eating anything. He had never heard such talk in his family. It made no sense.

"I don't get it," Carlton finally said. "Mama always said we're all God's children."

"And that's true," Elverse answered, hoping Carlton would leave it at that.

"So why did Mama say that? That's mixed up." Carlton stared at his father. He knew something was missing from the equation.

"Your Mama also believes in equal but separate. We all shouldn't socialize together," Elverse said guardedly.

"Why not?" Carlton pressed. "Socializing don't hurt anybody."

Elverse dropped his fork and rose from the table.

"Doesn't. You don't know everything, son," he said, agitated, and moved away from the table. Elverse walked to their bedroom door and knocked but didn't open it. He spoke through the door. "Isn't yours a fine Christian attitude, Amanda Jane? You're a hypocrite, Mrs. Turner."

Mandy opened the door and regarded her husband tearfully.

"If you're so set on having a house guest then let them be black."

"Oh, isn't that great? 'Hello, I'd like to offer my home but would you put Black Only after our name?' Good god, woman, these people are only here because they want to help us."

Mandy slammed the door again and spoke through it. "I don't want a white in my house."

Elverse angrily slammed the palm of his hand against the door then slowly returned to the kitchen where Carlton still sat at the table, confused and troubled. Elverse sat down and again tried to eat as Carlton studied his father.

"What don't I know, pa?"

Elverse looked hard at this son. Carlton lowered his head.

"It's up to your Mama to tell you," Elverse said finally.

"As a member of this family, I think I should know... whatever it is." Carlton kept his head down and spoke softly, knowing he was somehow moving into dangerous territory. He didn't want to anger his father but he really needed an explanation. He never expected to hear such words as his Mama had spoken.

Elverse looked pained and pushed his plate aside. He folded his hands together on the table as if he was getting ready to pray. He took a long time to speak.

"Maybe so," Elverse agreed. "Maybe so. OK." His chest rose as he took in air. "Son, Grand pappy Wilson isn't dead."

Carlton's head jerked up, stunned.

"He's not?" Carlton said, his eyes wide and incredulous.

"No, son. He's living with a white woman in New Mexico. When they ran off, the woman's husband came with some of his cronies and surrounded the house. They shot out every window. Your mother and Grandmother were inside."

Carlton's whole body shook. "Then what happened? Did they come into the house?"

"Yes," slipped out of Elverse's mouth before his brain thought to lie. He stopped, searching for the right words for which there were none. Carlton could hear the kitchen clock ticking. He waited.

"Tell me, Dad."

Elverse searched his son's face. He took another deep breath. "The husband—the white woman's husband—forced his way into the house and... and..." Elverse looked sadly at his son who shouldn't have to know of such things.

"And what, Dad?" Carlton's mind was racing. Had they hurt his mother? "What did he do?" His stomach churned.

"He had his way with your Grandmother."

Carlton's whole face registered disgust.

Elverse continued softly. "I'm sorry son. Things happen here in the South that are very wrong and very evil. Then try as we might, we can't all love those who persecute us as Jesus commands. Your Mama's fine with white women as long as they keep their distance."

Carlton fought back tears but one escaped onto his cheek anyway.

"But what about Grand pappy Wilson? He's the one who left."

Elverse rose and patted his son's shoulder.

"That's true, son. And you're right. He's got blame on his head that someday he'll have to answer for. But he's your mother's father."

Elverse headed back to the bedroom. He was glad he didn't tell the whole story, that the other man had held Mandy's head and forced her to watch. Maybe Carlton would never have to know that particular detail. Would never have to carry that image in his head about his mother. Elverse reached the bedroom, entered, and soundlessly closed the door.

Carlton sat staring at his food then rose abruptly. He carried his plate and violently scraped dinner into the trash, turned the water on full force, and allowed himself to cry.

The Turners weren't the only ones eating late that night. Over at the bowling alley, Choice, Sparky, and Rusty sat at a round table drinking beers. In the background sounds of pins being clobbered by fast rolling bowling balls were heard. The waitress, a gorgeous, slender girl with long chestnut colored hair brought over a freshly baked hot pizza.

"Here you go," she said as she slid the pizza onto the wire pizza stand in the middle of the table.

"Thank you, Carol Jean," Sparky said, pouring on his charm. "Say, how's your mother doing? Is she home from the hospital yet?"

"Why yes," replied Carol Jean. "She got home last Friday. Thanks for asking."

"You tell her we're praying she has a speedy recovery," Sparky said.

His two friends flashed idiotic smiles. Both secretly wished they could be as smooth as Sparky when it came to women. Carol Jean gave Sparky a luscious smile. She considered him so cute.

"I'll do that," she said. "That's so sweet."

"And," added Rusty, puffing up, "if you have any trouble with these Commies coming to town who think they can be served here, you just let us know."

"Oh, I think we're probably far enough away from that part of town so we won't have to worry," Carol Jean said.

"Well, if you do, you just let us know and we'll take care of it," said Sparky, taking command. Sparky took her hand and squeezed it. She giggled, squeezed back, and returned to the kitchen. All three men watched the bow of her apron sway seductively on her backside before they reached for a slice of the pie.

Choice was hungry and took a big bite. With his mouth full, he asked, "Did you hear the judge denied their injunction? Maybe they won't march tomorrow after all."

Rusty pulled a string of cheese off his piece and dangled it into his mouth. "Uncle says Judge Johnson's a nigger lover but maybe he was wrong?"

"Nah," countered Sparky. "Those jigaboos will march now that coon King is here. We should hit the bridge tomorrow just to watch the action. Maybe it'll be even better than Sunday. Hell! Maybe King will get his head busted, too. Bring it back down to size." Sparky always seemed able to predict future events.

"I got to work," said Rusty glumly.

"Too bad," Sparky said.

"Hey," Rusty complained, "I thought we said no onions?"

"Don't worry about it, Rusty," said Sparky. "Just pick 'um off."

"I'm free tomorrow," Choice said polishing off his first piece and reaching for another. He was still on disability from the meat packing factory accident and his chums figured that's how he got by without having to report to a job. They were all licking their fingers and washing down their pizza with beer.

"I'll keep you posted, Choice," Sparky said as he took another slice. "If no cars come to the shop expecting me to work a time miracle, you can come and pick me up. Niggers always start late, anyway."

"I wish I could go with you guys," Rusty said. "Hey, maybe I could call in sick."

"Nah," Sparky said. "You got family obligations and responsibilities now, little man. You can't take any chances on losing your job. Besides, that would be sure to cause an argument between you and Melanie Vi."

"She don't tell me what I can do," objected Rusty.

"Oh?" said Sparky. "Then why don't she let you out except for bowling night?"

"I choose to stay home," Rusty defended himself. "We watch our favorite TV programs together. Plus—and I don't expect you to understand this since you're not married—I like playing with my kid. She's so darn cute and does new stuff every day."

"Watch it," Choice warned, "or we'll have to start calling you Daddy Warbucks."

"Yah, right," said Rusty. "Like I got money."

"Hang in there with your Uncle," said Sparky. "You'll soon have money."

"Ah, shit," was all Rusty could think to say.

The next morning, Tuesday, Mother Nature cooperated yet again. No rain, just sunshine. It streamed through Annie Lee's kitchen window. Leslie was up and felt a little lost without Annie Lee's presence at the stove. She made coffee and poured herself a cup with shaking hands. Taking a sip, she walked to the telephone alcove, sat down and dialed.

"David!" Leslie exclaimed when her husband picked up. "Hi. Just thought I'd call before I left for the march." Her tone was forced. As she listened to her husband's voice, a frown crossed her forehead.

"David, we've been over this. You know I'm going to march today." He tried to interrupt her but she continued. "I told you. It's important to me that I walk in her place. I think she'll come back with me if I do. And I've got to support her."

On the other end of the line David grimaced.

"I know you do, but please be alert," he pleaded. "I don't want you ending up in the hospital, too, and not be able to come home. Besides. We miss you terribly. I'm barely keeping things together here."

A pang of guilt and loneliness surged through Leslie. She had never been separated from her family before. It was hard enough for her to justify taking her college night class once a week and now she had been gone almost two whole weeks.

"Oh, David, I know. I'm sorry, really I am. It's just that events keep postponing our plans."

"Promise me if it looks ugly you'll bow out," he beseeched. "You've seen first hand what they do to marchers."

"I promise," said Leslie softly. "But thousands are here now. Nothing's going to happen like Sunday, not with King and the press and the U.S. government and the whole world watching. Today will be different. Besides. No way are thousands of people going to take to the highways for Montgomery. I'm sure it will be a short march."

"That's what you said before Sunday's march," David reminded her.

"Please stop worrying," she entreated.

"I'm trying. Really I am. I love you, darling. I miss you like crazy."

A lump grew so large in Leslie's throat she could hardly respond. She kept swallowing, trying to find her voice.

Finally, she managed, "I love you, too. Hug the kids for me?" She was cradling the phone tightly as if she could pass a hug through the wire.

"I will," David answered tenderly. "They miss you, too. Mom's been great but she's not you."

Leslie bit her lip.

"Thank her again for me." She exhaled. "All right. Well, I must get going. So I need to say good-bye."

"Call us afterwards. We'll be watching on TV. I love you. Bye."

"Bye-bye, sweetheart."

Leslie slowly hung up the phone. She sat there a full minute more, then finished her coffee and stared into the empty cup. "Dear God," she whispered. "Please make it a safe march. Please protect us."

At the same Brown Chapel gathering grounds two days after Sunday's attack, instead of hundreds gathered, there were thousands. America's sense of outrage had banded together in direct violation of Wallace's proclamation and coalesced into a rallying force for civil disobedience. SCLC had requested a Court Order to prevent the police from interfering with this second march and most participants were confident Judge

Johnson would grant it. Instead, Judge Johnson handed down a Restraining Order against the march. The leadership was thrown into a panic when the injunction went against them. SCLC and the Committee knew Johnson to be sympathetic to their cause; Rusty's Uncle had been right about that at least. So what was the holdup? What was the reason? It put King between a rock and a hard place.

The thousands from all over the United States showing solidarity with the people of Selma intended to march at all costs. Yet the Doctor understood the need to honor the decision and cooperate with Judge Johnson if they were ever to be given a positive decree for a future march to Montgomery. He believed Johnson would ultimately hand down a decision permitting the march; he just wasn't going to be rushed.

It was obvious to King they couldn't begin to march to Montgomery with no preparation and so many people. It made sense to give Judge Johnson—and themselves—a bit more time. Yet the Steering Committee again refused King's request to wait a few more days to march; the leaders in Selma would wait no longer. So as a King Solomon compromise would have it, the great doctor determined they would march only until they reached an agreed upon point where they would be stopped peacefully by state troopers. At that point they would turn around. He could only hope the marchers would follow his lead and peacefully return to the church with him and avert another bloodbath.

With so many people arriving at Brown Chapel yard, Leslie didn't recognize anyone and felt adrift without Annie Lee. She stood alone, nervously waiting for direction.

Elverse, Mandy, and Carlton, gathered with Moses and Elmira, now sporting a cast on her broken arm. Carlton finished signing Elmira's cast and passed the pen to Mandy who likewise signed and passed the pen to Elverse. Under his name he wrote the date, March 9, 1965.

"This will be a day we remember all our lives," he said solemnly as he handed the pen back to Elmira.

"You're all now closer to my heart," she cooed in jest. Looking around, Elmira asked, "Anybody seen Leslie Cole?"

"Oh! We should have thought to tell her where to meet us," lamented Moses. "We got to do a better job of helping her since she's marching in Annie Lee's place."

"What makes you say that?" asked Mandy.

"Annie Lee told us when we visited with her yesterday," said Moses.

"Leslie's marching, too?" asked Carlton. "Cool!"

"Yes. Supposedly said that was the least she could do after what they did to Annie Lee," said Elmira. "Course, Annie Lee wasn't at all happy that Leslie decided to march in her stead."

"I see," said Mandy, studying her son's face. Elverse kept quiet.

A black nun wove her way through the crowd to Mandy and the two women greeted each other. "Ministers were overflowing in east wing last night. Your idea was brilliant. Bless you!"

The two women hugged briefly and then the nun rushed off while Elverse and Carlton registered bewilderment. Before they could ask Mandy what the nun meant, a murmur raced through the crowd and they heard someone shout, "The Doctor is here!" Carlton gasped and pushed forward to get a view of the podium and be up close to his hero.

Martin Luther King, Jr., stepped up to the soapbox and the crowd hushed. He looked over the thousands of faces. "The march is on," he claimed emphatically. The marchers gave a thunderous cheer. Mandy, Elverse, and Carlton clasped hands, overcome by the moment. King continued that it was a difficult and painful decision because he didn't know what might lie ahead. There could be more beatings. Who could predict what troopers might do? But he claimed they had a right to walk to Montgomery if their feet would get them there. His conscience gave him no choice.

Elverse turned to Moses, confused and anxious and said, "Surely we're not going to march into another confrontation?"

"It doesn't make sense with these thousands here," agreed Moses. "But I'll march on to Montgomery if they let us."

"Maybe Dr. King made a deal," Elmira mused. "People came from far away. They expected to march, ready or not."

King descended the soapbox and formed the first flank of five marchers. Realizing he couldn't hold the hand of the nun on his left who fingered her rosary or the rabbi on his right who held his prayer book, King instead linked their arms at the elbow and headed out for the street. Interlocking arms became the model for all the marchers who followed.

When the Turners and Washingtons formed their own flank and were told to link arms, Elmira moved to one end with her cast. Parade marshals walked beside the marchers and tensed when they saw a cordon of state troopers but a few blocks away. Instead of confronting the marchers, however, these troopers stepped aside. The parade marshals quickly spread word back through the marchers still waiting at the church.

"We are getting through!"

Winnie spotted Leslie and slid in next to her in order to march with a familiar face, not having found anyone from his airport ride. As the word of the forward movement reached the playground gate, Winnie linked Leslie's arm.

"We better get through," said Winnie amicably. "I came all the way from California to march."

Leslie barely reacted and gave him the slightest of smiles. Their flank exited onto the street. Winnie studied Leslie.

"You're not scared, are you?" he inquired politely.

"Scared?" Leslie replied. "No. I'm petrified."

"But today will be an inspirational high point in our lives. Just think. We're marching with Dr. King and we're changing the course of history," Winnie said.

"That's what my..." Leslie searched the right word to use. "...What the woman who raised me thought on Sunday when she marched. She's savoring her high point from a hospital bed."

"Oh," said Winnie. "I'm so sorry. Forgive me. I'm just a bleeding heart minister from the West coast. Winston Phillips is my name. Winnie naïve Phillips from California. Hi."

"As in 'the Pooh?" Leslie asked, allowing herself a small smile.

"The same," Winnie grinned. "But maybe not as smart."

"I'm Leslie Cole from Flint, Michigan. How do you do?"

The march proceeded to the base of the Pettus Bridge. A U.S. Federal Marshal stopped the parade before they could ascend the bridge and quickly read a portion of the Court Order.

"It is the order, judgment and decree of this Federal Court that herein for a temporary restraining order be and is hereby denied."

King looked squarely at the Marshal. "We are well aware of the order but we intend to march."

The Federal Marshal nodded and stated, "I do not intend to interfere with your movement." King returned the nod and the march moved forward. The flanks stretched all the way through the neighborhood back to Brown Chapel.

Late to the party, Choice drove his green Chevy well above the speed limit. Uncle was in the front and Sparky was in the back. They were singing "Dixie's Land" so loud, one could have seen their tonsils. The tires squealed as the car rounded a curve and passed a sign, "SELMA - 2 MILES." Maybe they could just make it before the marchers crossed the bridge.

King and his flank climbed Pettus Bridge and slowly crossed. The march extended a mile back. Again state troopers were waiting on the other side but today there were no volunteer posse men. No men on horses. No gas masks. Major Cloud was there, however, his bullhorn in hand. He turned it on.

"You are ordered to stop. This march will not continue," Cloud's voice crackled.

An aide handed King a bullhorn. He raised it and replied they had a right to march. The First Amendment protected their right to assemble. Two bullhorns speaking to each other. It would have been theater of the absurd had the stakes not been so high.

"You are ordered to stop where you are," Cloud answered.

King turned his bullhorn on again as he faced the Major and stated he respected Cloud's order. Could they pray?

Major Cloud's bullhorn clicked on. He told King the marchers could have their prayer but then they needed to return to their church.

King nodded to the troopers standing in front of him. He announced they would pray then handed the bullhorn back to his aide and kneeled on the pavement. The marchers looked like a football wave at a stadium as each flank took its cue from the one in front of them and knelt. Troopers continued to stand at attention, indifferent to the spectacle. There was an eerie silence. Breaking the silence, Cloud roared an order through his bullhorn.

"Troopers withdraw!" The troopers fell back to either side of the highway, creating an open path. Marchers rose to their feet, murmuring and confused.

"It's another Wallace trick," exclaimed Elmira. "They want us to break the law."

"That's right," agreed Moses. "They want us to defy the Federal Court Order so they can club us again."

"We will turn back, won't we?" asked Elverse. "We won't be dumb enough to march through those troopers again?"

"Fool us once, shame on them," Mandy concurred. "Fool us twice, shame on us."

King was again handed his bullhorn and turned to the crowd. "Let us return to our church and complete our fight in court."

With that, he swung his flank around and began to thread the marchers back along the open side of the bridge, returning to the church where they had started.

"Well, I guess that's it then," said Winnie, disappointed as they approached the point to turn around.

"I'm relieved," admitted Leslie. "It doesn't mean your trip was wasted. This show of people will have an impact. We'll be noticed just like when King organized his march on Washington."

"From your lips to God's ear. Maybe numbers will make a difference. Maybe our government will finally get behind voting rights. It's crazy that we're fighting in Vietnam and ignoring what's wrong right here. How can we say we're the leader of the free world if our own people aren't free to vote?"

"I feel so strongly about that," agreed Leslie. "We can't call our country a democracy if everyone doesn't have a vote."

"I think some people would be quite happy if we weren't a democracy. Gets in the way of their power."

Leslie and Winnie reached the point to turn around and saw close up the state troopers standing on either side of the road. Leslie sucked in her fear. Winnie took in their faces and tried to see what kind of human being was behind the uniform. Who were these men calling themselves peace officers?

There was some mumbling and grousing from fellow marchers but all cooperated and followed King's lead. They turned back.

Since the march ended early, Winnie had no particular place to be. Leslie planned to head for the hospital and told Winnie Annie Lee would want to hear all about it. It dawned on Leslie that she wanted to share every detail with Annie Lee. She was actually proud she had marched and began to see why it meant so much to Annie Lee. It also felt a bit safer. It was no longer a local issue; the country was now paying attention. If the march to Montgomery occurred in a few days, she would be content to postpone leaving.

"Would you like to go with me and meet Annie Lee?" Leslie asked Winnie.

"Sure," Winnie readily agreed. He was happy to meet someone who had been dedicated to the movement for so many years. Besides, it would distract him from the fact that he had already spent his daily food allowance on lunch. There would be no dinner beyond a possible cup of coffee.

When they walked into Annie Lee's hospital room, Leslie was relieved to see Annie Lee's eyes were no longer bandaged and Jackson was again by her bedside. He rose and introductions were made. Leslie and Winnie pulled up chairs and formed a circle around Annie Lee's bed.

"I practically had to hog tie her to the bed to keep her in this here room," Jackson said, chortling. "She kept saying, 'I want to go, let me go!' So I had to say, 'Yeah, well, people in Hell want ice water, too, but they don't get it.'" It was an old joke but everyone laughed congenially. Jackson did indeed know how to handle Annie Lee's determined willfulness.

Leslie described the march to Annie Lee, painting a picture of how thousands had created a long line that stretched all the way back to Brown Chapel once they reached Pettus Bridge and the troopers had obviously been instructed to stand down. There was to be no violence.

"I'm wondering if folks who came from so far away were mad they didn't get to march further?" Annie Lee asked pointedly, looking directly at Winnie.

"Well," Winnie offered, "it was a long way to come for such a short march. I noticed there were a number of people who did seem pretty peeved that we didn't push on to Montgomery but I have to trust there was a reason."

"I wonder if King agreed to something we don't know about?" Leslie said. "It seemed choreographed."

"I'd like to think that with so many people, even if it was symbolic, that our short march will impact getting your permission to march to Montgomery without any problems," said Winnie.

"It's definitely for the best you didn't go on today," said Jackson. "It's gonna take a whole lot of planning to get folks to Montgomery. You just can't expect to walk fifty some miles and eat wild berries and sleep by the side of the road with cute little bunnies. This ain't no fairytale."

"It's real, that's for sure," laughed Annie Lee, touching one of her bruises. "You see, brother Winnie, we're working for an injunction that'll keep our law enforcement from stopping our march to Montgomery. In the meantime, while we wait for the judge to issue it, we'll keep marchin' round town every day as we originally planned."

"Ah, now I understand. I heard some people talking about an injunction and saying it could take a long time," mused Winnie. "I don't know how things work in the South, but they seemed to think it won't come quickly."

"We're used to waiting," said Annie Lee.

"But we don't want to wait too long," interjected Leslie, her statement full of meaning. Annie Lee ignored it.

"Where you staying anyway, brother Winnie?" Annie Lee asked.

"Just down the hall, actually, in another wing," Winnie said, grinning.

"That so?" "I'd heard they turned over west wing to a dormitory but didn't believe it. How are you getting along?"

"Fine, just fine. It's the best ecumenical conference I've ever attended. I stayed up late last night with a priest, a fundamentalist circuit preacher, A Baptist minister, and a rabbi. We debated what the role of religion should be in political issues."

"Really," said Annie Lee, interested. "And what'd you decide?"

"No Matter what your view is, for or against, it can be backed up by Scripture."

That got a big laugh.

∽

EIGHT

Leslie and Winnie strolled down the main street in the black neighborhood filled with many marchers looking to catch a bite to eat somewhere. Disgruntled white restaurant owners, disgusted by their town's troublemaker invasion, were refusing service so choices were very limited.

"Annie Lee's quite a strong woman," Winnie noted. "A woman of conviction."

"Some would call it stubborn," said Leslie.

"I think she's admirable," Winnie said.

"She is that," Leslie allowed.

"So, will you be driving back to Michigan this weekend?" Winnie asked.

"I think so? I originally came to take Annie Lee back with me until things cool down here. But she won't budge. Even now, after all that's happened to her, she won't leave. It makes me sad to think she won't come with me but I need to get back to my children. I didn't come to march."

"Oh, no?" Winnie said. "Then why did you march today?"

"Why did I march today," Leslie pondered. "The real reason?"

"What ever reason you want to give me."

"I hoped by threatening to march, Annie Lee would agree to leave with me if I promised her I wouldn't. She was not in favor of me getting involved so I thought we could strike a bargain."

"But she didn't try to stop you?" asked Winnie gently.

"Oh, yes." Leslie looked pensive. "She did. She was very much against me marching. But it didn't make her agree to leave with me. So I didn't stop myself."

"Which means… what?"

Leslie was silent. "I don't know. I came down to pull Annie Lee out of all this trouble without understanding how much voting here means to her. How much it means to the country. I… I never realized that by her not voting she was being kept in her place." Leslie scoffed at herself. "Since I've been here and see how blatant the racism actually is, I'm embarrassed that I could have been so blind."

They walked on in silence as each wrestled with their actions: for Leslie, what it meant to march for herself, not just for Annie Lee, and for Winnie to go into debt and fly across the country to be part of the protest. Neither of them fully comprehended the deeper aspects of their actions.

"What about you?" Leslie queried. "How long do you plan to stay?"

"Just until tomorrow," said Winnie. "I'm on a very limited budget."

"Wow," said Leslie. "You really did come all the way across the country just to be here today?"

"Felt I had to, you know?" said Winnie sheepishly. "Not just talk the talk but walk the walk? Of course," he admitted ruefully, "I thought we'd be walking further. In fact, I thought we'd walk so far today I would need a day to recuperate so made my return ticket for tomorrow night's red-eye."

They snickered.

"I guess it is pretty far to come for symbolism," said Leslie.

"Yep," Winnie agreed. "I feel a little foolish. It was darn expensive to get here. Airlines don't give discounts for good intentions."

"You weren't foolish," countered Leslie. "Great numbers really do matter and you can say you marched with Martin Luther King, like you said."

"Yah. I guess the length of time shouldn't be the measure of the experience. It helps my impulsive decision to know our symbolic march might change what's really going on down here. In California I didn't have a clue."

"I was raised down here," Leslie said. "It's not really a surprise to me."

"Oh?" said Winnie. "When did you leave?"

"As soon as I could."

Winnie and Leslie continued walking down the street.

"So what's California like?" she asked. "I've never been but I sure would like to go sometime."

"It's a fantastic state," said Winnie. "It's got everything, a beautiful coastline with fabulous beaches, mountains, deserts—"

"—Hollywood!" interrupted Leslie.

Winnie laughed. "Hollywood," he allowed. "Great weather, lots of orange trees, interesting people who are open to new ideas, and peaceniks. Lots of people are against the war."

"Huh," considered Leslie. "Do you preach about the war from your pulpit?"

There was a long pause. "I don't have a pulpit currently," said Winnie.

Leslie was embarrassed for asking.

"Oh. I'm sorry. I didn't mean to pry."

"It's OK," said Winnie. "You didn't pry. It was a natural assumption. I resigned. I don't know if I'll get another church. I don't know if I even want another church. All I really know is I want to remain in California and be close to my daughter."

"Oh, so you're married?" said Leslie.

There was another long pause. "We're separated," Winnie revealed.

Now Leslie was really embarrassed.

"I keep asking the wrong questions, don't I?"

"No, actually you're asking the right questions. I just don't have the right answers yet. I see something like this... this activism for equality and trying to change the way our country is... it... it makes me realize that's how I want to be of use. Giving comfortable sermons to comfortable people seems a little hollow somehow compared to a minister like Dr. King who has dedicated his life's work to making other people's lives better."

"Well, we can't all be like Dr. King. Some of us have to be content with little steps."

"Don't get me wrong. I'm not comparing myself to Dr. King. I could never come close to being like him. But he is incredibly inspiring. He's helping me get clear about what the next chapter in my life should be."

Leslie didn't know what to say. She felt his confusion and could only nod as she listened. She thought how hard it must be for him to have chosen a profession only to realize it wasn't fulfilling him. And he had no family to sustain him while he searched for meaning. She offered up a quick prayer of thanks for her family and felt lucky to have such a supportive base. David may be worried about her but he would never stop her from acting on what she felt compelled to do.

They passed the Walker Café, a popular hangout in the Negro community that was filled to capacity with marchers. It seemed to be the only restaurant in town that would feed the ministers who weren't eating with their hosts. Seated at the front window table, the Turners and Washingtons were relishing ribs and greens.

"Oh, look," said Moses inside the restaurant, gazing up from his plate. "There's Leslie now." He knocked hard on the glass and both Leslie and Winnie turned in their direction. Moses, Elmira and Carlton waved. Leslie waved back.

"Leslie Cole is married, isn't she?" Mandy asked.

Elverse gave her a dark look and waved, too.

As Leslie and Winnie rounded a corner, Leslie shook off their pensive conversation.

"Hey," she said. "An ice cream shop. Let's stop and get some." They entered the store and there at the counter were Reverends Frey and Engel. Frey looked up and recognized Winnie.

"Hey, hey!" said Frey. "Good to see you again. Winnie, right?"

"That's right. And this was my flank partner, Mrs. Leslie Cole. Leslie, Reverends Jim Frey and Anton Engel." Engel extended his hand.

"Hi. Nice to see you again. I remember you from the lodging table. It must be a real challenge to be helping in this cause. There's so much racial tension."

Leslie shook his hand, then Frey's. Before she could correct the impression that she was a Selma resident, Jim spoke up.

"Wasn't the march astonishing?" he asked enthusiastically. "So much love. And what a turnout! I think the power we felt today will overpower racism. So, I'm buying. What'll you have?"

"Why, thank you," Leslie said. "Let's see." She studied the flavor chart. "How about a Rocky Road?"

"Ah, a woman after my own heart," Jim grinned. "You must have children? I have four and Rocky Road's the house favorite." Jim turned to Winnie. "And what would you like?"

Winnie laughed. "Sounds like I better pick the winner, Rocky Road?"

"Right you are," thundered Jim. He called out to the server. "Two more Rocky Road cones, please! There's a run on Rocky Road."

"Are you leaving tonight?" Winnie asked Jim.

"You know, my bag was in a car headed for the airport when I said, 'no, there's more to learn here' and I pulled it out. King also pleaded with us to stay on just in case the restraining order was lifted and the march would be allowed in the next day or so." Jim was thoughtful for a minute. "Anton agreed with me so we'll at least spend the night. The folks who put us up were kind enough to extend our stay. The people of Selma are so hospitable."

Anton was burning with his new resolve. "We're on our way to the SCLC office to talk about what we can do once we're back home to keep the momentum going. Even if we don't live in Selma, there are things we can do in our own states to keep the spotlight on Selma. Care to join us?"

Winnie looked questionably at Leslie as Jim walked over to the register to pay for the cones.

"Tell you what," Leslie said. "You three go on to your meeting and then come to the house for a little supper. I'm sure you haven't eaten. We're already having our dessert so I'll fix something light." She fished in her purse for a pen and slip of paper. "Here. I'll write down the address."

"Boy, that sounds great," enthused Anton. "So nice of you. Very cool! We get to taste some real down home Southern cooking."

Leslie smiled. "Well, not exactly," she replied as she handed them Annie Lee's address and phone number.

"Actually," Winnie said, "Leslie doesn't live here, either. She came from Flint, Michigan."

Jim joined them. "Shall we push out?"

Leslie didn't explain why she was in Selma and was just as glad. They parted company, saluting each other with their cones. The three ministers headed for the SCLC office, talking religion between bites of ice cream.

The ministers came to a cross street and turned right. As they discussed living by example they began to pass the Silver Moon Café, a rather unsavory dive of a diner, suspected to be a KKK hangout. Four white men emerged from the restaurant and stood glaring at the clerics as they passed, deep in their exchange. Winnie looked up and checked their surroundings. Anton took another lick of his cone.

"Then, he says I can't have both," exclaimed Anton.

"Did we take a wrong turn?" Winnie asked. "Did either of you bring the map they gave us when we signed in?"

The white men fell in behind the ministers. Jim was earnestly listening to Anton's tale and didn't register Winnie's question.

"Handing out food is as much a prayer as sitting in a pew," Jim contended forcefully.

"Right," Anton agreed. "I considered his statement such a narrow view of what the role of a minister should be."

The four men picked up their pace. Winnie saw them out of the corner of his eye and could smell the mist of alcohol enveloping them. If he didn't turn around, maybe the men would leave them alone. Instead, they came closer. Winnie whispered to Jim and Anton, "Walk a little faster."

"Hey, white niggers," the leader shouted menacingly as he closed in. "What the hell are you doing 'round here?"

Caught off guard, Anton turned around to see who was speaking and looked into the cold eyes of the speaker. The men rushed the ministers.

"Want to be a real nigger?" asked another and swung a baseball bat, striking Jim fiercely at the base of his skull. Jim slumped to the ground. The muggers quickly surrounded the ministers and knocked Anton and Winnie to the ground, too. Their ice cream cones went flying.

"Help!" Winnie screamed.

In a tight circle the attackers punched and kicked the ministers. Winnie and Anton rolled their bodies into balls, protecting themselves as they had been instructed, but Jim just lay there. As fast as the attack began, it ended with the hooligans dashing away under the cover of growing darkness. Anton immediately crawled over to Frey.

"Jim! Jim," he cried. "Are you all right?"

Winnie and Anton scrambled to their feet and slowly pulled Jim up. He staggered as he tried to speak.

"Dizzy. I feel so… head… pain." His speech was slurred.

Anton was alarmed. "We've got to find a hospital. Something is terribly wrong."

Winnie was suddenly very clear about which direction they needed to go. He took one of Jim's arms, Anton took the other, and they walked unsteadily, retracing their steps. Before they reached Good Samaritan Hospital they saw the Burwell Infirmary and rushed their stumbling friend inside there.

A distinguished black doctor greeted them and immediately saw he had an emergency on his hands. He escorted the men to the x-ray table in a tiny room off the small waiting room normally filled only with Negroes. Tonight it was empty. Gently, they laid Jim on the table.

"You men back up against the wall," the Doctor ordered.

Anton and Winnie stood against the wall as the doctor scurried behind a screen to take the image. Just as the doctor looked out through the little square window, Jim convulsed violently. The doctor, Winnie, and Anton rushed to his side.

"He may be bleeding internally," the doctor stated. "We don't have any blood here. I'll call for an ambulance."

The doctor ran to his cramped office while Winnie stroked Jim's head. Anton began to rummage madly through the mostly empty cupboards. The bloody Sunday march had taken its toll on their supplies and the shelves were bare.

"Hold on," Winnie said softly to Frey. "We're going to a hospital."

Anton was frantic. "Damn! Where's there a blanket? Where's anything around here?"

An antiquated ambulance sped out of town carrying Reverend Frey on a stretcher with Winnie and Anton at his side. Up in front with the young driver was the good doctor from Burwell. Suddenly there was a loud BANG and the ambulance lurched to a stop.

"What?" the doctor asked.

"Just got a flat," the driver explained as he jumped out of the driver's seat. He ran around to the back of the ambulance, the doctor following him, and they both starred down at the blown tire.

"Keep driving on the rim until we reach a phone," the doctor instructed. "We've got to keep going."

The driver nodded and banged on the side panel of the ambulance as the doctor scrambled back into the front seat.

"Got a flat!" he shouted. "It's gonna be a little rocky."

A mile down the road they limped into a gas station. The doctor leapt from the vehicle and raced to the freestanding phone booth. A sheriff's patrol car cruising down the road noticed the ambulance and pulled off the highway and drove up alongside the ambulance with its smoking tire. Two deputies got out of their squad car and approached the driver who jumped from his seat. Both deputies turned on their flashlights and fingered their guns with their other hand. They shined their flashlights on the black driver's anxious face. The driver kept his hands in the air as he spoke.

"Praise God you saw us, officers," he said respectfully. "Please help us. We were on our way to Birmingham Hospital when I got a flat. Got a patient in real bad condition."

The deputies didn't respond and instead sauntered around the ambulance to look at the back tire shot to hell. The older deputy shined his light on the tire while the younger deputy drew his gun and opened the back door of the ambulance. To his surprise he found three white men. He took in Jim. Winnie and Anton stared back.

"What's his problem?" the deputy inquired. "Drunk?"

"Whacked unconscious by a baseball bat," said Winnie.

Another ambulance screeched to a halt on the highway and made a wild turn into the gas station. It's elderly driver pulled up to the disabled ambulance and hopped out. The senior deputy approached him.

"You're driving' awful fast, boy," he said.

"Yes, sir," the old driver replied. "They said it was a bad emergency, sir."

The doctor rushed over to the men.

"Why didn't you use your siren?" asked the younger deputy suspiciously.

"It's broke, sir," the driver answered.

The doctor tried to take charge.

"Please," pleaded the doctor. "We have no time to lose. We need to move this patient to the other ambulance."

The deputies stepped aside, crossed their arms, and watched as Anton and Winnie struggled to slide Frey's stretcher to the waiting drivers and doctor outside the ambulance. Once Jim was out of the first ambulance, Winnie and Anton helped carry him into the second ambulance. The doctor addressed the deputies.

"Since this ambulance has no siren, will you escort us to Birmingham?"

"Well, now," the elder sheriff drawled. "That's not our job." The doctor looked hard at the deputies, searching for a shred of humanity in their faces.

"I'll radio ahead that you're coming," relented the younger deputy.

As the drivers, Winnie, and Anton struggled to put the stretcher arms into the cradles, it became clear the arms didn't match the newer ambulance. There was no way to lock the stretcher securely into place. Winnie slid in next to the stretcher and placed his hands around the arm and cradle.

"We'll hold them in place," Winnie offered. "Let's just go."

Anton nodded and slid in on the other side and clasped his hands around the other cradle.

"Right," the doctor agreed. Doors were slammed and the ambulance pealed out, the driver honking his horn insistently as the police stood and watched them go.

The sway of the stretcher rubbed both Winnie and Anton's palms. The ambulance rounded a curve and the arms slipped and pinched but the ministers never let go. Soon small blisters began to form as their skin was rubbed raw.

When the ambulance arrived at University Hospital in Birmingham, a medical team was waiting for them. The team blasted through the emergency doors and immediately moved Reverend Frey to a gurney. Two orderlies turned him on his side when they saw vomit and a nurse swiftly stuck a needle in his arm that was attached to an I.V. She ran along side the gurney, holding the I.V. bottle aloft as Frey was rushed inside. Anton and Winnie stood in a daze under the unnatural yellow light of the emergency entrance. They looked down at their blistered hands and realized they too needed a bit of medical attention and joined the emergency waiting room.

Leslie's light supper preparations were abruptly halted by a phone call from Winnie. He told her the news of the attack and where they were.

"Oh my goodness, Winnie," she said. "I'm so very sorry. Are you at the hospital now?"

"Yes. Reverend Frey is in radiation and Anton and I are waiting to be seen in the emergency room."

"The emergency room? What's wrong?"

"Nothing serious; just a few blisters on our hands. I'll explain later."

"How did you get there?"

"We came in the ambulance with Jim."

"Will it bring you back?"

"I'm pretty sure it left as soon as the hospital took Jim in."

"I'll leave right now and come and get you both."

"No, no, that's too much to ask. You could do me a big favor though, and call United Airlines and cancel my flight tonight."

"Of course," she said. Winnie gave her his flight number.

"Thanks, so much. I'll get a cab back to town. Anton contacted the Unitarians and they don't want him to return to Selma so he's remaining here in Birmingham."

"No. Don't call a cab. I'm on my way. Stay put." Leslie had gotten the picture that Winnie had very little money and an almost two hour cab ride back to Selma would have emptied his wallet. "Bye," she said and hung up before Winnie could protest.

Her mind racing, she stood a quick minute to figure out what she needed to do. First she called the airline. Next she found Annie Lee's phone directory and looked up the Turner's telephone number and called to relay the news. Next she called University Hospital and got directions, put the food she was preparing in the refrigerator, grabbed her coat, and rushed out the door.

Elverse replaced the phone receiver with a trembling hand. Mandy walked out from their bedroom in her nurse's uniform and Carlton looked up from reading his history book.

"Who was that?" Mandy asked.

"Leslie Cole."

"Leslie?"

"There's been more violence," answered Elverse. "A minister was clubbed tonight. A Reverend Frey."

"Oh my Lord. How hurt is he?" asked Mandy.

"Don't know. But I got a bad feeling about it. Some whites attacked him in front of a diner. Sounded like the Silver Moon."

"Oh, good gosh," scowled Mandy. "Why do you suppose he was on that street? The poor man. I wonder if they brought him to our hospital?"

"No. They took him to Birmingham. He was with two other ministers but evidently they weren't hurt as bad. Leslie's on her way to pick them up now."

"Birmingham," repeated Mandy. "Then he must be really hurt." Mandy moved to her husband and took his hand. Carlton rose from the couch and went to stand by his parents. Elverse shook his head slowly.

"So much madness. I'm not sure marches are the way to go anymore. After eight weeks we seem to be making things worse, not better."

"But Dad," Carlton said, "Jim Bevel says when you march that's how everybody takes notice."

"Dying is a big price to pay so others will take notice, son."

"Let us pray so this Reverend isn't added to the list," said Mandy. Elverse agreed and the three of them fell to their knees and formed a circle in the middle of their living room. Wordlessly, they bowed their heads and offered a prayer before Elverse took Mandy to work and called the other members of the Committee with the news.

It was well after midnight when Leslie pulled her Ford into Selma's Good Samaritan Hospital parking lot. She drove right to the side entrance of the wing that housed the ministers to drop Winnie off.

"I can't thank you enough, Leslie." Winnie reached over the seat and held her hand as best he could with his bandaged hand.

"Get some rest," Leslie said.

"It was way above the call of duty for you to drive all the way to Birmingham to pick me up."

"Don't be silly," said Leslie. "I'm just sorry the day ended like this. Reverend Frey was so excited about being a part of the effort down here, and the march went off so peacefully."

"I guess you never know what's seething underneath peace."

Leslie regarded Winnie who appeared to have aged years in one night.

"Will you reschedule your flight for tomorrow?"

"I won't leave now," Winnie said. "The authorities are bound to want to interview Anton and me. Maybe identify the guys once they're caught."

"Caught? I'm sorry to say down here it won't matter. It's catch and release," Leslie said with disgust. She patted his knee. "Well, Winnie, if I don't see you again, I'm glad we met and marched together, despite the horrible ending. Get some sleep. You've been through hell. Good night."

"I wish it was good," said Winnie sadly. He got out of the car but before he closed the door, he said, "Thanks again. And God bless."

"Good luck to you. Call me if you need any more help."

Winnie walked up to the hospital doors, grateful he had a place to sleep and had to knock on the glass as the doors were already locked. Leslie watched him go, in no hurry to drive home to an empty house. She sat there with the motor running, wishing she could visit Annie Lee and break the grim news to her. Annie Lee would be so upset. Her movement was unraveling. No, her movement was on fire and the flames were consuming her cause, just as Leslie had feared.

Once inside the hospital, Winnie greeted the night nurse and explained why he was entering so late. The night security watchman who let him in shook his head in shame for his town. He took Winnie's arm and told him not to worry; he would insure all the doors were locked tight and would stand guard all through the night. He would make sure Winnie was kept safe. Winnie signed in then tiptoed down the corridor, carefully stepping around ministers who had remained overnight and were fast asleep on the mattresses lined up end to end like freight cars on the floor.

Winnie went to the Men's room and realized how cold he felt. After using the urinal, he ran hot water over his fingertips, trying to avoid getting his bandages wet. He returned to the hall and searched for another empty mattress. Finding one, he crawled onto it, removed his shoes, unfolded the blanket a nun had carefully placed on top of a pillow, and tossed it over his legs. He leaned back against the wall. His head was pounding and he was certain lying down would make it worse. Sleep was not an option.

The door at the end of the hall opened and a shaft of light silhouetted a nurse carrying blankets. Mandy slipped softly into the hall and slowly checked each mattress as she passed. She spotted Winnie sitting up and picked her way around sleeping bodies until she reached him. She knelt down next to him.

"Extra blanket?" Mandy whispered.

"Yes, thank you," said Winnie. "I can't seem to warm up."

Mandy tucked a blanket around his shoulders and pulled up the one already on his legs to cover his midsection. She spread a third blanket over his feet and tucked in all the edges. He looked like a papoose.

"You've had a traumatic day," she spoke gently. "Your body is responding to all you've been through. How are your hands? Need some pain killers?" Winnie waved off the suggestion and shook his head.

"I had no idea the South was so, so savage," he whispered. "What you people must deal with. This is America?" Mandy sat back and lowered her head, allowing him to talk.

"And… and Jim Frey. Such a good man. I don't understand. Why?" Winnie fought breaking down and began to rock back and forth. Mandy, torn between empathy and the color barrier, gingerly put her arm around his shoulder. With her touch Winnie crumbled into her arms and began to cry in halting muffled sobs that escaped his best efforts to keep from waking anyone up. Mandy took him in her arms and comforted him. It was the most natural and right thing to do.

"It's OK," Mandy whispered. "Let it go. It's OK."

"I'm sorry," Winnie squeaked in between his stifled cries. "I just can't seem to wrap my head around the evil some people are capable of." Winnie pressed his head against Mandy's breastbone to muffle his heaving cries. She patted his back and held him as she would have held her son had Carlton needed consoling.

"Tell you what," Mandy said softly. "I'm taking you home when my shift is over. You need some privacy after what you've been through. You don't need to be trying to sleep here on the floor."

The next day anger hung over Selma like black putrid smoke. Leslie arrived at the hospital to see if Winnie needed anything only to be told that Winnie had left so she walked on to visit Annie Lee who had already learned of the attack from the early morning nursing shift. Word had spread quickly for people to meet at Brown Chapel and over a thousand defiant individuals arrived. Annie Lee was frustrated that she had to remain at the hospital and probably would have gotten up and left if Leslie hadn't arrived just as she was about to sneak out.

After a short service, people pored out of the chapel and made no attempt to hide the fact they were marching. It was another civil disobedient demonstration challenging the restraining order. They didn't care. No attempt was made to space out their flanks and marchers again linked arms to form short horizontal lines behind the front flank where Sisters Stella and Mary, and two others from Ohio, marched with Hosea Williams. Elmira, Elverse, and even Mandy, who looked exhausted with so little sleep, formed a flank. Yet Mandy had insisted Winnie stay home and sleep. Moses and Carlton were at school.

Leslie, after visiting Annie Lee, went directly to the SCLC office to answer phones and place calls so Elmira and the staff could participate in the spontaneous protest for Reverend Frey.

Selma Police Chief Baker was at the barbershop getting a trim of his already short hair. The barber had just finished shaving him when an out of breath patrolman yanked open the shop door.

"They're marching! Hundreds of them are coming!" he yelled to Baker. Baker ejected from the chair, threw off the cape and rushed to his sergeant.

"Find out where Clark is, quick," Baker ordered as he flew through the door and bolted for his Chrysler. The dumbfounded barber held his scissors in mid air, statue-like, as he watched his client disappear.

Baker immediately went into overdrive and ordered his patrolmen to run to Sylvan Street and form a blockade by creating a human wall line on the pavement in front of the marchers. Next he picked up the mayor and drove to the blockade and came to a screeching stop. Baker and the mayor jumped out of the car just as the marchers arrived at the police line. Smitherman raised the bullhorn he was carrying and addressed the marchers.

"Invoking the emergency powers of my office, I ban all marches. My Director of Public Safety completely agrees."

Smitherman then gratefully turned the bullhorn over to his chief. Nothing had prepared him for his city being torn apart and he was at a loss how to control the crowd.

Hosea Williams shouted back. "We want to march to the courthouse for Reverend Frey." His voice was shaking with anger.

Baker lifted the bullhorn and replied, "We are stopping all demonstrations. It is too risky under the present circumstances."

"Then we'll hold a vigil right here," Williams answered defiantly. He turned to the marchers behind him. "Let us pray for Reverend Frey. Let us pray here, on this very spot."

The nuns immediately knelt down on the pavement, caring not one wit about getting their habits dirty. The hundreds behind them followed suit. Baker sighed and returned to his car to confer with Smitherman who was leaning against the hood. The police line shifted their weight nervously as they waited for more orders.

Baker went to the trunk of his car and pulled out a rope. He walked toward the protesters as a circuit preacher stood up and railed against him and his police line.

"What is law and order if it is used to protect evil, Mr. Baker?" the preacher demanded.

Baker did not respond and strode to one side of the street and tied the end of his rope around a tree. He then unraveled the rope as he crossed the street. People were now watching his actions.

"It will take more than a rope to stop us," the preacher shouted. "We will keep vigil until our fallen comrade is out of danger."

Baker tied the other end of the rope to an iron fence and pulled the knot tight. He barked orders for his men to continue standing watch just on the other side of the rope. He strode back to Smitherman. They got back into his car and slowly drove away.

"What do you think they'll do?" Smitherman asked nervously. "Do you think they'll stay behind the rope?"

"Don't know. But we took the wind out of their sails so I think we'll be OK. In a few hours I'll call most of the men away and then I'll rotate a few of them to on-line duty until the march breaks up. They'll get bored just standing there pretty quick."

But the marchers did not break up. Demonstrators came and went and returned. They took bathroom breaks and slipped out for a quick meal, or left to change into a heavier coat or wrap themselves in a blanket, but it became clear they intended to remain throughout the night at the rope. Winnie arrived in the afternoon looking more rested and was also determined to remain through the night. The spot had become a vigil.

Elverse, however, insisted on taking Mandy home. It was a rare day off for her and she desperately needed to rejuvenate herself if she was to continue her double shift pace. They retired early that evening to reconnect and simply hold each other close.

Mandy lay in her husband's arms and stroked them tenderly.

Elverse said quietly, "So many people willing to put their lives on hold and stand up for our cause. I can hardly believe it. It's just so powerful."

"I feel like we're stealing time away from the rope," said Mandy. "But I'm so tired, I knew sleeping on the curb tonight wasn't going to cut it."

"You had to take a break." Elverse caressed her face. "I'm so proud of you," he said softly.

"Me? Why?"

"Because you're totally committed now. And you did a real charitable thing to bring Reverend Phillips home."

Mandy shrugged. "He needed it after being attacked. He was in shock."

Elverse kissed her head and tightened his arms around her trim waist. "Mandy… I hope you're proud of me, too," Elverse said haltingly.

Mandy was taken aback and turned to touch her husband's cheek. "Of course I'm proud of you. Why wouldn't I be?"

"The violence, it… I seem to lack courage. I've had to realize I'm not so brave when it comes to these confrontations. I'm not setting a good enough example for Carlton."

"Honey. You're scared and you march anyway. That's the definition of courage! I'd worry about your sanity if you weren't scared. Besides. You and Carlton are quick. You can run if things get violent again. That's not being weak. That's being smart. Aunty Annie Lee, now, she is a worry. Leslie's right about that."

"You're agreeing with Leslie?"

"Just giving credit where credit's due."

Elverse kissed her. "I'm glad we're in this together."

"It's pretty basic."

Elverse kissed her again. "I'm all for getting back to basics." He nuzzled her neck. "I love you, Mandy Jane. I love you so much."

They kissed more passionately. Mandy unbuttoned her gown and Elverse slipped into his wife's waiting arms.

ॐ

NINE

The next day Leslie was trying to control the stress that kept her stomach churning as she drove out of the Good Samaritan Hospital parking lot. She had parked in the lot just long enough to run up to Annie Lee's room and gather up Annie Lee's things only to find Annie Lee arguing with the nurse about having to be wheeled to the exit.

"I'll get the car and meet you at the front entrance," Leslie said and whisked out of the room with the shopping bag of Annie Lee's belongings before Annie Lee could turn on her. Now that Annie Lee was being discharged, Leslie worried Annie Lee might discharge *her* and insist she return to Flint alone.

Leslie drove up to the entrance and ran around to the passenger side to open the door, smiling her best smile as Annie Lee approached in a wheel chair. It had been a tough couple of days visiting Annie Lee who was constantly cross. Annie Lee was done being a patient and wanted only to be in the streets marching again with her friends. The nurse wheeled Annie Lee to the car and Annie Lee started to rise.

"You wait," snapped the nun as she set the break.

"Heavens to Betsy, don't know why I had to be wheeled out like a cripple," Annie Lee grumbled. "I can walk."

"Hospital policy," the nurse replied, exasperation in her voice. It was obvious she was relieved to see her patient leave; they had locked horns all morning. With great dignity Annie Lee rose from the chair and plopped into the front seat. Leslie closed the car door and turned to the nurse who was adjusting her wimple.

"Thank you," Leslie said gratefully, her gaze heavy with meaning. The nurse only nodded and wheeled the chair back into the hospital as Leslie took the driver's seat and left.

Leslie headed toward Annie Lee's house and kept trying to think of a way to approach the question burning inside her: would Annie Lee now leave with her? They rode in silence until Annie Lee said, "Let's drop by the vigil first."

Relieved for the distraction, Leslie readily agreed. "Great idea," she said. "You can see our 'Berlin Wall.'"

Leslie changed course and arrived at Sylvan Street and parked the car. A few boisterous teenage boys were teaching a group of nuns a newly worded rendition of "Joshua Fit The Battle of Jericho" behind the rope.

THE BERLIN WALL SONG – (*to the tune of "Joshua Fit the Battle of Jericho"*)
"We've got a rope that's a Berlin wall,
Berlin wall, Berlin wall.
We've got a rope that's a Berlin wall,
In Selma, Alabama."

There were several verses describing the conflict but the last verse was upbeat. Civil rights music always strove to end on a positive note.
"Love is the thing that will make it fall.
Make it fall, make it fall.
Love is the thing that will make it fall.
In Selma, Alabama!"

Leslie and Annie Lee alighted from the car and walked toward the clapping and singing of the hundreds assembled in back of the rope. For a vigil, it was quite joyous. Many were swaying as if they were in the Brown Chapel AME Church choir. The nuns who had joined in the song were swinging their veils wildly to and fro, having the most fun.

Annie Lee broke into a great big grin at the sight; it was the first time she appeared truly happy in days. They walked around the tree to the other side of the rope where the stationed line of police still stood.

Winnie saw them and ambled up. He attempted to be heard above the singing. "Hi!" He yelled. "Glad to see you're out of the hospital, Annie Lee." They hugged.

"Hi yourself," said Annie Lee. "Will you look at this!" A self-satisfied smile broke into her hearty laugh.

"You're still here," said Leslie to Winnie.

The song ended and a cheer filled the air. Even the police couldn't help but grin. Winnie no longer had to shout.

"The Turners were kind enough to invite me to stay with them so I guess I'll be around a little while longer," explained Winnie.

"Bless you," enthused Annie Lee. "You been to visit your Reverend Frey friend since that despicable night?"

"I've thought about it," admitted Winnie. "They flew his wife in yesterday so I don't know if I'd be intruding? I really would like to let him know how much we're all pulling for him here in Selma. He was the first person I met when I came and I feel, well… I'm not sure what I feel except he's already like a good friend to me." Leslie and Annie Lee nodded.

"I'd be happy to drive you over there after I take Annie Lee home," said Leslie.

"Y'all can go on. I want to soak this in for a while. I'll find a ride," said Annie Lee.

"No way," objected Leslie. "You need to go home and rest your first day out."

"Leslie May?" scolded Annie Lee. "You wouldn't be telling me what to do now, would you?"

Leslie smiled apologetically and flushed. "No, of course not."

"Good. So run along then. I'll be fine."

Leslie and Winnie departed and Annie Lee wove her way through the crowd, stopping every few feet to be greeted by those who knew she had been in the hospital. She was given great big bear hugs just as she was known to do.

On the other side of the crowded vigil street Elverse, Carlton, and Moses sat on the curb, eating sandwiches. Moses shook his head as he wiped his mouth with a paper napkin.

"Those attackers are already out on bail," he said.

"You mean they got to go free?" Carlton asked, incredulous.

"Might as well have," explained Elverse. "They put up money—it's called bail—to get out of jail. They still have to stand trial, but that'll be just a formality. They'll be let go."

"But that's so wrong," objected Carlton.

"Which is why we're here, son. Which is why we're making noise," said Moses.

It was mid afternoon by the time Leslie and Winnie arrived at University Hospital in Birmingham. Leslie wondered why they had brought the Reverend to this hospital when Montgomery was so much closer to Selma? Like so many things in the South, it seemed to make no sense. They entered the hospital and were told Reverend Frey was in intensive care. Up on the intensive care floor, Leslie hung back.

"You go on," she said quietly. "I'll wait for you in the waiting area."

Winnie looked at her and saw she was anxious and ill at ease. He didn't press her.

"All right," he said kindly, and rounded the corner to the nurse's station while Leslie found a seat next to a man asleep in a chair. She folded her hands in her lap and offered up a prayer for Reverend Frey and stilled her memories of her father who had been in the very same hospital right before he died.

"Good afternoon," said Winnie to the nurse on duty. "I'm Winston Phillips and I'm wondering if it would be possible to see Reverend Frey."

The nurse looked up from her charts. "I'm sorry," she said. "He's not allowed visitors. Only his wife and father are allowed in the room and they're with him now." Winnie nodded.

"I was with him when he was clubbed," he explained. "Three of us were attacked but he was the one really hurt. I came hoping to see him but I understand. Thank you."

"You're one of the men who came with him in the ambulance?" she asked, suddenly more interested.

"Yes. Reverend Engel and I were in the ambulance."

"And you kept the stretcher in place."

Winnie was startled that she knew this fact. "Why, yes."

"We all heard about that."

Winnie blushed and gave a slight shrug. "Listen. Would you please pass along a message to Mrs. Frey and Reverend Frey's father that everyone in Selma is praying for the Reverend? We're keeping a twenty-four hour vigil for him."

The nurse rose. "Just a minute," she said. "Wait here."

With that she left the station and walked down the hall to a darkened, large circular room where critical patients were being monitored around the clock. She spoke to the nurse on duty and then to Mrs. Frey. She left the intensive care room and walked out into the hall and beckoned for Winnie to come. He quickly walked down the hall to her.

"Come with me. You may see him but only for a minute."

Winnie steeled himself and slipped inside the unit.

Reverend Frey was lying in a coma but tubes were no longer attached to him except for life support. Reverend Frey's wife and father sat by the side of his bed. Winnie tiptoed over to them and pressed each of their hands between his own.

"I'm so very sorry," he whispered. "Everyone in Selma is praying for his recovery. We're keeping a continuous vigil."

Wife and father nodded and Frey's wife formed the silent words, "thank you." Winnie stepped to the end of the bed and softly laid a hand on the sheet covering Jim's foot. He closed his eyes and prayed that energy from his body would flow through to Frey and give him strength to stay alive. He lowered his head and offered, "We're with you, Jim. Keep fighting. You're not alone. God bless you." He then turned, tenderly squeezed Frey's wife's hand and his father's shoulder, and thanked them for allowing him the moment. He nodded a thank you to the intensive care nurse as he left.

Winnie found Leslie sitting quietly in a chair, staring at her clasped hands. She looked up and saw Winnie's sorrowful face and knew his news would not be good. Wordlessly she rose and took his hand. They stood there noting the man who was still asleep in his chair, now snoring.

"Let's go get some coffee before we return," Winnie suggested softly.

Leslie agreed and they found their way to the empty cafeteria. They helped themselves to tepid coffee from half filled glass pots that more than likely had been sitting for hours and purchased a package of peanut butter crackers from a vending machine. The cafeteria remained deserted: no visitors, no workers. They had their choice of any Formica table and sat down. Leslie studied Winnie's brooding face.

"Were you able to talk to him?" Leslie asked gently, opening the package of crackers.

"No. He's in a coma. It looked like he's on life support. His wife and father are sitting with him."

"How are they doing?" Leslie reached for a cracker and took a bite.

Winnie took a cracker, too. "Stoic. I guess. Waiting for a miracle."

"Is there any hope?" Leslie asked.

"There's always hope, I suppose." Winnie took a sip of the stale coffee that had turned bitter. He chewed on a cracker thoughtfully. Leslie waited.

"Hope's a funny word," he said finally.

"Oh? How so?" Leslie asked.

He thought for a long time as he ate another cracker and gazed into his coffee cup.

"A little kid hopes for a bicycle at Christmas. A teenage girl hopes a boy will invite her to the prom. A farmer hopes the seeds he plants will yield a good crop. A struggling family hopes they can pay the rent and put food on the table. I hoped my marriage could be saved and last forever. You're hoping Annie Lee will return home with you. And now we're all hoping Reverend Frey will somehow pull through. We're hoping for a miracle with life and death hanging in the balance. Hope means almost nothing and everything." He stopped and stared down at the cracker crumbs. "Hope is too encompassing, too nebulous, too general. You can pin anything on it."

"Well," said Leslie. "Maybe that's the good thing about it, too. Hope can be applied to anybody's specific need. Hope is whatever it needs to be."

Winnie considered her words as he drew a line through his cracker crumbs on the table with his finger.

"Maybe," he allowed. "But maybe there should be degrees of hope or more than the one kind of hope. Some hopes are so much more consequential than others."

Leslie considered this idea as he continued.

"My problem is hope seems too much like a wish… or a daydream… maybe even a fantasy. It's optimism rather than realism. Maybe we should have to 'work' for a miracle. Hope seems passive. Work is active. Work could make you earn a miracle. The trouble is we often don't even know what that work should be. We don't have a clue." Winnie stopped abruptly. "*I* don't have a clue."

He finished his cracker. Sorry," he said quietly. I'm blithering."

"Who's to say what's dreaming and what's being realistic? Someone once told me if it wasn't for the optimists, the realists would have us still living in caves," quoted Leslie.

Winnie thought about that. "Maybe we still do."

Leslie took in her troubled friend. He was struggling so hard to discover his place in life. She smiled at him and he gave a weak smile back.

"I think we better get going," she said. "This hospital is making you depressed on top of everything else."

"You're right," he agreed. "Sorry," he said again.

They both downed the rest of their coffee and rose.

Leslie wanted to lighten things up. "Or maybe it's because this coffee is so bad!" Winnie grinned and nodded as he gathered up their trash and they headed for the exit.

Back in Selma, on the other side of town from the Berlin Wall, yet another kind of hope was apparent at the Echo Bowling Alley. Choice and Sparky were passing time and Sparky was having a hot streak of luck. He stood at the head of his lane, holding the ball as if he was lining up a canon, then made a swift motion and flung the ball speeding down the lane until it smashed into the pins. STRIKE!

Choice sat at the table and recorded the points all the while shaking his head. "You're the big winner tonight," he said to Sparky who swaggered back to the bench.

"I felt it tonight," agreed Sparky. "How much was my highest score ever?"

"Don't remember but it would have to go some to beat tonight."

"I can score more 'n' that, bubba," Sparky said darkly. "What say we take a ride by the nigger rope?"

Choice shrugged and picked up the score sheet. They returned their shoes and left the alleys, passing the cocktail lounge where a table of women were sitting together and laughing. Choice nudged Sparky.

"Hey, hey, Spark," he said, eying the women. "Want to see if we can score here instead?"

"I done told you I got bigger plans," said Sparky, annoyed. "Get your mind off sex for god's sake."

They approached the men's room.

"OK, OK," said Choice. "Lemme make a quick pit stop. I'll catch up with you at the car."

"You're turning into a sieve, Choice. You better see a doctor—or get a hose."

Choice forced a laugh and waved Sparky off as he entered the john. It smelled of urine and Clorox. There was no one standing at the urinals. Choice began to sweat as he checked under the one stall to make certain he was in fact alone. He pulled out a crumpled paper from his wallet and deposited coins in the wall pay phone. Their jingling rings bounced off the tile walls, breaking the sound barrier to his flushed ears. He dialed quickly, dropped the receiver, and left it to dangle as he hobbled out.

It was already dark and began to sprinkle as Leslie and Winnie drove back toward Selma. Their car became a comforting cocoon in the night. The windshield wipers kept metronome time to the soft, classical station Leslie had turned on and they spoke little. A newscaster broke into a Braham's concerto.

"We interrupt this program to announce that Reverend James Frey has died in Birmingham."

Leslie gasped and immediately pulled off the road to a stop. Both she and Winnie stared at the radio dash light.

The newscaster continued, "Reverend Frey, a Unitarian minister from Boston, went to Selma, Alabama, at the request of Dr. Martin Luther King Junior to participate in the voting drive when he was clubbed down. He leaves behind a wife and four children. Again—"

Leslie snapped off the radio. They stared out through the windshield into the darkness, trying to accept the finality of what they had prayed to prevent. The certainty of hearing it over the airwaves was still a shock. Minutes ago Jim Frey was a living human being. Now he was dead. They sat on a patch of highway shoulder in the rain, aware of their breathing. In and out; they were alive. Winnie watched the wipers keep a steady beat. A shiver slid down Leslie's spine.

"His poor children," she said.

"I guess the South was short on miracles," Winnie said bitterly. They continued to stare straight ahead but their hands groped, met, and their fingers touched.

"You mind if I say a prayer?" Winnie asked.

"Of course not."

Winnie gathered his thoughts, which wasn't easy as he tried to break through the piercing pain of the news. His voice was soft, unsteady as he began slowly.

"Dear God," he prayed, "Bless Reverend Frey and all those who have prayed for him. Bless his wife and father who kept vigil by his side and will now need Your strength more than ever. Especially bless his children. May You comfort them for losing their Daddy."

Winnie swallowed hard and tears sprang to Leslie's eyes. "May we always remember why he was here and continue to march on his behalf. Forgive us our shortcomings and guide us in this cause. May his death not be in vain."

Leslie and Winnie whispered, 'amen' together.

Choice slowed his car to a stop when he and Sparky heard the bulletin on their pop radio station.

"We repeat, the Reverend Frey has died at University—"
Sparky flipped off the radio and slammed his fist on the dash.

"Shit!" he said. "Cops will be out in full force now. We can't catch a break. No way will we get close to those niggers at the damn rope. Damn! Damn! Shit!"

"Might as well forget it," Choice said glumly. "Let's get something to eat."

He turned the car around and an FBI car tailing him followed at a very careful distance.

In Selma it rained harder as the night wore on and the hundreds keeping vigil at the 'Berlin Wall' hunkered down. Mandy, Elverse, and Carlton struggled to juggle their umbrellas while keeping their blankets wrapped around their bodies for warmth. They were glad Moses and Elmira took Annie Lee home. It would have been insane for her to be out in such a storm her first day released from the hospital.

Sheriff Baker's car pulled up and Baker respectfully walked up to the demonstrators who strained at the rope to hear why he had come.

"Reverend Frey has died in Birmingham," he said simply.

There were shrieks and cries of No, and Oh, God! Baker slipped back to his car and slowly drove away. Elverse reached for Mandy's hand and Mandy reached for Carlton's. They joined the other demonstrators who silently knelt down on the wet pavement to pray. Elverse held his umbrella high over his family, offering a shield of protection to those he cherished so dearly.

Sheriff Clark, meanwhile, missed hearing the announcement at the time it beamed over the airwaves as he had stayed late at his office. On the wall behind his desk he was busy taping up all the telegrams he'd received. Pro, con, it didn't matter; they had his name on them all and filled his office with fame. Clark fumbled with his tape dispenser and added one last telegram to cover a small bare spot. He replaced the dispenser so it sat exactly parallel to the edge of his spotless desk. He stood back to regard his handiwork. He crossed his arms and filled his lungs with a deep satisfied sigh. Notoriety agreed with him.

The Berlin Wall rope remained the focal gathering place for demonstrators the next morning. Reverend Frey was now considered the second martyr in their cause and the simple act of marching to the Selma courthouse took on even bigger significance. Annie Lee did not join the demonstration, however; she was obligated to re-establish her work schedule. Leslie dropped her off at a client's home then drove to Montgomery to purchase "Montgomery Rebel" shirts, baseball jerseys she planned to bring back to her sons and little Annie who would be thrilled to look like her brothers. It was an errand to take her mind off the tragic events and fulfill bringing her children gifts when she returned home.

Later in the afternoon, they returned home to prepare dinner. Leslie stood at the O'Keefe and Merritt gas stove, Annie Lee's pride and joy, frying chicken in a large, black iron skillet. Annie Lee searched for her hot pads in a drawer next to Leslie.

"Do you think the injunction will come through now?" Leslie asked, pointing to the drawer where she had put the hot pads when she straightened the house for Annie Lee's return. "Or will Jim Frey's death be in vain just like Jimmie Lee's?"

"Oh, it'll come through all right, honey," said Annie Lee forcefully, taking out two hot pads. "They're not gonna have the blood of this white minister on their hands."

Annie Lee told herself to be grateful Leslie had tidied up and put her hot pads away, even if they were in the wrong drawer. She excused herself and nudged Leslie aside as she opened the oven door and took out a pan of cornbread. She carried it to the counter while Leslie turned the oven off.

"You've got to stop thinking in terms of black and white, Annie Lee. We'll never get over the color barrier if you keep making such distinctions," said Leslie. "It's not right."

"It may not be right, but it's true. You watch. The Reverend's death will get a whole lot more attention and action than Jimmie Lee's."

"That may be so," Leslie allowed, "but I don't think it's because he was white."

"What then?" challenged Annie Lee.

"I think it's because he was a minister who risked coming down here from the North and marched with Dr. King. Jimmie Lee lived here. It was quite a selfless act."

"Like you, honey?" Annie Lee slipped in. Annie Lee took a picnic basket from a shelf and added a plastic bowl that fit perfectly.

"No, not like me," rebutted Leslie. "You know I came because I was worried about you. He came on principle."

"And you stayed on after I said I wouldn't leave. So I guess you got a little principle in your bones, too." They exchanged looks and smiled at each other.

"Well, as a matter of fact, I have been thinking," said Leslie. We've come this far; it would be a real shame to miss marching to Montgomery. I think it might happen real soon."

Annie Lee added napkins and plastic silverware to the basket. "I've been thinking, too," admitted Annie Lee. "Had plenty of time in my hospital bed for ideas to roll around in my head like a game of marbles. My thinking said, maybe I do need to take a short break. Maybe a visit to Flint would be real nice and I could see the children again." Leslie's face lit up and her eyes widened.

"You mean you'll come home with me?"

"I missed all my cleaning houses last week," Annie Lee elaborated. "I need to catch up and give my customers some notice. I'm thinking that if the injunction comes through this week, then we stay and march and leave afterward. But if it don't, we leave anyway. No more waiting."

"Oh, Annie Lee," Leslie gushed, even as she tried to tamp down her excitement. "I know how hard it is for you to leave. I hope you're sure."

"I'm sure."

Leslie set down her cooking fork and gave Annie Lee a quick hug and kissed her on her cheek. She then turned back to her chicken and suppressed her impulse to jump up and down and shout halleluiah! Annie Lee, equally desiring to keep the decision nonchalant, fussed with the basket.

"Funny how you can get used to waiting," said Leslie. "This past week I actually thought, well, with just a little more time…. Oh, Annie Lee, your decision means so much to me. Thank you. Thank you so much."

Leslie turned off the fire underneath the frying pan of her juicy, golden fried chicken. She hadn't lost her Southern touch after all.

"Can't promise for how long," warned Annie Lee. She handed Leslie the basket. "Here."

"What's this for?" Leslie asked, perplexed.

"The chicken. Just leave two pieces aside. Take it to the good folk at the rope and keep them company." Leslie wasn't understanding Annie Lee's intent. "Jackson's coming to dinner tonight, sugar," Annie Lee said matter-of-factly. "We'd like a little 'lone time."

Leslie blushed and took the basket while Annie Lee shuffled over to the cooling cornbread and began cutting it into pieces.

Leslie arrived at the Berlin Wall with the brimming dinner basket in tow. She spotted Elverse and Winnie and invited them to join her in some finger licking. Together they sat on the curb, lustily biting into crunchy pieces of Southern fried chicken in between bites of cornbread.

"You gonna stay the night, too?" Elverse inquired.

"I'll be protesting right here with you until we march to the courthouse in memory of Reverend Frey," Leslie said between bites.

"I hope that happens tomorrow along with the service," said Winnie. There was that word again. He smiled inwardly at the irony of using it so casually. The English language did have its shortcomings.

Mandy arrived with Carlton and four mason jars filled with beans in a cloth bag. Elverse jumped up and kissed her.

"Hi there, Mrs. Cole," Mandy greeted. "I didn't know you'd be here. I'm sorry I only brought four jars of beans."

"That's no problem. You all need it more than I do, working long hours like you do. Your beans will go great with the chicken I brought. Please help yourself."

Carlton didn't need a second invitation and sat down on the curb next to Winnie after sliding a plump wing from the basket.

"Well, we can share at least," replied Mandy as she passed out the jars to the men. "Here. You take mine. I'll share with Elverse."

Leslie was about to object when they saw Baker arrive in his white Chrysler. Dinner immediately halted and they all stood up to see why he was there. Without a word, Baker walked up to the rope and cut it. A big exhilarating shout arose. Leslie, Winnie, and the Turners pressed forward to see the rope cut in two, lying on the ground. Baker turned to the demonstrators.

"You still can't march," he instructed firmly.

A Reverend, suspicious of his actions, asked, "Then Mr. Wilson, sir, why did you cut down the rope?"

"I put it up, I can cut it down," Baker retorted and returned to his car. Before he could even drive away, a boy with a pocketknife began cutting the rope into sections. There was a scramble for the pieces and Carlton fought through the crowd to grab one. He danced back to his family.

"Got me some rope!" He cried out happily. "Got me some rope!"

"Carlton!" Mandy spoke harshly. "Drop that! This is not a carnival with souvenirs. A man died for you last night. Show some respect."

"But Ma," Carlton pleaded. "I can show it to my own kids some day."

"Carlton!" Elverse said sternly. "You heard your Mama. Toss it back." Carlton reluctantly tossed his rope back into the clamor.

"Hey," interjected Winnie. "I seem to remember we were all enjoying some mighty fine chicken and beans."

Thankful for the change of subject, they returned to the curb and polished off dinner.

"You planning on spending the night with us, Mrs. Cole?" Carlton asked innocently.

"Absolutely," Leslie said, smiling at the boy.

Mandy looked over at Leslie and viewed her with new respect. She smiled. Leslie smiled back, more to acknowledge they were both in for a difficult night. They managed to spend a restless night wrapped in blankets with dozens of others, leaning against the curb and calling the street their bed.

Leslie arrived back at Annie Lee's at dawn. Without a tent, a canopy, or even a sleeping bag, keeping vigil through the night was hardly a feat to romanticize. Leslie was cold and stiff and grateful to be back in the house. She removed her street clothes and wrapped herself in her comforting robe after taking a long, hot shower. Her aches reminded her of how much she missed her own bed—and David. She wanted to hear his familiar voice.

Even though it was barely morning, she phoned home while the rates were still low. Justin answered, much to her surprise. He explained he was up early studying for a history test. Everyone else was still asleep.

"Well, you can tell everyone the news when they wake up," Leslie said, "Annie Lee and I are finally coming home."

"Really, Mom? Annie Lee finally agreed?"

"Yes, she did. Just yesterday. And today is the memorial for Reverend Frey."

"We talked about him in class yesterday. A lot of kids didn't really get what it meant for him to die. It's so sad."

"Yes. Very sad and more than that, it's despicable. He was a remarkable minister. Dedicated. Not like the wicked men who attacked him. I actually met him briefly."

"You did?"

"Yes. He was a friendly man, upbeat, optimistic. I hope we'll celebrate his life and remember his spirit and not dwell on the attack. Those men don't deserve any mention."

"I sure wish I could be there with you."

"Oh, honey, I wish you were here, too. I feel like I'm witnessing history. You would find it so meaningful."

"When do you think you'll head back?"

"Annie Lee and I both want the injunction to come through this week so we can be part of the march to Montgomery."

"And an injunction is… ah…."

"A court order that says Wallace can't stop us."

"Oh, right."

"But if it doesn't come through then we'll leave as soon as we can, maybe even this weekend."

"Oh, that's so great, Mom. I'll start moving my stuff out of my bedroom and in with Alex so Annie Lee can have my room as soon as you arrive."

"What a great kid you are. Thank you, honey. Good luck on your test today. I'll call back again tonight to talk to everybody."

"Ok. We'll be waiting. We all miss you. I love you, Mom."

"I love you, too, Justin. So much. Bye-bye, sweetheart."

Leslie hung up and began to make some coffee for herself and Annie Lee. The song, "The Sound Of Silence," randomly popped into her head and she hummed the tune as she filled the coffee pot. The sun shone through the window as it rose in the sky and added a warmth and brightness that helped Leslie forget her overnight aches and pains. She was ready to join the vigil with renewed energy. Her trip was finally paying off. Everything was coming together.

Annie Lee had slept in, a rare treat for her. Once up, the two women sat down to a breakfast of grits and fried eggs. They then tidied up the kitchen and left to participate in whatever the leaders thought appropriate before Reverend Frey's memorial service.

The day's temperature continued to rise, and it quickly evolved into an unusually warm day for March. Hosea Williams gathered up the supporters at the Chapel, telling them they would try to march to the courthouse steps before the memorial service began, which was slated to start at two. People rose from the pews and again formed flanks as they departed the churchyard. The Turners, Washingtons, Winnie, Annie Lee, and Leslie formed their own very broad flank. Moses, in the middle, stepped high as they walked.

"I got a good feeling we'll make it to the courthouse today," Moses said happily. "They have to let us protest Reverend Frey's death," he decreed. They rounded the corner.

"Or not," corrected Elverse.

Sheriff Clark and his posse were posed just beyond the corner. The posse stretched across the width of Sylvan Street. Clark moseyed into the middle of the street and planted his great hulk with authority. Looking over the vast numbers, he noticed newsmen on the sidelines. He raised the bullhorn to his lips and addressed them.

"Newsmen. Clear the area!" he hollered. He turned to the demonstrators. "There will be no marching. You have thirty seconds to disperse."

Not one marcher moved. A photographer raised his camera, ready to capture the result of the standoff. Up the street Baker was in his Chrysler, talking on his car radio. Clark checked his watch, strolled back to his squad car and sat down, leaving his door open. His face was impassive as if he had just said, "Good morning, marchers. Great day to gather in the street."

"We shouldn't challenge him," whispered Elverse. "He's too crazy."

"What should we do?" Winnie asked.

"Shh," admonished Annie Lee. "Wait it out."

Leslie wasn't so sure. She hung her head and looked at her shoes as if not seeing Clark could negate his demand. She thought of David and her promises to him. Over and over she heard Justin's voice from the morning's conversation say, "We'll be waiting. I love you, Mom." How angry David would be if he knew that she was standing up to the bully sheriff.

The marchers stood firm and watched as Mayor Smitherman arrived at a run, followed by city police. The mayor rushed over to Sheriff Clark's open car door. The two men engaged in a heated but inaudible argument. While Smitherman distracted Clark, Baker went into action. He whistled and his policemen jumped to form a line between the marchers and Clark's posse. Once his men were in place, he confronted Hosea.

"I plead with you to remain lawful. The court order bans all marching," he intoned.

Tall, distinguished Reverend Greeley stepped forward, ready to respond on behalf of Hosea.

"Mr. Baker," he began. "There is a higher court than the court of the land, God's court, and we must listen to His laws. Our cause dictates that we arrive at the steps of the House of Justice on behalf of Reverend Frey. It is a small concession compared to the concession this man made to insure that all Negroes may someday walk freely to the courthouse and there become registered voters."

Greeley's eloquent words had their desired affect. Baker was visibly moved. His tone was quieter.

"I have to uphold the Alabama Constitution, Reverend Greeley."

"And what about the Constitution of the United States?" questioned the Unitarian Reverend.

Baker, always good at thinking fast of his feet, said, "Go back to your church and hold your memorial service for Reverend Frey. With all my might I'll try to negotiate a march to the courthouse steps afterwards."

Greeley and Hosea signaled agreement.

Baker turned and faced his men. "About Face!" Baker barked and his police line reversed their stand and faced the surprised posse men; they formed a protective shield between the posse and the marchers who were dispersing. Enraged, Clark jumped from his car and slammed his fist on the fender, shouting an expletive that was probably heard in Perry County.

Well before two in the afternoon, the throng gathered at Brown Chapel as planned, but the service did not immediately begin. Many people of faith were there to pay their respects and be counted, even though most of them had never marched and had no intention of remaining to march after the service. Annie Lee called them vicarious participants. Quite a few kept checking their watches while they waited, concerned perhaps the delay could cause them to miss their flights booked to leave that same evening.

It was now stifling hot and all the stained glass windows were open, including the one broken by the boy who had been thrown through it. Many women employed colorful fans they had brought from home while others utilized the cardboard fans provided in the pews with handles like tongue depressors. Men kept reaching for their handkerchiefs to catch the sweat that trickled down their temples. Because it was such a somber occasion they wore suits only to be forced to remove their jackets so as not to suffer a heat stroke. The folks sitting in the balcony were sweltering even more, proving a law of physics.

Up in the middle of the balcony and avoiding recognition by blending in with the crowd sat Anton Engel. He had met with Dr. King in Birmingham to relate the details of the attack and insisted on returning to Selma to be present to memorialize his friend. Winnie spotted him and caught his eye. They smiled and nodded to each other. Winnie nudged Leslie who looked up and gave Anton a tiny wave and smile.

As often happened when Reverend Martin Luther King, Jr. was to be the main speaker, the actual service began an hour late. With good reason. King was in Montgomery that morning giving testimony in Judge Johnson's chambers, urging the judge to lift the city and state bans against marching. He sought a Federal injunction that would allow a march to Montgomery. Not surprising, King's schedule was always impossibly tight.

The Turners, Washingtons, Winnie, Leslie, and Annie Lee all arrived early to insure they would secure a seat. They spent the hour waiting for Dr. King by singing hymns and freedom songs along with a fervent congregation. They swayed and clapped as they sang "Rock A My Soul," and "Study War No More," and "Welcome, Happy Morning." It truly was a joyous celebration of a life.

When King did arrive, a cheer went up. Men of God from all faiths who had prepared speeches and eulogies sat among an ecumenical rainbow of speakers on the chancel: a Monsignor, chief Ministers, a Catholic Bishop, a robed Greek Orthodox Primate, a Rabbi. Sweat poured off all their faces equally as they paid tribute to Reverend Frey in rapid succession.

Then it was King's turn to speak. He began with a quote from Shakespeare:

"And if he should die,
Take his body, and cut it into little stars.
He will make the face of heaven so fine
That all the world will be in love with night."

King compared these eloquent words from Romeo And Juliet to the radiant life of Reverend Frey. He then asked the same questions he had asked at Jimmie Lee Jackson's memorial, challenging the congregated to be committed to change. King's words struck a deep chord with Winnie. He decided then and there to dedicate his ministry to outreach rather than pastoring a congregation. How he would do that without being assigned to a church he did not know, but he had faith a way would open.

King's words electrified Leslie when he brought his words home to the state of Alabama. Was it possible the state in which she was born could actually shake off its racist shackles? She couldn't help but wonder.

Elverse and Annie Lee paid special attention to King's recitation of the famous and the faceless, anonymous, relentless people, black and white who stormed the barricades of racism. They were the foot soldiers. King reminded those gathered that all the children of God were created from one blood. Each person present must work with all their heart to create a society where all people respect the worth and dignity of every human being. Annie Lee nodded vigorously in agreement. Her soul was on fire with dedication and purpose.

King concluded his eulogy with these words, "So we thank God for the life of James Frey. We thank God for his goodness. We thank God that he was willing to lay down his life in order to redeem the soul of our nation. So I say—so Horatio said as he stood over the dead body of Hamlet— 'Good night sweet prince; may the flight of angels take thee to thy eternal rest.'"

Annie Lee let out a loud "alleluia" and "amen." Elverse looked upon Mandy who had a tear trickling down her cheek and kissed it. And Winnie and Leslie smiled at each other, acknowledging their friend had been memorialized brilliantly.

King returned to his seat, quite spent. A Methodist minister rose next and walked to the dais to introduce Rabbi Reuben from Canada.

"Rabbi Reuben will deliver the mourner's Kaddish to be followed by 'We Shall Overcome.'"

But as Rabbi Reuben stood up, the Greek Orthodox Primate who appeared slightly deaf thought they were to begin singing and led off with the first line of "We Shall Overcome." The congregation joined him and soon voices filled the air with the song that had come to symbolize the movement, even though Reverend Tindley had written it in 1901.

"We shall overcome. We shall overcome. We shall overcome, some day. Oh, deep in my heart, I do believe.... We shall overcome, some day."

The worshipers began to hum the melody that became a stirring accompaniment to the Kaddish. The Rabbi's strong voice resonated over the humming, sonorous and beautiful. It did not matter that no one understood the words. The emotion was profoundly felt.

At the conclusion of the memorial, the entire congregation lined up behind Doctor King and other clergy dignitaries. They again set out for the courthouse steps. Dr. King carried a funeral spray made up of white roses and mums encircled by palm fronds. This time their march was unimpeded and they reached the green marble steps without incident. King placed the wreath at the courthouse door and knelt in prayer with other dignitaries while those behind bowed their heads.

Baker watched from afar in his Chrysler. He now had the law on his side; he had convinced Judge Thomas to back him up and allow the conclusion of the service to end at the steps of the courthouse. Baker had pulled off another improbable feat.

Reverend Engel returned to Brown Chapel with his Unitarian Board members and found Winnie and Leslie. He was flying back to Boston that evening and wanted to say goodbye.

"I'll never forget either of you," he said, choking up. He turned to Winnie. "Are you going to stay as long as it takes to march to Montgomery?"

"That's my plan now," said Winnie. "You have a church and responsibilities to return to. I'm... well... let's just say I have a lot of free time on my hands right now."

"Well, I wish you the best. Be very careful. I feel like we're marked men for witnessing such brutality. You could become a target by staying on."

Winnie nodded. It was a chance he was willing to take.

Anton turned to Leslie. "And thank you for all your kindness, Leslie. I'm sorry you had to be part of such tragedy."

"We're all in this together, Reverend Engel. We all wish that evening could have been different. Take good care and have a safe journey home."

They hugged one more time, and then Anton was gone.

ᴄᴓ

TEN

The whole town was buzzing after the memorial service because the President of the United States would be addressing a joint session of Congress that night. Every television and radio in Selma would be tuned in to hear if President Johnson would mention Selma in his remarks. The Committee gathered together to share a potluck meal and hear the President speak to the nation.

They began arriving at Moses and Elmira's house; it could hold more people than most. Even so, if the walls could have bulged, they would have. In addition to the Committee members and their families, there were the clergy guests staying with committee members, clergy camped at the hospital, plus a few clergy stragglers staying in motels who were not leaving until the following day.

Elverse stood in the living room second-guessing what the President's topic would be with other Committee members.

"For my money, the President probably intends to talk more about Vietnam," said Elverse.

"No, I think he'll talk about what we're doing down here, what with Reverend Frey's death and all," disagreed Annie Lee.

Winnie nodded in agreement. "Well, he should talk about down here. Wake up our country and move it to action."

"Wallace was just in D.C. over the weekend," said Amelia Boynton who was finally out of the hospital. "You know they weren't discussing Southeast Asia."

"But with so many lawyers jawin' in front of Judge Johnson, it could be ages before we're allowed to march to Montgomery," said Moses.

"Maybe not," said Annie Lee. "We could be surprised."

"Surprised? Down here? See justice done? That would be a surprise," lamented Moses.

Another boy was chasing Carlton and they both tried to weave through the crowd gathered in the living room. Elverse grabbed Carlton's arm and stopped him.

"Hey, hey, son. No running in the house. Where are your manners?" Carlton looked shamefaced at his father and grinned at the boy chasing him.

"We were just on our way to check out what desserts there are. Sorry, Dad. We'll slow down." Elverse loosened his grip and the two boys threw their arms around each other's necks and threaded their way on to the dining room.

The dining room table was laden with scrumptious homemade baked goods. There were apple, sweet potato, pecan, and cherry pies, a pear cobbler, angel food cake, a chocolate bundt, spice sheet cakes, and cupcakes for little fingers. Mandy and Elmira were rearranging these delicious offerings in a futile attempt to create more space. Leslie joined them, bringing yet another pie from the kitchen.

"Thank you, Mrs. Cole... Leslie," said Mandy, catching her own formality. "I don't know where we'll put that?"

"Hot ziggity dog," exclaimed Elmira. "We could open a bakery. We just don't have any more room, honey. Wait! Let me clear some space on the sideboard and we'll put more desserts there."

Elmira stacked her milk glass collection while Leslie waited agreeably to put the pie on top of the cabinet. The women realized how prized each offering was considered to be by their bakers and made sure every homemade gift made it to the dessert table. Especially if it was a luscious, picture perfect lemon meringue pie.

Carlton and his friend hung around the dining room entrance, eyeing all the goodies. Mandy saw him and read his sugary thoughts. "Carlton," she instructed. "Please go and tell

the folks in the living room to come and form a line to shuffle through the kitchen to take their meal. And Carlton, you
eat your greens first before you even think about this dessert
table."

Dinner was a feast with more than enough delicious
Southern dishes to feed everyone present. The guests dug into
black-eyed peas, Southern fried chicken, greens with ham
hocks, gumbo with rice, corn bread of course, and macaroni
salad.

The President was not speaking until nine o'clock so there
was plenty of time to enjoy the food and thrash out ideas for
their crusade.

The Committee members were particularly animated as
they began to believe success was actually within their reach
after so many years of going up against the Southern establishment and being knocked down. The national attention
they were now receiving would surely make the difference.
Maybe, just maybe, the President of the United States would
use his bully pulpit to shine a light on Alabama and include
their movement in his remarks, even if just a little.

Suddenly, the television volume was turned up for all to
hear. "MR. SPEAKER? THE PRESIDENT OF THE UNITED
STATES!"

Women rushed from the kitchen and men ran from discussions in the dining room and den to press into the living
room and glimpse the small TV screen. Moses adjusted the
rabbit ears antenna, trying to improve the image. The gathered alternated between laying bets about the content of the
speech as the President walked down the aisle and telling people to hush so as not to miss what members of Congress
might be saying to the President as he headed for the podium.

President Johnson took to the platform, Speaker McCor-
mack and Vice President Humphrey at his back, his Texas
stature in full command. "Mr. Speaker, Mr. Vice President,
Members of Congress. I speak to you tonight for the dignity
of man and the destiny of democracy."

Mrs. Boynton couldn't restrain herself. "That's right, Mr.
President. You tell it."
Shh!

"At times, history and fate meet at a single time in a single place to shape a turning point in man's unending search for freedom. So it was at Lexington and Concord. So it was a century ago at Appomattox. So it was last week in Selma, Alabama."

The room held its collective breath. They could hardly believe the word "Selma" actually passed across the lips of their President to the televised nation.

"There, long suffering men and women peacefully protested the denial of their rights as Americans. Many were brutally assaulted. One good man–a man of God–was killed.

'There is no cause for pride in what has happened in Selma. There is no cause for self-satisfaction in the long denial of equal rights of millions of Americans. But there is cause for hope and for faith in our democracy in what is happening here tonight."

"OK, Lyndon!" Shouted Jackson. "Get down to it."

Shh!

Leslie and Annie Lee hugged, overjoyed by the President's eloquent references.

"For the cries of pain and the hymns and protests of oppressed people have summoned into convocation all the majesty of this great Government–the government of the greatest nation on earth. Our mission is at once the oldest and the most basic of this country: to right wrong, to do justice, to serve man."

"My Lord," Elverse exclaimed. "The President of the United States is only talking about us. His whole speech is about Selma!"

"Glory, hallelujah!" tagged on Annie Lee. "We're gonna march for sure."

People hushed them so as not to miss a single word of President Lyndon Baines Johnson's endorsement.

Not all of Alabama was pleased with the President's pronouncements. In sharp contract to Moses' home, Rusty Denton's living room was like a wake. The TV they looked at might as well have been a dead body in need of burial. The youngest of this group of friends, Rusty sat stoically on his swayback couch, his arm around his young bride, Melanie Vi, who held their little baby girl, Sandra De. Choice sat glumly next to them. Uncle Parker and his wife, Allie April, a nervous woman who kept playing with the corner of her paper napkin, sat on chrome kitchen chairs that had been brought into the living room. Sparky sat hunched over on the floor. All the KKK buddies were drinking whiskey and spitting expletives at the TV.

The President's speech continued. "Many of the issues of civil rights are very complex and most difficult. But about this there can and should be no argument. Every American citizen must have an equal right to vote. There is no reason which can excuse the denial of that right. There is no duty which weighs more heavily on us than the duty we have to ensure that right. Yet the harsh fact is that in many places in this country men and women are kept from voting simply because they are Negroes."

The Denton house turned even gloomier.

"Shit!" said Sparky. "Shit, shit, shit! Equal rights my ass. Niggers aren't meant to be equal to us. Don't he know that Niggers aren't the same as whites? The Bible says they're not. He's messin' up God's order of things."

"Damn commie President," hissed Rusty.

"We could turn it off," Melanie Vi offered.

"Shh. No, we got to hear what the bastard's going to do," said Uncle.

"Experience has clearly shown that the existing process of law cannot overcome systematic and ingenious discrimination. No law that we now have on the books—and I have helped to put three of them there—can ensure the right to vote when local officials are determined to deny it.

"In such a case our duty must be clear to all of us. The Constitution says that no person shall be kept from voting because of his race or his color. We have all sworn an oath before God to support and to defend that Constitution. We must now act in obedience to that oath."

"What a turncoat ass kisser," complained Allie April. "This guy's a Southerner?"

Melanie Vi hugged her baby closer and kissed her little head. She never liked their talk when they'd been drinking. It scared her. Uncle Parker and Allie April were so generous and helpful, she knew underneath they weren't mean people, just people who believed in the ways of the South. And those ways were good ways. Why, when she got pregnant, they didn't run her off. They told Rusty to stand up and be a man and do the right thing. Not like in movies where Northern girls are treated like dirt if they make a mistake. They supported her and made sure Rusty got a job. She was grateful. And although she kind of wished it had been Sparky she'd ended up with because he was so handsome, he never seemed to pay her much mind. Except that one time when they accidentally ran into each other at the drug store and Sparky bought her a soda pop. But Rusty would be OK once he grew into his manhood a little more. He loved their daughter and wanted to be a good father. That mattered more to Melanie Vi than anything else. Marriage was all right even if a bit boring.

The President reached the section in his speech that told what action he would be taking.

"Wednesday I will send to Congress a law designed to eliminate illegal barriers to the right to vote.

"It will provide for citizens to be registered by officials of the United States Government if the State officials refuse to register them. Finally, this legislation will ensure that properly registered individuals are not prohibited from voting."

Allie April ripped her napkin in half.

"Oh, great," she said, looking to Uncle Parker for approval. "Another law to choke off our state's rights. First they pass a law that says their rights have to be equal. And now they'll vote, too? What about our rights?"

Uncle Parker just shook his head and took another swallow of whiskey. He hadn't been fooled by this President now speaking, which is why he had voted for Goldwater.

"But even if we pass this bill, the battle will not be over. What happened in Selma is part of a far larger movement that reaches into every section and State of America. It is the effort of American Negroes to secure for themselves the full blessings of American life.

"Their cause must be our cause too. Because it is not just Negroes, but really it is all of us, who must overcome the crippling legacy of bigotry and injustice. AND WE SHALL OVERCOME!"

Uncle Parker, his outrage dulled by liquor, slurred his words as he rhymed, "Overcome... troublesome... mettlesome... slum. They'll never be equal. I'll never be slum with 'um. They'll see. Jus' wait!" And he drained the rest of his bourbon from his glass.

When the President's speech was over, the Committee engaged in an animated dialogue. Winnie surmised a march was no longer necessary; a Federal bill would give them the vote. Elverse and Moses thought that even with the introduction of a bill, they must keep up some pressure to make sure it passed. And then there was the contingent, among them Amelia and Annie Lee, who had little faith in the government and insisted they move forward with their plans because it would take a big showing like the march to achieve passage. Still, even with differing views, everyone was enthralled as they left, their empty potluck dishes in tow. Mandy was still flabbergasted that the President made an entire speech about their town. All were in awe of the recognition Selma had received and there was a feeling of pride they'd never known before.

For Mayor Smitherman and his law enforcement officers, however, they heard that their job would get harder after President Johnson's speech. To their way of thinking, he encouraged the Negro to go ahead and break their laws.

Clark, Baker, and Smitherman met in Clark's office. Clark sat rocking in his big oak desk chair, his feet up on the top of his desk. Smitherman kept pacing the room, and Baker stared out the window into the darkness.

"We made it through Frey's funeral," Smitherman seethed. "Now we got the President fanning the flames. We got to expect more trouble."

"It'd be easy enough to take care of if I could be left alone to do my damn job," complained Clark.

"Yeah, like when you were itching to crack more heads this morning," Baker said without turning around.

"We were doin' jus' fine till you fenced your way in-between us," retorted Clark. Baker turned around slowly.

"And why do you suppose we did that?"

Clark swung his feet off the desk.

"Because you're a smug ass who can't mind his own business."

Baker strode across the room to Clark's desk and leaned across it to look Clark directly in his eyes.

"Those marchers weren't going to disperse and you knew it. They were determined to march to the Courthouse for Frey. You were deliberately creating a confrontation," Baker said in an even, steely tone.

Clark rose and the two men faced off on opposite sides of the desk. Smitherman stopped pacing and looked at the two.

"OK, OK, hold it fellas."

Ignoring him, Clark answered, "At least my men respect the law and don't kiss no marchers' asses."

Baker slammed his hand on the desk.

"There's more to law enforcement than brute force, you moron! We're trying to keep—"

Clark lunged for Baker but Baker reared back and readied his fists. "Listen you arrogant son-of-a-bitch," Clark warned as he leaned over his desk. "If you and your police force interfere with my authority again, I swear I'll arrest you!"

"You touch me and I'll kill you," hissed Baker.

Smitherman rushed to the desk and shoved them apart as they continued their stare down. The two men snorted, their mutual hate on red alert.

"Jesus!" Smitherman said, exasperated. "Haven't we got enough trouble with the damned marchers? Cool it, for god's sake."

The next day many of the visitors who remained, committed to marching to Montgomery, were frustrated by the Southern sense of time. How long, they wondered, would they need to wait until the wheels of justice turned to decree an injunction permitting the march? It was a tight neighborhood and the restaurants and grocery stores were straining to accommodate the swollen numbers. Families who had taken in strangers continued to do so willingly but those being hosted feared they had become a burden and felt guilty that they were creating hardship and wearing out their welcome.

Sisters Mary and Stella were among those who extended their stay and came to Brown Chapel following morning prayers. Leslie was already there after dropping off Annie Lee at a client's house. Mandy was at the hospital; Moses and Carlton were in school; Elverse was back at his hardware store after dropping Winnie off; and Elmira was indoors volunteering in the church office, working as best she could with her cast.

Committee members had gotten back to their daily routines but the out-of-towners had nothing in particular to do. So they gathered on the steps of Brown Chapel and thought of themselves as an informal demonstration of solidarity. They felt their numbers could make the march a reality and saw their simple act of gathering outdoors as an act of protest.

On Wednesday folks again milled about greeting and chatting. An amateur guitarist rather badly played the Beatles' song, "I feel Fine." As folks began to recognize the melody they tried to remember the words and sing along. When the guitarist came to the bridge of the song, some people rose and began to do a sort of square dance. Winnie smiled wickedly and drew Leslie to her feet and started to swing her around. They laughed breathlessly.

"Stop," cried Leslie.

"Never," Winnie yelled. When the song ended the invigorated crowd stood laughing and didn't notice John Lewis approaching. He weaved his way through the crowd and advanced to the steps. Once noticed, everyone hushed and looked expectantly as he climbed to the top. He turned to the group.

"The decision came down today," he announced. "WE'RE MARCHING ON MONTGOMERY!"

People went wild. They shouted and whistled and applauded and jumped up and down and grabbed and kissed each other. Winnie kissed Leslie and was stunned by his sudden rush of feeling. He stood there and watched as other people grabbed and kissed her, too. He wanted to hold her in his arms again. What was going on with him? He knew she was a married woman. It must be the dramatic events. He would have to watch himself and not allow the excitement of the moment to carry away his ethics. A small inner voice opposing his conscience countered that "ethics" spoiled spontaneity.

When the enthusiasm quieted, Lewis unfolded a piece of paper. "I have here a copy of the injunction and would like to read the last paragraph to you."

The crowd pressed in to better hear. "It seems basic to our constitutional principles that the extent of the right to assemble, demonstrate, and march peacefully along the highways and streets in an orderly manner should be commensurate with the enormity of the wrongs that are being protested and petitioned against. In this case, the wrongs are enormous. The extent of the right to demonstrate against these wrongs should be determined accordingly."

The group murmured their approval while Lewis slipped the paper back into his pocket. He smiled at those gathered.

"Today Judge Johnson accepted our plan for the march and issued this injunction against Wallace. However, he was concerned about where the highway narrows through Lowndes County. We offered to limit the number of marchers to three hundred when the road becomes two lanes and he accepted that offer. We will reach that part of the highway on Monday. It will take us two days to walk through Lowndes. Those who want to be one of the three hundred who keep marching need to submit their names to the Committee to be considered. All others are encouraged to march every day except Monday and Tuesday. We will shuttle marchers back and forth. We will leave Selma this Sunday and arrive at the Capitol steps by Thursday. There's a lot to organize so let's get busy."

"Oh, I'm so excited," said Leslie to Winnie. "I can hardly wait to tell Annie Lee tonight when I pick her up."

Just then, Carlton and Moses arrived from school.

"You just missed it," said Winnie. "John Lewis announced the march is on. We'll start out this coming Sunday."

Leslie grabbed Carlton and gave him a big hug.

"Wait till my boys hear about this, Carlton. They'll be wanting to come down and join you."

"That would be real fine, Miss Leslie," Carlton replied, grinning and slightly embarrassed by her enthusiastic show of affection.

"Lord, lord, lord!" shouted Moses. "Have we got our work cut out for us. Four days? To move thousands down the highway? Good thing I believe with God, all things are possible."

"Don't know if there'll be thousands. And only three hundred will be allowed to march on Monday and Tuesday when the road narrows through some County; I can't remember the name. But it's a huge challenge no matter how many there are, that's for sure," said Winnie. "Yikes! I just realized that number doesn't include a support crew," he added.

Still, they didn't allow reality to dampen their visions. They hugged again and grabbed hands and danced around in a circle. More shouts and laughter. Now that it was really going to happen, people could hardly believe it. As Lewis descended the steps, marchers ran up to him and hugged him and shook his hand. When they asked what they could do to help, he told them to go to the SNCC office and volunteer. They would need many hands to pull off a successful march in four days.

"Let's go see what we can do," said Winnie.

"We'll need all the volunteers we can get," agreed Moses. "Elmira's already been contacting businesses who might donate supplies and food, but it'll have to be all rounded up."

Carlton took off at a run. "I'm going to go tell Dad," he called over his shoulder. "Meet you there!"

They laughed at his exuberance.

"What a great kid," said Winnie.

"The best," agreed Moses.

They began heading for the office.

"The Committee has worked out an overall plan anticipating this day, right Moses?" asked Leslie. Her thoughts had been so consumed about Annie Lee she hadn't given much thought about preparations for the eventuality of the march. Obviously, they would be in big trouble if they were starting from square one.

"For sure," said Moses. "SCLC and SNCC both have been helping us figure out what we'll need and how to do it. Thank God they're both on board and Dr. King has deep pockets. SCLC has knowledge of how these big marches work, especially after the March on Washington. And I wouldn't be surprised if the government pitches in some bucks now that our President has spoken in favor of us."

Leslie suddenly stopped in her tracks.

"You know? You guys have really done it. After this march you will actually be given the right to vote in Alabama!" Both Winnie and Moses laughed at her epiphany. Moses threw his arm around her. "Well, of course, honey," he hooted. "If you never give up, things have got to change. The old ways just finally wear themselves out from the weight of their own wickedness."

It rained that evening but that didn't dampen the spirits of the marchers in Selma. The lights burned brightly long into the night at the church as the Committee organized what obviously would be a gargantuan effort.

It was along the side of a dark road that Choice again met with the FBI agent. Neither was in a good mood having to meet under rainy conditions. Choice had been looking forward to sliding a few more days to earn more money and was disappointed the injunction had come down so soon. The FBI agent was agitated the Federal government would now be breathing down his neck and he would be held more accountable.

"Wallace can't stop these fool marchers now," the FBI agent said. "You got to be extra sharp—determine who is just talk and who's real action."

"The guys are out for blood," Choice said ominously.

"Yeah, well spread the word that there's going to be a hell of a lot of Federal Troops down here: National Guard, The Army, more FBI, you name it, they'll be here. Maybe thousands of them. There'll be more forces assigned to this parade than Kennedy had in Fort Worth. A lot more. Every little nook and cranny will be covered. Johnson isn't going to take

ELEVEN

Annie Lee and Leslie rose early the next morning, showered, ate a quick breakfast, and allowed the dishes to drip-dry. Leslie drove Annie Lee to one of her employer's houses where Annie Lee intended to give notice that she would be leaving for a spell. She also doubled up her schedule to fit everyone in before she took time off to be a marcher on Sunday, the first day of the march, and Thursday, the last day of the march. She accepted her ankles would not allow her to march the entire pilgrimage to Montgomery. She didn't need to walk every day. As long as she began and ended the march she was content. Moreover, she knew Jackson would not be allowed any days off and she needed him for support when she walked. The week would allow her time to pack her things. She would be ready to accompany Leslie back to Michigan once the march ended.

Jackson was glad for her. He believed she needed a little rest from juggling full time cleaning houses that took a toll on her joints and being an active, protesting member of the Committee. They'd been separated before. Their love was always there. The separation would be temporary.

After dropping off Annie Lee, Leslie drove on to Brown Chapel to volunteer wherever they needed her. More tables had been added to the ones still standing from the influx of the second march. A telephone worker was installing more phones, and women were making charts that they tacked up on the walls. It was a beehive of activity.

Elmira was already seated behind a long metal table and waved a greeting to Leslie with her arm in the cast. Leslie stood in front of the table, waiting for Elmira to finish her call.

Mandy arrived to help plan meals as much as she could before she left for her shift. She continued to double up on work so the family could afford to take the entire week off and march together. They laughed and called it their walking vacation. Tucked under Mandy's arm was a cookbook, "Feeding the Multitudes." She scurried up to Elmira's table and exchanged greetings with Leslie.

"Morning, sisters," said Elmira as she hung up the phone. She spoke fast, like a person relaying as much information as possible in a three minute call before the operator came on and asked for more money. "Glad to see you brought that cookbook, Mandy. I want you and Leslie to sit down and finish planning out the menus. Here's a list of what we got so far." She waved a piece of paper at them without taking a breath. "You know what we like, Mandy, and you, Leslie, should know what Northerners will eat. Once you've got the meal plans all set, let me know and I'll make calls to order the food from markets that agreed to help us. Let me know by this afternoon how much we'll need to feed three hundred marchers every day and night, and—"

"—Right, boss!" Mandy joked.

"Sorry," said Elmira good-naturedly. "I'm just so wound up. The good Reverend Williams handed me a list a mile long of things that need to be done."

"Don't worry, Elmira. We'll get it all done somehow," said Leslie. She took the food collection list and smiled at Mandy. The women found a small alcove a bit removed from the chaos. Leslie had a notebook and pen, ready to write down their ideas.

"Let's see," said Mandy. "Obviously, we've got to keep the cost down and we probably need to have a lot of carbohydrates to give us marchers energy. Let's start with breakfast."

"I love fried potatoes," blurted out Leslie.

"Good heavens, Leslie! We'd need hundreds of pounds of potatoes. Think how heavy that would be and how much space that would take up. No, we need to stick to good ole Southern grits."

"Well, we'll have to doctor them up with lots of butter or cheese. Most Northerners I know aren't keen on them when they first taste them."

"Maybe you're right. We can serve them for dinner when there are other choices." Leslie nodded and made a page for dinner items and wrote down "grits." Mandy read a few recipes and then, as if they'd both heard the voice of inspiration, they said simultaneously,

"Oatmeal!"

"With raisons," Added Leslie.

"For iron," agreed Mandy with a giggle.

A few of the out-of-towners, like Winnie, found a way to be helpful. But most of the remaining visitors who decided to stay until the Big March were at loose ends. They didn't know how to help with preparations in a town unfamiliar to them that had its own way of doing things. To fill their time they continued to demonstrate with short marches, wanting to believe they were being a constant reminder to the South that there would be no justice until every eligible voter was registered.

On Thursday, while preparations were bustling in the black section of Selma, over thirty visiting white marchers decided to march from Brown Chapel into an all white neighborhood, carrying signs, "Voting Rights For All."

Sister Stella arrived at the gathering bristling. She turned to a young priest.

"Did you hear what Bishop Toolan said about our efforts?"

The priest shook his head.

"He said he didn't believe we're equipped to lead groups in disobedience to the laws of this state. That we're doing a great injustice to Alabama acting like crusaders. Really?"

"Isn't he the Bishop who integrated all the Catholic schools last year here in Alabama?"

"Yes. Bishop Thomas Toolan. And he built the first hospital where black and white doctors work together. That's why his words are so stinging. He's done so much good but can't quite take that last leap to see the Negro race as equal, the paternalistic old goat."

"Now, now, Sister," the priest gently chided. "He has achieved a lot. We're the next generation and can be grateful to build on what he's accomplished. Let's be joyful in our work."

Sister Stella flashed him a big, fake smile, then relented. "Well," she said. Actually, she felt better having vented.

An inexperienced SCLC volunteer guided the white marchers into an all white community to confront the town's segregation and white population. The group strolled down the sidewalk, chatting amicably and greeting passing white residents who regarded them scornfully. Sister Stella was in the lead with the priest and SCLC worker.

"Hey Sister," a man across the street yelled. Sister Stella turned his way.

"What are you doing to the white race?"

"Educating it!" Sister Stella yelled back. The priest smiled appreciatively but the man went into a rage.

You stink!" he screamed. "You should be in a whorehouse!" He scurried off when he saw Baker's Chrysler speeding up the street to the marchers and careen to a stop. Baker jumped out and blocked their path on the sidewalk. He was livid.

"You told me if I got you to the Courthouse after Reverend Frey's memorial service you wouldn't march. You should call yourselves the Southern Stupid Leadership Conference. You're all under arrest!"

A school bus rumbled into view and stopped. Baker picked out the young priest and pointed his finger as he walked up to the man and grabbed his jacket front.

"Do you know where the hell you are?" The priest was unnerved and shook his head. The SCLC volunteer stepped up to Baker.

"Sir, with all due respect, we are—"

"—Shut up!" Commanded Baker. He moved the priest toward the bus by his collar. "I'm taking you all into protective custody. I should take you to a mental institution. You're crazy to march in a white neighborhood." He loosened the grip on the priest and turned to the rest of the demonstrators following him. "You're all sick," he continued, infuriated. "You don't have enough sense to know when your lives are in danger!"

The marchers grew silent and became contrite as they crossed the street to the bus. Once Baker had loaded all the marchers on the bus, he told the driver to head for the jail and took the seat next to Sister Stella.

"This has ceased to be a Negro movement. It's become a misfit white movement," he told her.

"Thank you for not calling us all Communists," Sister Stella snapped back.

Some marchers at the back of the bus began singing "We Shall Overcome." Others attempted to join in but they were off key. The sour notes made Baker wince. He turned to the Sister. "At least when it was only Negroes demonstrating we had good music."

By Friday morning volunteers who had worked practically through the night began to show signs of fatigue. Winnie spent all of Thursday collecting food from donating stores and churches and organized it in the Green Street Baptist Church kitchen basement. He made hundreds of trips up and down the church stairs. By Friday the basement took on the appearance of an overstocked grocery warehouse.

Leslie had been reassigned to hospitality and helped find lodging for the steady stream of people who kept coming to participate at the beginning and end of the march. She was also assigned to the transportation Committee and spent long hours on the road raking up miles between Selma and the airports in both Montgomery and Birmingham.

There was no inspiration for the job Elmira tackled. The yellow pages were flipped open on her desk to construction equipment and she was going down the short list. She dialed another number.

"Good morning," she greeted amicably. "I'm trying to find portable toilets. Do you rent them?"

"Sure do," came the answer. "How many do you need?"

"That's mighty fine. We need a dozen."

"A dozen? My god, woman! You building the Taj Mahal?"

"Something even bigger," said Elmira proudly. "We need them for five days, starting this Sunday."

"Say," the man drawled. "Are these for that damn march?"

"Yes, sir, they are. And we will pay cash in advance."

The man slammed down his receiver and Elmira jerked the phone away from her ear. She sighed and checked off another name. She was almost ready to admit defeat when the last place she called agreed to rent to her.

"But we're closed tomorrow," he admonished. "Aren't open on weekends. You'll have to pick them up by closing time today and pay for seven days starting today. That's if you get 'um back by next Thursday night before we close at five. If you don't get them back in time, you'll be charged another day."

"Do you have a weekly rate?" Elmira asked politely.

"Hell, no," replied the man emphatically. "And you'll need to pay cash in advance."

"Thank you, sir," replied Elmira, fuming underneath her politeness. "We have every intention to pay cash in advance. We will have a truck at your establishment to pick up a dozen portable toilets lickety-split."

While the white churches acted as if nothing of note was happening in their community, the black churches in Selma were working overtime. At the Green Street Baptist Church, Elverse and Winnie carried shinny newly purchased galvanized garbage cans down the stairs into the basement kitchen. These cans would deliver food every evening filled with enough dinner helpings to feed the three hundred hungry bodies marching the entire way. Elverse carried his garbage can hoisted on his shoulder and over his back. Winnie carried his can in front of him like a protruding stomach. The huge cans were so unwieldy it was a toss-up which was the better method.

"Did you hear?" Elverse asked. "A Russian walked in space yesterday."

"You're kidding!" said Winnie. "Really? I'm so out of touch with the rest of the world, all I know are these church walls. I had no idea. That's incredible!"

"Sure is," said Elverse enthusiastically. "Their astronaut actually stepped out into space. I can't imagine what that must have felt like floating in the cosmos and being attached to the ship only by a tether. Carlton, on the other hand, was just jazzed by it. He had no problem seeing himself doing it."

"I'm with you," laughed Winnie. "I'd want a guarantee I'd get back into the ship, not to mention back to earth."

They carried the cans to the kitchen and passed 3,000 lunch sacks lining the walls in the huge fellowship hall, already partially filled to meet the demand for the first day. The Committee wasn't certain how many people would march on Sunday, but from the inquiries they'd received, they realized there would be thousands. Folks kept arriving not just from Alabama or the South, or even the United States; people from all over the globe were flying in to take part. This march had touched a nerve with citizens throughout the world who understood something very big was happening in a small town named Selma. They wanted to be able to say they'd been a part of it. The very cloth of long held accepted customs, conventions and beliefs was coming apart at the seams, making way for a new experiment in liberty.

Elverse and Winnie trudged back up the stairs.

"You know, I'm glad you came to stay with us," confided Elverse. "It's been great for my family. We've learned a lot from you."

"Me? No, no, please," objected Winnie. "I've learned so much from you. And I'm so grateful for the lodging. I couldn't have stayed otherwise. I owe y'all a lot." Winnie began to chuckle.

"What?" asked Elverse.

"I just said, y'all! Slipped right off my tongue. If I stay much longer I'll be talking like a real Southerner!"

"Stay as long as you like. In fact, I think I can speak for my family. We're going to miss you when the march is over."

They reached the top and each grabbed another shinny can and headed back down the stairs except this time Winnie tried Elverse's method. They both looked like old-fashioned ice deliverymen or piano movers. Elverse rolled his arm to look at his watch and almost missed a step.

"Sweet Jesus," he exclaimed. "We're supposed to pick up the portables at a construction yard. Elmira said it had to be done this afternoon."

Elverse secured a large truck with a hydraulic tailgate from the hospital, which they drove to the construction company yard where Leslie was already sweet-talking the owner.
She stood with him at a tall lectern he used as his outdoor counter underneath a Southern Sugar Maple. Leslie finished signing rental papers and handed the pen back to him with a bright smile.

"I can't thank you enough, Mr. Rawlings," Leslie gushed in her best Southern drawl. "You're a man of vision."

Mr. Rawlings was clearly taken with Leslie and played down his reluctance as he gazed into her blue eyes.

"Well, now, it's my pleasure, ma'am. Business is business. I got to keep up with the times—and they're surely changing."

"How very true and perceptive of you, Mr. Rawlings. But it will be to your betterment, you wait and see."

Elverse and Winnie showed up with the truck and jumped out of the cab. They strode over to Leslie and the owner.

"Ah! Here are my volunteers. Hi, fellows. I'd like you to meet the owner of this construction yard, Mr. Joshua Jacob Rawlings," introduced Leslie as if she'd known him all her life and was proud to call him friend.

"A pleasure," said Winnie, extending his hand. "Winston Phillips." The men shook hands.

"Happy to meet you," said Elverse, also extending his hand. "I'm Elverse Turner." After a perceptible pause, Mr. Rawlings also shook Elverse's hand.

"We really appreciate your help, Mr. Rawlings. Really appreciate it." Elverse said, smoothing over the awkward moment. "I have a hardware store in town and if you have any business cards, I'd be happy to prominently display them to send more business your way."

Mr. Rawlings was not sure what to say. He'd certainly been doing OK without having to do business with niggers. He looked slightly befuddled so Leslie stepped in and said tactfully, "Mr. Rawlings. Why don't you tell these gentlemen where they need to drive the truck to load up and we'll finish our transaction?"

"For sure," replied Mr. Rawlings. "Drive 'round back of the building and you'll see the portables at the far end of the yard. Take the number you need."

"Thank you, sir," said Elverse politely. Winnie nodded and they returned to the truck and drove to the back lot.

"I saw how he hesitated to shake your hand," said Winnie with a frown. "Even in a business deal it exists."

"Ah, that wasn't even worth noticing. Had plenty of interactions a whole lot worse. Why, once a white man called up the store looking for a rare kind of nail and I told him I carried them? He was so grateful because he'd called all over the county. Coming from up north, I don't have as strong a southern accent as some so I don't think he realized who he was talking to. I gave him directions and when he arrived, he asked for the owner. Said he didn't deal with 'no niggers.' When I told him I was the owner, his eyes looked like they'd pop out of his head, cartoon like! He looked me up and down, turned on his heel, and walked out the store—without buying his nails."

"Really?" said Winnie. "So, even though he needed these nails and couldn't find them anywhere else, he wouldn't allow himself to buy them from you."

"That's right," Elverse nodded. "Kind of pathetic, isn't it?"

Leslie, meanwhile, completed the order with Mr. Rawlings. She took out her wallet and handed him large bills. "Thank you, again, sir. It's been such a pleasure doing business with you."

Mr. Rawlings smiled at her. "Call me JJ. I know you're renting them for seven days but if you like, you can return them Friday morning. I won't charge you for the extra day."

"Why, thank you, JJ! That's extremely generous of you." The words easily slid off Leslie's tongue while she thought, yah, you know they'll just sitting on our trucks until Sunday. Big of you.

"Thank you so much for all your help," she restated.

Like people who avoid speaking real feelings yet want to fill in silent spaces, JJ said yet again, "It's been my pleasure, ma'am. After all, business is business and times are changing."

Leslie gave him a sweet smile and thought better of any further reply. She had achieved what they came for, and she could see the man was really struggling with those changes.

When people come together in a common cause, miracles are possible. With so little time to prepare, the churches of the Selma black community along with the experience of SCLC and SNCC doggedly brought it all together. They planned for the thousands who would begin the march and made arrangements for them to return to Selma at the end of the first leg with the exception of the 300 people who would continue marching Monday and Tuesday through Lowndes County. They also planned for the thousands who would end the march and arranged for a staging area near the state capitol where transportation would be provided so the marchers could quickly exit Montgomery after the rally was over.

All applicants who wished to march every day had to be examined by a doctor and given a clean bill of health to be one of the 300 chosen. The Turner family, Amelia Boynton, and Moses passed with flying colors but Elmira was asked to remain behind. Elmira, her arm still in a cast, took not marching in stride and continued to work the phones. She would remain busy until Thursday when she would join Moses in Montgomery for the victorious march into the city. Annie Lee, having not applied, looked forward to arriving on Thursday, too, when she would witness standing up to Wallace and the entire state of Alabama. Nor did Jackson apply; he understood he would be fired if he took even one day off. Leslie and Winnie would be part of the support crew.

There was a certain naivety among some marchers who wished the Judge had allowed all the people to march the entire route. The more experienced organizers realized with great relief how much safer the march would be with fewer people, especially when they entered the county known for its vicious racism and swamps. The narrow road became a perfect excuse to keep the numbers down.

As Sunday approached, not every assignment had gone smoothly. There had been numerous setbacks. The Negro woman who offered her farm to pitch their tents on the first night turned out not to own the land even though she'd farmed it for decades. Owned by a white Southerner, the landowner stepped in and secured an injunction prohibiting the marchers from using his fields. The Committee scrambled to find a replacement. A grocery store in a nearby town offered to sell them large cans of tomatoes at a huge discount but when they went to pick them up, Elmira noticed the dates on the cans had long expired.

Winnie, who had accompanied her, said, "What do they take us for? Stupid?"

Elmira laughed and shook it off, stating, "Well, if we think a bargain's too good to be true, we better count on it being too good to be true. We'll stick to the stores we know from now on."

There was one small town between Selma and Montgomery—Lowndes Borough—but the organizers knew it would have nothing to do with the marchers. Lodging and every single meal would have to be supplied by the movement.

By Saturday there was a small lull in all the activity as the hundreds of details were either in the works or had been dealt with and crossed off the list. Fifty support vehicles had been secured, among them a 60-gallon water truck, a mobile health clinic, trash pickup trucks, a half dozen ambulances, and an entire fleet of command cars. All camping locations had been secured and the collected food had teams that would cook it. The SCLC would end up spending over thirty thousand dollars for the five-day march. Considering the national annual wage in 1965 was $4,659.00, that cost put a considerable dent in King's coffers.

Leslie sat at the transportation table, her eyes closed, her shoes off.

Hi," said Winnie who stood before her. She blinked open. "Catching a quick cat nap?"

Leslie smiled ruefully. "Just resting my eyes. You look a bit exhausted yourself."

"I'm sleep walking. It's amazing how really few hours I need, but it wrecks havoc on my appearance. But more than sleep, I need a break. I noticed 'The Sound of Music' is playing downtown. Want to sneak away for a couple of hours and see it with me?"

Leslie laughed. "Oh! Doesn't that sound like fun? But I think I better stay here and mind the table."

"Oh, come on. Just ask any one of these people running around here to take your place for a few hours. We've earned it."

Leslie regarded this tall, lanky, adorable man standing in front of her. He was so enthusiastic and playful with that engaging Warren Beatty appeal. Who did he remind her of? Not David, her husband, who was much more serious and almost a father figure. Justin? Of course not because she admitted there was a slight attraction. That was it! A certain teasing attraction like her first boyfriend had possessed. She hadn't thought about Johnnie Hennington in years. It wasn't a serious attraction with Winnie, just fun, a little spice added to their friendship. Like it had been with Johnnie.

Leslie grinned. "You're tempting me."

"Good. I accept the role of tempter. Grab your sweater."

Leslie slid her black flats back on, found someone to take her place, and the two of them dashed out the door like teenagers playing hooky.

The theater was all but empty for a Saturday matinee so they sat right in the middle. Winnie even bought popcorn to share. They were transported far away from Selma. The music was so uplifting they both fairly danced out of the theater when the credits rolled.

"Thanks for pulling me away, Winnie. I wouldn't have thought of it. I've been on such a treadmill."

He slid his arm through hers as they headed back to the church. "I just knew I needed to do something that had nothing to do with the march because starting tomorrow, that's all we'll be thinking about."

"I can't believe how it's all come together. We pulled off something no one believed was possible."

"Yes, the hills are alive," he shouted. Leslie giggled as he continued. "And I'm going to try to remember the songs Julie sang when I'm heaving garbage cans full of food for the next four days."

"And when I can't sit in a car one minute longer, I'll jump out and pretend to be on top of an Austrian mountaintop!" She did a little pirouette.

Winnie caught her in his arms and spun her around again, making her laugh. He looked at her, happy to be with her, happy to have these few stolen moments together.

"Life is good," he said softly.

Leslie gave him a quick kiss on his cheek, the kind a sister would give a brother.

"It'll be even better next week when Annie Lee and I finally head home. Come on, we need to get back."

"OK," sighed Winnie and wistfully dropped his arm from Leslie's waist after a quick squeeze. "No rest for the weary."

"Or the tempter," declared Leslie as they skipped back to work.

The Federal government, too, was busy organizing. Governor Wallace unequivocally stated if he were forced to permit the march, despite the injunction by Judge Johnson, his state of Alabama would not pay the $360,000.00 price tag for parade security. Wallace would make certain Alabama didn't pay one dime for protection, claiming Alabama couldn't afford it. The Alabama State Legislature backed Wallace up with a commendation letter praising him and claiming how unfair it would be for Alabama to bear the burden of all the trouble that had been stirred up in their fair state.

"The United States government has created a highly explosive situation and then seeks to put the burden of policing such a dangerous condition on local and state law enforcement officers," the letter complained.

President Johnson outsmarted Wallace and the state legislature by calling up the Alabama National Guard and deputizing them to take orders from the Federal Government. Many in the Guard who were avowed segregationists now found themselves in the role of protectorates. Ironically, the Selma City Council President was called up by the Guard to protect this march that his City Council had voted to stop.

John Doar, Assistant Attorney General for Civil Rights, was put in charge of securing the safety of the marchers. Along with nineteen hundred Alabama National guardsmen, one thousand federal military soldiers, a small battalion of FBI agents and U.S. Marshals, and another thousand U.S. soldiers on alert, Doar created a nearly impenetrable shield. The Federal government was going to insure safekeeping absolutely.

❧

PART FOUR

HOW LONG?

TWELVE

On Sunday, March 21, 1965, a brilliant orange sun slowly rose in the chilly eastern horizon as green combat army jeeps rolled silently into the city. Soldiers jumped off at every cross street along the parade route and carried a rifle with a fixed but sheathed bayonet. There was to be no doubt that a powerful United States government would protect the marchers. No doubt at all.

Deputy Attorney General, Ramsey Clark, from the Department of Justice, flew down to command the army, National Guardsmen, FBI agents, and U.S. Marshals from his post set up in Selma's Federal building. John Doar, meanwhile, would accompany the march the entire way on foot: he would walk, eat, and sleep with the marchers, and from the field he would send daily reports directly to Ramsey Clark and President Johnson.

It was no surprise that the march did not leave on time. Considering the leadership had organized as much as possible in four and a half days, there were still last minute details that demanded attention. The logistics were horrendous, every bit as challenging as going to war but with one big difference. They were marching in peace.

Marchers began to gather in front of Brown Chapel around eight o'clock despite the morning chill. The Turners arrived immediately after church once they'd rushed home to change their clothes and shoes. They were too excited to dawdle at home. Mandy was probably the most excited of all. Exhausted from working double shifts, she looked forward to simply putting one foot in front of the other and spending full days and nights with her husband and child. The Turners stood one behind the other: Elverse adjusted a strap on Mandy's backpack while Mandy straightened Carlton's sweater underneath his backpack.

Since Elmira wasn't marching, she already was inside the Chapel wielding the phone and finalizing specifics. Moses spotted the Turners and danced over to their circle.

"Got me some new winged tips!" he gloated, a twinkle in his eye. Mandy was about to object when he pinched up his pant legs to show off new sneakers. The men guffawed and slapped each other playfully. Moses looked around.

"How many do you reckon are here?"

Elverse did some quick calculations in his head based on the number that were at the second march and how much space they had taken up on the lawns.

"I'd say at least two thousand," he guessed. "Maybe more?"

Moses nodded. "And they're still coming," he said. "I bet we could have over four thousand by the time we head out, not counting the support teams who aren't even marching."

"Isn't it amazing," marveled Elverse.

"We've definitely come a long way from our straggle-ass lines down at the courthouse," said Moses.

"Ain't that the truth," exclaimed Annie Lee as she walked up to the group with Jackson and Leslie. "I've never seen so many people, praise the Lord!" Annie Lee was so excited she could have been a Macy's parade balloon levitating in the sky had she not been a live human being. It was a dream come true.

"What a glorious day," Leslie enthused, caught up in Annie Lee's euphoria and ignoring the cold. "If I hadn't promised David, I'd march, too."

That claim wasn't close to being true for even though she had made such a promise to David, she had come to realize it was Annie Lee's moment, Annie Lee's time to express what she had lived and breathed and worked toward for so many years.

It was the people of Selma who deserved their time in the sun. Leslie would remain in the background as support. She was still a part of the effort; she just wasn't using her feet.

"Good thing tomorrow is limited to three hundred. Can you imagine how hard it would be to keep all these folks together the entire way?" Annie Lee assessed as she looked over the ever-growing crowd proudly.

"Not to mention how hard it would be for us all to keep up," chortled Jackson.

"Where's brother Winnie?" asked Annie Lee.

"We dropped him off at First Baptist. He's probably already elbow deep in spaghetti sauce for tonight," explained Elverse.

"He's so driven to help," said Mandy. "Sometimes I worry about him."

"Why, Mama?" asked Carlton. "He told me this march has become his new ministry since he don't have a church of his own."

"Doesn't," corrected Mandy. "I am grateful he's here. We can be sure we'll be well fed tonight with him on the job." They all gaily agreed.

An ecumenical service prior to the march began and the gathered, now numbering almost four thousand, were ready to be inspired. The service started late but eventually Ralph Abernathy introduced King with his own rosy version of what the march was accomplishing.

"When we get to Montgomery we are going to go up to Governor Wallace's door and say, 'George, it's all over now. We've got the ballot!'" The assembled roared with laughter and cheered.

Dr. Martin Luther King, Jr., their beloved leader, then told them they were creating a new chapter in their nation, and while they might not have much and may know poverty, they had their bodies, their feet, and their souls to enable them to walk to the promise land. America would be a new America.

Filled with motivation, the marchers set out. The thousands of lunch bags were passed out. The churchwomen had filled each bag with either a peanut butter or American cheese sandwich, an orange, a few cookies, and a napkin.

Taking the lead at the front of the long parade that would stretch over a mile was John Lewis who, despite his doctors efforts to curtail him, would walk the entire way. Others were Sister Stella, who had decided to stay on in Selma despite her Mother Superior's instructions to return to Chicago; Ralph Abernathy; Martin Luther King, Jr. and his wife, Coretta; Cager Lee, Jimmy Lee Jackson's grandfather; fellow Nobel Peace Prize Laureate, Dr. Ralph Bunche; Rabbis Abraham Joshua Herschel and Maurice Davis; and civil rights pioneer, Fred Shuttlesworth. And, of course, there was John Doar, marching as the sentinel next to the line, keeping a watch out for trouble.

The march departed a few minutes before one in the afternoon. Beautiful, fragrant orchid leis flown in from Hawaii were placed around the heads of those in the front flank. As they stepped out, the leis swayed like a Hawaiian ocean breeze, bouncing on their suit jackets and coats. Coretta clasped hands with her husband as they set the pace. She asked him, "Do you really think we can walk to Montgomery by Thursday?"

King smiled at her and replied, "A piece of cake."

Two jeeps drove ahead of the marchers, clearing the way, much like the famous Pasadena Rose Parade in California. But instead of floats, there were people, people, and more people.

On their way out of town the thousands marched passed a record store whose loudspeaker blasted into the street, "Bye Bye Blackbird." A car passed with a sign, "Yankee Trash Go Home." When they again crossed Pettus Bridge, helicopters hovered overhead and almost drowned them out as they sang, "This Little Light Of Mine."

Most whites stayed away from the spectacle altogether, as requested by Mayor Smitherman and Governor Wallace. Still, on the other side of the bridge, positioned again in front of the Chick-N-Treat Café were hard-core hecklers. They held up signs like, "Too Bad Frey," "I Hate Niggers," "Nigga King Go Home," and "Martin Luther Coon," signs that said more about the persons holding them than the march. Yet such a display of racism could not dampen the soaring spirit of the marchers whose sheer force of numbers made a powerful counterpoint to the flimsy, crude scrawled signs.

Choice and his KKK buddies were among this group, naturally. As the leading two jeeps filled with guardsmen whizzed past, Sparky spit in disgust and sulked off.

"Shit!" he drawled. "There are more troopers than marchers." Uncle patted his arm. Choice and Rusty exchanged woeful looks.

"Damn," hissed Rusty. "I can't believe they're actually letting these nigger spooks take over our state."

"Take over my ass," huffed Uncle. "There's plenty of us to stop 'um, just you wait and see. Hey! The South will rise again." They put their heads together as if they were a football huddle and shouted in unison, "THE SOUTH WILL RISE AGAIN!"

The South might rise again but these friends couldn't. The length of the march had effectively locked them into their spot and they couldn't leave until the road reopened. They would have to wait for the whole parade to pass. Choice finally sat down on the curb; his foot hurt. Rusty worried about Melanie Vi and the Sunday family time he was missing and began to pace. Sparky defiantly turned his back on the marchers and kept drinking. Only Uncle Parker stood watching the entire parade. The image of the march seared into his brain, it would forever be a reminder of the day he believed the South as he knew it had died.

There was no way the march could hit its original eleven-mile goal on the first day, but what was important was they were on their way. It remained a huge achievement considering how many people were participating. They would make it to Montgomery by Thursday and hold what they were now calling their Freedom Rally.

Unlike an individual who sets her or his own pace to walk, it's infinitely more difficult and tiring to walk with a mass of people. Annie Lee and Jackson fell further and further behind until they brought up the rear. They were gratified to see Amtrak sitting placidly in the middle of the countryside when the day came to an end. John Doar had realized they didn't have enough buses and cars to return the Sunday marchers to Selma before nightfall, so he called upon a train that would take the tail end of the marchers back to town.

Annie Lee was puffing hard and her ankles were horribly swollen as she and Jackson headed for an Amtrak car.

"Jus' a little further, sugar. We made it, honey!" said Jackson.

"Truth be told," replied Annie Lee, "I'm grateful they figured out this here train. I couldn't walk another step." She limped up to the train and dumped her weary bones into the partially filled car while Jackson paid the SCLC volunteer marshal their fares of seventy-five cents each.

The huge tents for the first camp were pitched on a farm property owned by David Hall, a black hardihood who allowed the marchers to use his eighty-acre land after he learned the original site had fallen through. David Hall knew he could face retaliation for helping the march so he shipped his eight children off to relatives to keep them out of danger. They would not be able to witness the march even though the marchers would camp on their own property.

"What about your own safety?" John Doar had asked when he visited the farm to work out logistics. David looked at John who obviously was putting himself at risk, too.

"The Lord will provide," David Hall had answered simply.

Mandy, Elverse, Carlton, and Moses filed into camp, thankful for the tents already erected by the roustabout team: seminarians and professors from the San Francisco Theological Seminary in San Anselmo, California, and actors, Gary Merrill and Pernell Roberts. Winnie was at his food station ready to dish out dinner from his garbage can "pot" filled with spaghetti. Next to him was another volunteer, Reverend Hank Anberg. He stood behind the portable tables offering heaping spoonfuls of pork and beans. Winnie smiled at the Turners when they arrived and held out their plates.

"How'd it go on your first day?" he asked.

"No problem," proclaimed Carlton. "Easy as pie." They gave each other a high five.

"Of course, this camp isn't as far as what we were originally supposed to cover every day," said Mandy. "Do you know how many miles this farm is from Selma?"

"I heard it was just a little over seven miles. Not bad considering what time the march started," said Winnie.

"It'll be easier tomorrow when there are less people," Elverse said. "We'll be able to make up some time."

I'm not too worried that we'll get there by Thursday, stated Mandy, "especially if we have enough energy food to keep us going. I have to say, Winnie, I was really looking forward to your spaghetti tonight."

"Me, too!" Agreed Carlton as Winnie plopped a large portion onto his plate.

"Nice to know my cooking is appreciated," grinned Winnie.

"Oh, it is, brother," hooted Elverse, "it is."

After dinner Carlton watched the communications vehicle set up its portable radio station. It had a fifteen-foot antenna that was operated by a SNCC member. SNCC was able to broadcast from the march each night on a short wave frequency that had been approved by the FCC for the duration of the march. When the technician noticed how interested this young marcher was, he asked Carlton if he would like to say something over the airwaves. Carlton's eyes widened and adrenalin pumped through his body.

"No thank you, sir," said Carlton, suddenly very self-conscious. The technician patted his shoulder and smiled. "Maybe another night," he said. "Didn't mean to spring it on you."

Carlton never did feel able to speak into the microphone. Like his father, he was modest and couldn't conceive of speaking to the entire nation. But every night thereafter he swung by the truck to watch their station connect with the country and listen to the broadcast.

The organizers, ever mindful of white suspicions about inappropriate sexual behavior, handled sleeping quarters by rigging one tent for the men and one tent for the women. Since more than the designated 300 persons wanted to spend the first night in the encampment, they agreed to sleep out-side the tents. Even so, the tents were crowded. Fortunately, most marchers were more interested in sleep than comfort and managed with very little space. Carlton and Moses found spots and immediately fell asleep. Elverse escorted his wife to the female tent. He cupped her delicate face in his hands when they reached the entrance.

"Good night, Mr. Turner," said Mandy. "I've had a lovely time. Please do call again." Her eyes shone as she looked at her husband. It had been a long time since they'd spent an entire day and evening together. He held her tight and kissed her on the lips.

"You bet I will. Good night, Mrs. Turner."

As Elverse walked to the men's tent, he passed a small group of marchers who obviously thought it was party time. They were creating a ruckus around a bon fire built in an oil drum and passed a thermos between them that Elverse knew didn't contain coffee. He thought to ask them to respect those trying to sleep but instead simply went to bed himself. He found Carlton and Moses, unrolled his sleeping bag in what little space was left and crawled in, still wearing his clothes. It was too cold to do otherwise. There were no blankets that first night. Through some glitch, blankets donated by a closed hospital in Boston didn't arrive. Everyone had to make do.

At his doctors' insistence, John Lewis, still recovering from his concussion, returned to Selma every night to sleep in a bed. Dr. King slept in a trailer parked in the middle of the camp for better protection. The army created a perimeter ring around the camp by building bon fires every couple of yards and kept watch over the marchers throughout the night. From the movement itself, two teams of unarmed freedom march veterans patrolled the inner and outer perimeters of the army ring. They were on the look out for any would-be KKK snipers and overly zealous Alabama guardsmen who might disobey their duty to the United States government. To be nationalized didn't mean these Southerners would change their segrega-tionist stripes. The movement leadership didn't trust them.

⁂

THIRTEEN

The next morning, the marchers cleaned up after a breakfast of hot oatmeal, toast, and coffee. Andrew Young
took charge of sorting out who would wear one of the 300
identifying orange vests. There were still almost 400 marchers
in camp and some confusion arose over who the 300 were
supposed to be. The roll call sheet had gone missing.

"Those who cut up last night and showed no deference to
others trying to sleep ought to return to Selma," Young began.
There were murmurs of agreement.

"Now then, on your honor. A doctor must have already
screened you in Selma. First priority is for all those who
marched on March 7th or were there as part of the support
team back at the church on that terrible day. Please step forward." Close to 200 marchers stepped forward and were
handed vests. Moses and the Turners took their vests and
unfolded them with care. Carlton treated his vest like it was
spun gold, not cheap nylon, and would keep it forever. He
was so proud to be one of the chosen. So proud he was being
treated as an equal, not a boy.

"Next will be the volunteer folks who have been working
on our committees to make this march come together, including office staff from both SNCC and SCLC." Young handed
out more vests.

"We welcome all clergy to join us who have come to
march the entire way and also ask you to wear a vest." Rabbis,
ministers, nuns, and a Buddhist monk stepped forward and
were given their vests.

"And last but not least, those who contacted our office from other states and countries and informed us they were prepared to come to Alabama and march the entire way with us."

All three hundred orange vests were passed out and the "hard core" as they became known helped one another put them on over their jackets, sweaters, coats, religious robes and habits. The vests were not particularly attractive, but everyone donned them with pride. They symbolized something so much more important than fashion.

The 300 vested marchers were eager to get moving. Leslie arrived as part of the transportation team just as they were breaking camp. She dropped off John Lewis near the tents that would soon be taken down and found a parking space near the command cars. She hopped out of the car and began searching for the Turners. When she spotted them, she loped over to say hello. "Good morning, I see you all got the same memo about what to wear today."

"Yes, aren't they chic?" said Mandy.

"It's so we'll keep together and they can identify us for protection," said Carlton.

"Or make it easier for snipers to identify us. We might as well have a bulls-eye on our backs," said Moses drolly.

"Moses! There'll be no talk like that," chided Mandy.

"You're here early," said Elverse looking at his watch. "It's not even eight o'clock yet."

"It's not early according to John Lewis. He wanted to be sure to be here before you headed out. I'll be taking marchers back who I heard stayed the night even though they're not marching this next leg."

"They were the rowdies who partied because they knew they didn't have to march today," said Carlton. "At least they had a fire to keep warm."

"Yah, I heard the blankets didn't arrive," said Leslie. "I hope you weren't chilled to the bone. I think the temperature dropped below freezing last night."

"Let's just say Mandy and I would have liked to have been together to keep each other warm," grinned Elverse.

"Elmira tracked down the problem so blankets will definitely be at your next camp site tonight."

"I wonder how long it'll take us to get to the camp?" asked Mandy.

"The radio said it's going to be a long day today, trying to make up for yesterday," said Carlton.

"I sure hope our feet won't suffer," said Moses. "I'll be holding my breath that my new shoes won't cause my dogs to bark!"

"And I'll be holding my breath that you get through Lowndes county in record time," said Leslie.

"You and me both," agreed Mandy. "Today will be one day down and one more to go before we're past the swamps."

"Well, I hope you got enough sleep to keep you going. Good luck." Leslie gave each of them a quick hug, including Mandy.

Leslie found Winnie loading up his empty cans to return to the Baptist church for the next hot meal.

"Morning," she said.

Winnie straightened up and grinned broadly. There were dried bits of oatmeal on his shirt that he tried to brush off.

"Good morning to you," he said, his exhausted face brightening.

"You're pulling off an amazing feat to feed so many," said Leslie.

Winnie nodded. "Thanks to the incredible women working back at First Baptist!" he said. "These next two days will be a whole lot easier when we're only feeding the three hundred."

"Only three hundred," said Leslie with a laugh.

Winnie took in this woman he had such feeling for in the compressed time they had known each other.

"How are you and Annie Lee coming along for your trip?"

"I don't see her much with all the running around I do," said Leslie. "But she told me she plans to pack a box every day. Now that's she's actually decided to go, she just might be looking forward to it, although I don't think she would admit that to me."

"That's terrific. I'm happy for you, Leslie. You're finally getting your wish."

"I guess so," Leslie mused. "Sounds funny to say that now. I don't seem to have just one goal anymore."

"I can relate," beamed Winnie.

They stood there smiling a bit awkwardly at each other.

"Well," Leslie broke the moment, "I guess I better round up the bodies I'm supposed to take back to Selma."

"Right," agreed Winnie. "And I've got to get this truck packed up and head back to help with dinner." Winnie snorted. "It never ends."

"After this experience you'll be able to hire yourself out as a cook," she teased.

"Great idea. It'll be my new ministry," he smirked. "Bring folks to the Lord through their stomachs. Halleluiah!"

Lowndes County consisted mostly of pastureland with an occasional cotton or cornfield alternating between long stretches of swampland that hosted Loblolly Pine trees dripping with Spanish moss and dark, slimy water. Two helicopters flying overhead announced the march's arrival long before the march could be seen. The 300 marchers looked like streaked-backed Oriole birds in their bright orange vests as they walked through Lowndes County that was eighty-one percent black yet did not have one single black registered voter.

In the lead, on each side of the march, were trooper cars with flashing warning lights. They moved at the same pace as those walking. Behind the trooper cars were the army jeeps hauling riffled soldiers. At the tail end of the march were news vans, followed by medical vans, trucks carrying the portable toilets and supplies, then even more army jeeps with soldiers, and finally one more trooper car with flashing lights acting as the caboose. As the marchers walked through one of the most notoriously racist counties in Alabama, the government's protective show of strength made it clear the Federal government took the threat of violence seriously. Very, very seriously.

Yet one small plane that was not part of the protection plan entered the air space over the marchers and dropped yellow segregationist leaflets on them. These leaflets claimed to be from the "Confederate Air Force" and were a warning to all marchers that they stood to lose their jobs and perhaps their homes if they participated. Moses was particularly spooked that a hostile plane so easily penetrated the airspace over their protected entourage.

Maintaining the pace at the head of the march was Dr. King, (Coretta would return to the march that night), John Lewis, a blind man led by his mother, and Jim Letherer, a social worker from Saginaw, Michigan who came and marched on crutches. As a polio victim in his youth, he was missing one leg. When the march left town the day before, ignoramuses that had formed a pack to give each other courage heckled Letherer. They shouted at him as he passed, "Left! Left! Left! Left!" Obviously it did not occur to them the amount of bravery and strength it took for this white man to walk on crutches for fifty-four miles.

The National Guard stationed along the route had been instructed not to face the marchers but to face the swamps where evil could be lurking. Some did about-face but most did not, perhaps as a protest, perhaps because they wanted to witness history in the making with their own eyes.

The helicopters hovered even lower as the marchers swiftly passed by dark, shadowy swamps, drowning out any singing and creating great gusts of wind. Carlton had always thought he'd like to ride in a helicopter but the piercing clatter and hurricane-like force of air changed his mind. He knew the choppers were there for his own safety but he wished they wouldn't hang right over their heads like the sword of Damocles. It was unnerving. A team of army demolition experts, always ahead of the march, inspected every bridge and suspecting fence as the marchers moved east, which heightened the marchers' trepidation of potential danger.

As the march approached a hill, John Doar stepped up to Jim Letherer and asked if he would like to take a little break and sit with him by the side of the road? Jim agreed and the two chatted while the march continued up and over the hill.

John then hailed one of the jeeps and the two were driven back to their places in the march. It was a small incident that spoke volumes about how observant and sensitive Doar was to the people he was there to protect.

There were other poignant scenes, too. As the marchers passed an all white Southside High School, students ran to the fence and waved. A few cheered. Carlton smiled at them and waved back. Perhaps his generation would be more accepting of equality. Perhaps his age group would worry more about a war build-up in Vietnam than racial differences.

When they marched past a few scattered shacks, black mothers with their heads wrapped in rags and holding babies on their hips, stepped outside and just stared, not comprehending what was taking place.

A white family reclining on lawn chairs in front of their brick mansion laughed at the parade along with their black maid who was serving them bourbon hot toddies. A very small boy ran to the edge of the property and chanted, "nigger, nigger, nigger" and shook his tiny fist. Without missing a step, Mandy flipped him the peace sign.

Further down the road a boy came running through a field to watch them pass. Elverse and Carlton stepped out of line and went to say hello.

"Hi there," said Elverse. "Nice of you to cheer us on. This here's my son, Carlton." The boys shook hands. "How old are you son?"

"Twelve."

"I see. I would have thought you were thirteen at least." The boy grinned and puffed up his chest.

"What do you raise on this farm?" asked Carlton.

"We don't raise nothin'. We can't have a garden or anything. Mr. Reilly, he live up in that white house yonder, he raises cotton. We pick it."

"I see," said Elverse. "What do you think of our march?"

"Oh, I think it's a good thing. White and black ought to be mixing. This march will make things better."

"What things would those be?" asked Elverse.

"Things that are bad."

"Well, we hope we'll turn bad into good," said Elverse.

"Oh and one more thing," said the boy. No matter how old they are, people ought to be able to vote."

"Like you, for instance?"

"Yah. Right. Like me."

"If you could vote, who would you vote for President?" asked Carlton.

"Wallace."

"Wallace?" said Carlton in dismay.

"Johnson! Johnson, I mean to say Johnson. I don't think much of Wallace." Elverse and Carlton laughed.

"Neither do we! Well, you may not vote until you're twenty-one but by the time you are, we'll make sure your able to."

"Thank you, sir," said the boy respectfully.

Elverse and Carlton then shook his hand good-bye and trotted off to catch up with Mandy and Moses.

Morning drifted into afternoon and it began to drizzle, but the spirit of the march was not dampened, even if marchers' caps and scarves were. Moses put his arm around Carlton as they took in the countryside and passed a decrepit building. It had a rusty tin roof with whole sections missing and big holes in the walls. Moses and Carlton stopped when children appeared from what was little more than a shack and ran down to the road. The multi-aged group stood in a line and solemnly sang, "We Shall Overcome."

When they finished singing, Carlton and Moses shook their hands.

"How do," said Moses. "Mighty fine singing."

"Thank you, sir," said the tallest boy.

"Thanks for being supportive of our march," said Carlton.

"Oh, yah!" said another boy. "Our school even took up a collection to help pay for your food while you march."

Carlton eyed the dilapidated structure up on the rise. "Is that your school?" he asked incredulously. The children nodded and one pointed back toward the hill. "Yah, that be Rolen School. That's our school."

Carlton looked at the students before him who were so obviously poor in their ill fitting, faded clothes. "Gosh. Well, thank you for your collection. That was mighty generous. I'll thank you every time I eat."

"That would be real fine," said the tallest boy, smiling. "If your belly will remember us, it'll make us part of the march, too."

"Don't let any building stop you from learning," said Moses. "That's the important thing. You study and do all your work and someday you'll be able to come back to your neighborhood and build a brand new right proper school." He added, "Keep studying hard, boys, and "we shall overcome!"

Moses made one of his fancy dance steps in front of them, much to their delight. Then Carlton and Moses waved over their shoulders as they raced to catch up with the march.

That night the pitched tents were waiting in a pasture for the tired marchers who walked sixteen miles to arrive at Rosie Steele's farm. There was a long line at the huge mobile hospital on loan from the Ladies Garment Workers Union. King had limped into camp with several blisters; his feet were the first to be treated and bandaged because he soon would be flying to Cleveland for a speaking engagement. King hoped to raise money from sympathetic northerners to help defray some of the cost of the march.

Others had blisters, too, but the main complaint was sunburn. The morning sky had been overcast and many hadn't bothered to put on any sunscreen. They stood patiently waiting their turn as the drizzle began to turn to real rain.

Not far away in the small town of Lowndesboro, Rusty's wife, Melanie Vi, prayed her husband and his buddies would forget about the march and celebrate her daughter's second birthday. She had hung pink crepe paper across their living room ceiling, and balloons decorated the doorway corners. On the pass through ledge to the kitchen sat a delicious looking praline pecan cake from Priesters, the famous pecan company where Rusty worked a fork lift, and a large pitcher of Southern Comfort punch, now almost half gone.

Choice and Sparky had already arrived and the four adults each held the corner of a blanket to toss baby Sandra De up into the air.

"Wheeeeee!" they all chanted to her squealing delight. They tossed her a few more times before ending the game and downing more punch. Melanie Vi took her baby, put her on her hip and gave her a kiss before taking dainty sips of the punch.

Allie April, Uncle's wife, sailed through the front door, shook off raindrops, and stopped in her tracks as she took in the decorations. "Why Melanie Vi, just look what you did! How festive!" She walked over to Melanie Vi and gave her and the baby kisses. "Hi y'all!"

"Hey, hey, Auntie Allie April. Evening. Can I get you some punch?" asked Rusty happily. He was proud he and his wife could host a party for their cherished daughter.

"I do believe I will have a glass. My, my, and you're serving my favorite cake, too." Rusty poured her a plastic cup of punch and handed it to her.

"So where's Uncle?" asked Sparky.

"He's out in the car. I'm to tell you boys to get on out there. Says you're gonna get Sandy De here her best present ever!"

Melanie Vi held her baby tighter as her festive mood deflated and she watched the three men grab their jackets to flee out the door.

"Thanks for the punch Melanie Vi. Guess we'll get some cake another time," said Sparky.

"Yah. Thanks so much. Happy birthday to little Sandy De," said Choice.

"Bye, honey," said Rusty and gave his wife a quick peck on the cheek before he cut out after his buddies. The door slammed and they were gone. The party was over.

"Well," said Allie April brightly, "I guess that means more cake for us."

Uncle drove his caddie real slow past Rosie Steele's farm and every man took in the camp, swiveling their heads as they passed and trying to make out the lay of things through the rain streaked windows. No one spoke. Only the sound of the windshield wipers made rhythmic, muffled thumps. There were sentinels at the edge of the highway and a ring of bon fires surrounding the camp. Flames licked the sky, sizzling from the rain, and lit up the many soldiers surrounding each barrel.

"Shit!" said Uncle. It's like Fort Knox here."

Once safely down the road beyond the camp, Uncle turned his car around, careful to avoid the ditch. He headed back for Lowndesboro, passing the FBI car that had been following at a safe distance. Leslie had just missed passing them when she had picked up a woman who was sick and needed to be taken back to Selma. The men were in a foul mood. But at least their aborted intentions would be offset by praline pecan cake.

The marchers awoke the next morning to a constant, hard rain. It was going to be their toughest day yet. The pasture had turned to mud and people struggled to walk from their tents to the latrine trucks. Elverse and Mandy wrapped their hands around hot cups of coffee and were grateful for the warmth, even though breakfast itself wasn't hot. The ladies at First Baptist were too exhausted to change the menu to accommodate the weather.

After a breakfast of corn flakes, Carlton, along with a few other younger marchers, took the empty boxes and tore them open to make rain hats. The hats worked for a few hours until the cardboard became too soggy to be useful. Others, who hadn't brought any rain gear, were given thin, clear, plastic sheet ponchos that barely kept a body dry. The rain turned into a downpour and water could not drain off the road fast enough. When a drop hit the slushy pavement it bounced back up almost a foot. Marchers hunkered down and kept their eyes on their shoes. Rain dripped from their noses and spattered their backs. Rivulets slid down their slick raincoat sleeves.

Mandy, Elverse, and Moses walked in a flank, each with their own umbrella. There was no linking arms or holding hands. To keep their spirits from completely drowning, they joined in a chant, "Free-dom, free-dom." But it was hard to chant when rain restricted one's every step and the chant died down quickly. There was less singing, too, even though Moses and Carlton tried to keep the music going to avoid total misery. At one point, Moses closed his umbrella briefly and filled his mouth with rainwater and tried to gargle the melody, which Carlton found hysterically funny.

John Doar was completely drenched but never complained. In the afternoon a truck pulled alongside the marchers and began to toss oranges to waving hands, slowly working its way down the line. Laughing marchers scrambled to catch—or in some cases chase—the appreciated fruit. They momentarily forgot their wretched rain misery.

In the early evening their soaked bodies turned onto Robert Gardner's farm, a pasture that had turned into a huge mud hole. The bomb squad had covered every inch of the pasture that morning but by mid afternoon it wasn't habitable. The roustabouts went further up the hill and managed to raise the tents there, but the damage had already been done to that ground and any sleeping bag with the weight of a body inside would sink into the sodden mess.

Back in Selma, Elmira tried to solve the problem by delivering air mattresses to be used underneath the sleeping bags. But they, too, sunk and were of little help. Portable heaters were brought to the site and people gathered around them to dry out and warm up as best they could.

Moses, Carlton, and Elverse, along with a few northern soldiers, tried to spread hay over the mud but that didn't help; there was not enough hay to make a difference. When people walked, their shoes sunk into the mud and care had to be taken that the mud didn't suck their shoes off completely. If they didn't pay close attention, when they took their next step they would find mud oozing between their toes.

Everyone was cranky and hungry. A guardsman spit on a priest and Doar promptly removed him. It was the low point of the march—until dinner.

"OK, marchers," shouted Winnie when dinner was set up. He and the other ministers on the food crew instantly became the most popular men in camp as that evening's hot meal did not disappoint. There was barbecued chicken, hash, peas and carrots, corn bread, plus candy bars for desert. The women at First Baptist had outdone themselves and Winnie felt like a chosen servant to be privileged to serve such grateful patrons. After a day of slogging eleven miles through the rain, the marchers had more than earned every hot morsel.

ᘓ

FOURTEEN

As miserable and difficult as it was to march in the pouring rain the day before, Wednesday was their reward. It was sunny and bright and some mud caked marchers even got too hot. Then, in the afternoon there was a sudden cloudburst that drenched everyone briefly and washed a lot of the mud away. It was God providing showers.

As soon as they passed the Lowndes county line, the highway widened and became four lanes again. All afternoon cars pulled up and let off people who wanted to march this last leg. Leslie was busy ferrying people from Selma to the march, each time dropping her passengers off several miles further up the sixteen-mile distance the march covered that day. The numbers quickly grew to over a thousand and kept growing. A huge bus pulled up with a banner on its side that read, "Montgomery or Bust—Canadians Love Y'all" and unloaded its one hundred Canadian supporters eager to join the parade.

This journey had become international news, just as Gandhi's march to the sea was beamed throughout the world. A determined change was definitely taking place in America and the eyes of the world were upon the state of Alabama to see how that change would play out. Sadly, the march wasn't being reported locally. The Atlantic Constitution, Montgomery's leading newspaper that was the largest newspaper in the South and claimed it "covers Dixie like the dew," boycotted the event. Their publisher maintained the march wasn't news.

The marchers turned into St. Jude compound, a triumphant assemblage of dirty, happy demonstrators who had used their feet to challenge power. Behind them were excited, freshly clean supporters eager to take up the cause with them. Thankfully, St. Jude had room for them all. The city of Montgomery had been less gracious. The City Council had refused a request to use their stadium. St. Jude saved the day by inviting the march to camp on its property. The City Council then countered by refusing to allow the use of the parking lot at the George Washington Carver High School directly across the street from St. Jude. Any roadblock to the voting rights cause was an acceptable tactic.

St. Jude, however, was living its mission. The compound, opened in the mid 1930's to assist black and white alike, became known as the "City of St. Jude." This city welcomed all marchers and supporters with open arms. People bedded down for the night where they could. Additional tents were pitched on the athletic field even though the ground was still waterlogged from the rain. But for the hard core 300 marchers, that was no big deal.

The numbers swelled to an astonishing ten thousand and spirits were high. A social worker from New York conducted continuous classes on safety for visitors as they arrived. They were told, "Don't talk to people you don't know. Don't answer back. And go straight home immediately after the mass Freedom rally is over. Do not remain on the streets."

Winnie and the food crew had more difficulty creating an area that would serve the hard core yet not look like a food station for anyone passing by. Hank, who had worked by Winnie's side all week, inquired, "How are we going to know which ones to feed? The ones with the most mud caked on them?"

Winnie shrugged. "We'll feed anyone who comes to our station and is hungry. Maybe we'll even pull off a feeding of the multitudes—like the fish and loaves."

Hank chuckled. "That shouldn't be too hard with beans."

"Let's pray our newcomers will respect the orange vested marchers and let them be served first and will wait to see what's left over. We'll stretch it as best we can."

"Should we make a sign asking people to wait until the marchers have been served?" suggested Hank.

"Sure. Do you have a poster board?"

"No, I sure don't."

"Any paper?"

"No."

"A marker pen?"

"No."

They looked at each other and cracked up.

"Right! We'll just tell them," conceded Hank with a snort.

Leslie walked up to them and saluted.

"I'm sorry miss but you'll have to wait until the orange vests have been served first," said Winnie solemnly. Hank snickered which turned into chortles as Leslie cocked her head, bewildered.

"Yah, the orange vests want to eat. They have very big stomachs, being orange and all." It made no sense but that set the two men off again with peals of laughter. Leslie grinned at them.

"I know two men who are pun-chy!"

"Sorry. We don't have any punch tonight," Hank said and they burst out laughing again.

Winnie pulled himself together and grinned at Leslie. "You're right. I'm dead tired. Don't ask me my name because I don't think I remember it."

"I just want you to pass along a message to the Turners and Moses when they come to get dinner," Leslie said. "I'll never spot them with so many people here."

"Sure."

"Tell them to meet Annie Lee, Elmira and me tomorrow in front of the Winter Building. Then we can be together for the Freedom rally and we'll all go back to Selma together. The Committee's worried about having enough transportation to get everyone out of town before dark."

"OK. The Winter Building. Where is it?"

"I'm not sure but Annie Lee seemed to think they will know. I guess it's close to the Capitol on Dexter Avenue," said Leslie.

"I'm happy to deliver the message. I'm sure they'll be here soon because they haven't missed a meal yet."

"Thanks, Winnie," Leslie said warmly.

A few orange vested marchers came up and Leslie stepped aside while they were served. Leslie watched this man with whom she had been through so much in such a short span of time. What an incredible morality play they had shared. Did they really meet only two weeks ago? It suddenly hit her how much she looked forward to seeing him every day. She was going to miss him.

The marchers moved on down the line to collect corn bread and Leslie stepped back to Winnie.

"Will you be able to join us on Dexter Avenue tomorrow?" Leslie asked.

"Absolutely. Hank plans to join up with members of his church and I want to be with you guys. The Turners have become my second family. We'll probably pack all this stuff up after the rally's over."

"Good. We should all be together. You deserve to witness the rally, too, after all your work."

"Thanks. Are you staying for the big Stars of Freedom show tonight?"

"No. I'm exhausted and want to help Annie Lee finalize what she thinks she can't live without from her kitchen before we turn in."

"Tell her she doesn't need as much as she thinks she does. I've really learned how less is more on this job."

They smiled at each other.

"Where will you sleep tonight?" Leslie asked.

"At the Turners, like I do every night after I turn in the cans. We've still got one more breakfast meal."

Winnie wondered why she'd asked?

"You've worked so hard," she said.

He gazed upon her fondly. "So have you," he said. It seemed like they'd known each other forever. What the heck. He came around the table and gave her a big, long hug and she hugged him back. There was a quick kiss. A marcher strolled up to the table looking for dinner. "See you tomorrow," he said softly.

"See you tomorrow."

It wasn't long after Leslie left that the Turners and Moses did show up. Carlton, as usual, was still full of energy, his parents less so.

"Hey, hey," Winnie greeted them.

Carlton was about ready to burst. "Can you believe all the stars that are here? I just saw Peter, Paul, and Mary. And Nipsey. Nipsey Russell is here! I can't believe it."

"Wait till you hear the whole line-up," said Winnie. "It's pretty unbelievable. Harry Belafonte's been amazing pulling so many acts together."

"I understand Sammy Davis, Junior is here," said Moses, doing a little dance step in imitation of his hero.

"Him, and Pete Seeger, and Leonard Bernstein," said Mandy. "It's fantastic how many came."

"Ah, and the ladies!" said Elverse. "Is it really true that Lena Horne and Mahalia Jackson and Nina are here?"

"I think it's true," said Winnie. "I saw a list back at the office and couldn't believe how many are supposed to come. Tony Bennett, Joan Baez, Dick Gregory, and, and, let's see, who haven't we mentioned?"

"Elvis? Mandy asked, hopefully.

"No, sorry," Winnie laughed, "he wasn't on the list. He's probably busy making another movie. He's been cranking 'um out one after another since he got back from the Army. Still, there's more talent here than Vegas. It's going to be a great show."

The show was great and not just a little symbolic that the stage on which it was performed consisted of stacked coffins donated by a local mortuary. The jerry-rigged sound system occasionally sputtered but the show went on long into the night. Even more stars than Winnie could remember lined up to add their talent to the night's program: Odetta, Ella Fitzgerald, Billy Eckstein, Frankie Lane, actors Ossie Davis, and Ruby Dee, Sidney Poitier, Shelley Winters, comedian Alan King, and writer James Baldwin. Stars who knew they had to be there, had to contribute in some way. Had to lend their fame to history.

Winnie and Hank almost forgot how tired they were as they hiked the equipment back to the truck while Harry Belafonte sang "Day O," the Banana Boat song. It was a night the marchers and volunteers would never forget. And it didn't rain.

೫

FIFTEEN

The early morning of the Freedom Rally was not as fortunate. It was raining on the triumphant Thursday they were to march into the Montgomery city limits to the seat of power. Raindrops were splashing in puddles, and workmen, up since dawn, were drenched as they placed plywood over a star plaque embedded in the state capitol lawn. The star commemorated the spot where Jefferson Davis had stood when he became President of the Confederacy and the city did not want it sullied by any marchers.

A television crew sent to cover the milestone march waited glumly while their producer argued with the city's Police Chief. They had begun to set up on Dexter Avenue when the chief arrived and forbid it.

"You're interfering with the free press," exclaimed the producer. "Our country has a right to witness today's events!"

"And I'm telling you the city has issued no permits for filming," retorted the Chief, his voice raised in anger.

"Newspaper reporters are here. What's the difference?" demanded the Producer.

"I'm warning you," the Police Chief threatened. "You set up I'll have you all arrested and confiscate your film!"

At that moment a well-dressed man walked up to them. It was Bill Jones.

"Excuse me, gentlemen," he said politely. "I'm the Governor's press secretary?" He turned to the Producer. "Governor Wallace invites you to set up on the Capitol lawn, which is state property and not controlled by the city." He nodded to the stunned Producer while the Police Chief walked off in a disgusted huff.

"Governor Wallace invited us?" asked the Producer incredulously.

"That's correct, sir," replied Mr. Jones with no further explanation.

The crew wasted no time in shifting onto the Capitol grounds.

As more and more marchers poured into St. Jude, most of the regular Army, National Guard, and U.S. Marshals were deployed to Montgomery, the capitol city of Alabama. Sentries were dropped off every twenty-five feet along the parade route in back of wooden barricades set up the day before. Additionally, an Army marksman lookout was assigned to every tall building. Over three thousand troops were put in position. It was a complete military invasion. The few who remained behind at the St. Jude campground were soldiers stationed to guard the entrance. They were told to block any left hand turns into the compound.

King, who returned from Cleveland the day before had spent most of the night at a nearby home meeting with his staff. When his car attempted to return to St. Jude by turning left into the driveway, they were stopped by a sergeant and not allowed to pass. Andrew Young tried to explain to the sergeant he was looking at Martin Luther King's car but the sergeant wouldn't budge. He had his orders. Dr. Ralph Bunche, also in the car, tried. "I'm Dr. Ralph Bunche, undersecretary of the United Nations. I'm here for the march."

"I'm sorry, sir. This is not the United Nations. My orders are no left turns."

Finally, King himself got out of the car to try and resolve the matter when a Montgomery police officer showed up and called the sergeant a fool.

"This is the man! Let him through," he ordered.

Dr. King and his associates joined the march.

The marchers themselves and those who just arrived to be a witness to the final triumph weren't thinking about security.

There were so many gathered, so much camaraderie, and so much U.S. government support behind them, people felt comfortable and safe. The power and strength of over twenty five thousand strong was palpable. There was a giddiness, a joyfulness, a true sense of community sharing a common purpose, despite the confusion of where the procession began and ended. People continuously poured into St. Jude and formed several lines they thought were exiting to the street only to find the line didn't move. Eventually the exit was sorted out and everyone funneled through the gates to begin the three-mile trek to the Capitol.

Carlton, aware of the history his family was making, convinced his Mom and Dad to let him climb up the St. Jude tower and watch the parade move out. He would catch up to them, knowing they would be at the front of the parade, proudly wearing their orange vests. To be on the safe side, Moses winked at Mandy and stated he, too, would like to see that view and stayed behind to climb the tower steps with Carlton.

Leslie had picked up Annie Lee and Elmira and drove to St. Jude. The rain stopped and she was able to turn off her windshield wipers just as they pulled into the makeshift parking lot—making a right turn.

"I can't believe Jackson's company wouldn't give him even one day off," Leslie said, knowing how disappointed Annie Lee was that he wasn't going to share this momentous occasion with her.

"Those nincompoops are as nervous as long tailed cats in a room full of rocking chairs," Annie Lee sputtered. "They think there's gonna be a riot and said he had to stand guard or be fired."

"That's ridiculous," said Elmira. "All these rumors are just to scare people."

"Don't I know it," agreed Annie Lee. "They can't stand that our nonviolence makes them out to be liars."

"Look!" Leslie said. "The sun's going to shine." Streaks of sunlight brightened the sky.

"Praise the Lord, He's smiling down on us," Annie Lee exclaimed.

"And He's giving me a parking space, too," Leslie cracked as she pulled into a spot.

They entered the campground and Leslie went to find Winnie. She walked to the supplies tent and spied Hank stacking boxes.

"Good morning, Hank. How was it last night?"

"Hi there, Leslie. Incredible! Just incredible. The best show I've ever seen. Did make our shut-eye rather short, however. You looking for Winnie?"

"Yes."

"We tossed a coin this morning to see who would do an early run back to Selma. We figured it would be worth the extra trip this morning to return some of the big things and give us more room when we're rushing to load the trucks later. He won the toss but said he didn't mind going and left with the driver." He raised his eyebrows as he gazed at the boxes. "Our stuff kind of grew as the week passed."

"I can see how it would," said Leslie. "Is he due back soon?"

"Guess it depends on how long it will take them to unload. I think maybe he was secretly hoping he could sneak in a shower before he comes back. He said if you showed up before he returned that he knows to meet you at the Winter building."

"Oh, OK. Thanks. I hope you know where to meet your friends? Can you believe how many are here? I think the march is already moving out."

"Really? Thanks. Just want to finish this bit of packing. It's been a great joy to meet you, Leslie."

"It was nice knowing you, too, Hank. Take care."

After some searching, Leslie located Annie Lee and Elmira. They had not found the Turners or Moses but moved on out, knowing they had a meeting place.

As the colossal march wound its way toward the Capitol, even more marchers were dropped off on the road itself as they pressed on to Dexter Avenue. First they walked through the black neighborhood that, while poor, was not poor in spirit. Children ran along side the marchers laughing and shouting; adults sat on their porches waving small American flags. The mood was as jubilant as a fourth of July parade. As they walked deeper into downtown, the black neighborhood morphed into a poor white neighborhood. Few people were in the street but those who were expressed restrained, seething hostility. The secure safety the marchers had felt at St. Jude's switched to a subdued concern for safe passage.

Downtown Montgomery was eerily deserted. Wallace had given all women government workers the day off, proclaiming it a "danger holiday." Local businesses also took up Wallace's proclamation and encouraged employees and shoppers to stay home. The only time the local newspaper mentioned the march was to endorse staying away from downtown.

Even as the march was making history, it was passing locations that had already made civil rights history. Moses and Carlton caught up with the Turners, and Moses pointed out recent famous locations. In the lead, Dr. King and Coretta turned down Oak Street to walk by Holt Street Baptist Church where Dr. King had addressed the first mass meeting nine years prior. His sermon kicked off the bus boycott inspired by Rosa Parks' refusal to move to the back of the bus. The march circled around the Court Square fountain where Mrs. Parks had been arrested.

The route then opened to a wide boulevard for the last six blocks that displayed a gracious vista of the white domed Alabama state capitol. It was impossible to reconcile that the gigantic flag waving in front of the capitol was Confederate. The front flank marching in front of the orange vests carried their own eclectic array of flags besides an American flag. There was a U.N. flag, peace sign flags, and a state of Nebraska flag. The flags flew high as the carriers hiked the last stretch to the Capitol grounds.

Carlton was sent to find Leslie, Annie Lee, and Elmira waiting at the Winter Building. He streaked away from his family and soon was united with the women. They hugged him as Carlton exclaimed, "We did it! We really did it!"

"Yes we did, son," Annie Lee laughed. "Yes, we certainly did." Everyone was so happy.

"Come on," Carlton said. "I'll take you to where Mom and Dad and Moses are. We're right in front with all the orange vests."

"Wait," said Leslie. "Winnie isn't here yet."

"Oh," said Carlton. "Cool. He'll be with us, too?"

"He said he was. He made a run to Selma this morning to return some equipment but left me a message that he'd meet us here."

"We'll wait five minutes," said Elmira, "and then if he doesn't show I think we should move on down with Carlton. I want to be along side my Moses when Martin speaks."

It was a long five minutes. Winnie didn't show. Reluctantly, the group left their spot in front of the Winter Building and threaded their way to the front of the parade. When they reached the others, Carlton pushed them all together to snap a picture with his new camera that he bought for the occasion.

"Steady hand, Mr. Future Voter," Elverse advised. "This will be a picture for posterity." Carlton snapped his camera.

Leslie stepped out from the group.

"Here," she said to Carlton. "Now you join your family and I'll take a picture of all of you."

They stood proudly together and Leslie, looking through the viewfinder at the people who had become so important to her, felt a rush of emotion. She snapped the picture and gave the camera back to Carlton as she wiped tears from her eyes.

"I really can't believe this is happening," she said. "You all should be so proud." They joined in a big group hug.

It took the march a half hour for the tail end of the participants to come to a stop after the front of the march had reached the Capitol grounds where Dexter Avenue ended. Alabama wouldn't allow a stage to be set up on the eight-lane Boulevard so the organizers improvised a stage on a flatbed truck. The dignitaries were arranged on the flatbed and sat behind a makeshift podium and sound system. Beyond the truck, a line of Montgomery police created a further barrier between the marchers and the Capitol. Even though the marchers were not allowed on the steps of the Capitol, it still made a fine backdrop for their Freedom Rally.

Martin Luther King settled in with John Lewis, Roy Wilkins of the N.A.A.C.P., James Bevel, Ralph Abernathy, U.N. Undersecretary Dr. Ralph Bunche, Whitney Young of the National Urban League, A. Philip Randolph from the Brotherhood Sleeping Car Porters, Rosa Parks of the bus boycott fame, and the Committee's own Amelia Boynton.

Entertainers also became part of the rally program. There was Joan Baez, Harry Belafonte, Peter, Paul and Mary, and writer James Baldwin among others offering up their talents in between speeches. Mary, of Peter, Paul and Mary, even kissed Harry Belafonte on stage, which was televised on national TV. The station's switchboard immediately lit up with outraged TV viewers demanding the filming be shut down immediately. They were insulted the station dared show a white woman kissing a black man.

Wallace had agreed to meet with the leaders that carried the petition; the ensemble intended to personally hand it to him. It was their manifesto of sorts. But when the small group attempted to go to his office, the guards turned them away. When they tried a second time, they were told Wallace's office was "closed." What was open were Wallace's eyes as he hid behind his office doors. He peeked through his window blinds and looked down upon the twenty-five thousand people filling the boulevard.

"That's a lot of votes down there," he said to press secretary Jones.

The leaders returned to the rally without presenting the petition, the original reason for the march. But Amelia Boynton took the opportunity to read the petition aloud from the stage. At least the people would hear their demands even if the Governor would not.

"We have come not only five days and fifty miles, but we have come from three centuries of suffering and hardship," she read. "We have come to you, the Governor of Alabama, to declare that we must have our freedom now. We must have the right to vote; we must have equal protection of the law, and an end to police brutality."

The crowd shouted its approval. They also gave a sustained ovation to Rosa Parks when she rose and spoke briefly despite her reluctance to draw attention to herself.

There were many speeches. They went on for over two hours before the man they were all waiting to hear, Dr. Martin Luther King, Jr., raised from his chair. The euphoric crowd sent up a cheer that rumbled down the avenue. He looked beyond the six microphones clipped to the lectern at the mass turnout. Then over the loudspeakers came their leader's familiar voice.

He spoke of the thousands of demonstrators who began the walk. He told of the sweltering sun and sleeping in mud. Yet, the marchers who were told they would never make it had indeed made it and no one could turn them back. The quarter of a million people bellowed their approval.

Winnie appeared, out of breath and winded. He had run miles to be with his friends and they greeted him with relief.

"We were worried about you," said Mandy.

"It wouldn't have been the same without you," said Carlton.

"Sorry guys. I got hung up in Selma."

"Dr. King has just started. I'm glad you made it," said Leslie. The group smiled affectionately; they were now complete and linked hands in solidarity.

Back in Selma on Jefferson Davis Street, Uncle Parker had run a red light and a sheriff's car pulled out from a side street and stopped them. Rusty, riding shotgun, quickly locked the glove compartment, and began to hyperventilate. It was the first time he had ever called in sick, and he panicked. Maybe the cop would recognize him and know he wasn't at work and would call his boss as if he was still a kid and the cop was a truant officer. Sparky and Choice slouched down in the back seat and turned their heads away. The sheriff ambled up to their car and tipped his hat.

"Gentlemen," he said.

"Why ain't you doing something about these coon black-birds flyin' 'round our state instead of hiding?" said Uncle who wasn't used to being stopped. He was steamed. The Sheriff leaned into the car in sympathy.

"It's a black day for sure with the federal government rammin' these commies down our throats, but we still got to obey the law. Tomorrow it'll be all over," he said.

Sparky sprang forward from the back seat. "Like hell it will," he challenged. "Those jigaboos are drunk with the own importance. They're gonna keep pushing and pushing and pushing their way into our town!"

"Yah," said Rusty, finding his tongue. "How come they get to push us around and march on our streets and nobody seems to pay them no mind?"

Uncle agreed. "It's plum nuts to have to watch our South turn into a Commie slum and not do anything to stop it. Damn crazy!"

The Sheriff sighed. "I know how you feel. Just mind the speed limit—and the lights." He walked away without giving them a ticket.

On Dexter Avenue, Dr. King had warmed up and gazed out at the thousands assembled. All those dedicated bodies inspired him to give the most eloquent words he could draw forth from his vast repertoire. So many people had worked so hard for this moment; some had even died. He must go beyond rhetoric. He must match their determination and will. He must reach down into his own soul to touch theirs. And so he continued.

Carlton listened intently, standing on tiptoe to look over orange vests in front of him so he could see his preacher man hero with his own eyes, and hear his leader's words with his own ears as King expounded, "truth pressed to earth will rise again."

Elverse and Mandy held each other tightly. Leslie clasped her hands to her lips in prayer. Tears streamed down Annie Lee's broad cheeks. Moses danced a little warrior step and Elmira raised her cast in a power salute when King implored them it would not be long before lies fell away and they reaped what they had sown.

Winnie mouthed the words from *"The Battle Hymn of the Republic"* along with Dr. King as this great man entreated, "How long? Not long, because mine eyes have seen the glory of the coming of the Lord, trampling out the vintage where the grapes of wrath are stored. He has loosed the fateful lightening of his terrible swift sword. His truth is marching on! He has sounded forth the trumpets that shall never call retreat. He is lifting up the hearts of man before His judgment seat. Oh, be swift my soul to answer Him. Be jubilant my feet. Our God is marching on. Glory hallelujah, glory hallelujah! His truth is marching on!"

Even before King finished his entreaty, a roar mightier than a thousand lions vibrated down through the street and into every heart. Their lives would never quite be the same.

It was truly phenomenal how quickly over twenty-five thousand people could disperse. Everyone took the admonition to get out of town seriously and headed for the buses, trucks, and cars a block away at the staging area, or quickened their pace to walk back to St. Jude. The Washingtons, Turners, Annie Lee, Leslie, and Winnie were silent as they walked back to Leslie's car. It was as if each needed to emotionally process what they just witnessed, what they were a part of, what they helped achieve. One thing was certain: they achieved it together and the respect and love they felt for one another needed no words.

When they arrived at St. Jude the roustabouts had already pulled down the big tents. Their effort had come to an end.

"Maybe you all should come over for breakfast tomorrow," invited Annie Lee. "We'll make it a farewell party."

"I'm back at school tomorrow," said Moses. "Maybe Saturday?"

"When do you think you'll leave?" asked Mandy.

Leslie held her breath and looked down, wondering how Annie Lee would answer. Since Annie Lee had agreed to leave, Leslie had been careful not to push or even ask for a date when they would finally get on the road.

"Well," drawled Annie Lee. "I'm not going to need a lot if I'm going to be living for a time in a house already nicely furnished. There are a few things I got to take from my kitchen, like my favorite frying pan, things like that, and, and maybe a few knick knacks to make me feel at home. My Bible. Other than that? Just some clothes and my tooth brush."

Leslie let out the breath she had been holding and gave a quick prayer of thanks.

"So," Mandy pressed, passing a look of understanding to Leslie. "How long do you think it will take you to pack your toothbrush?"

"Seems to me we'll be able to leave by this weekend. Either Saturday or Sunday at the latest," said Annie Lee.

"Yes!" said Leslie under her breath.

"I'm good for a breakfast farewell if it works out and you don't leave until Sunday," said Winnie. "But right now I've got to go. There's still a lot to pack up."

"I'll help you with the final clean up," said Elverse as he turned to the others. "So we'll catch you back in Selma."

"Me, too," offered Moses. "Many hands make light work." The two men kissed their wives and charged off with Winnie to the school building where many of the supplies had been stored.

The women and Carlton piled into Leslie's car. Carlton wished he had offered, too. After all, he felt like one of the men having marched the whole week with the adults.

It was a jubilant exit from the parking lot with car horns honking in celebration. They had changed their state—heck, maybe their country. Maybe even the world.

Pulling into a liquor store lot in Selma was Uncle and his buddies. They had run out of alcohol. Not exactly inebriated but certainly not clearheaded, they strolled into the store. Lagging behind was Choice who darted to the side of the building where a phone hung, dialed the emergency number, and let the receiver hang down as he hobbled back to catch up with the others before they noticed he was missing.

৵৯

SIXTEEN

Leslie pulled into the Washington's driveway and Elmira gleefully jumped out, happy to stretch her cramped legs. Leslie walked around the car and took Moses' backpack from her trunk and handed it to her.

"So will you come around for breakfast Saturday?" Leslie asked.

"Honey pie, you two are going to be real busy, but Moses and I will come of course... that is, if you're not already gone," Elmira said with a twinkle.

Leslie grinned and hugged her.

"No, I'm sure Annie Lee will take her time deciding what last things to pack. I don't expect we'll leave before Sunday."

"Thanks for the ride back, Leslie. It sure has been gratifying to know you. You'll let us know if we should make it Saturday," said Elmira. "We'll be in touch."

Leslie jumped back into the driver's seat and they took off for Annie Lee's place, which was not far. Leslie ran to Annie Lee's side to help her out of the car. Standing that many hours on Dexter Avenue did its damage to Annie Lee's ankles, now swollen and painful. She rose with difficulty. Carlton hopped out and offered to help her to her door but she waved him off.

"OK, y'all," Annie Lee waved. "I hope to see you Turners Saturday morning. Take care!"

"Keep packing," Leslie shouted as she and Carlton jumped back into the Ford. As they drove off she hollered out her window to Annie Lee, "Love you!" Annie Lee waved over her shoulder as she limped to her front door.

Leslie drove to the Turners home and pulled into their broad driveway. Mandy and Carlton stretched while Leslie opened the trunk and removed their backpacks and orange vests. She handed off their things but found it hard to leave. They stood there lingering a moment longer.

"Well," Carlton spoke up. "Everything turned out right fine, didn't it? A perfect day."

"It's hard to believe you actually did it after all these years," said Leslie.

"It's been a pleasure having you be a part of it, Leslie," said Mandy sincerely.

"It's been thrilling," said Leslie. "If you ever find yourselves North in Elverse's home state again, please come visit. And Carlton? I expect you to come and spend some time with my son, Justin. Maybe this summer?"

"Really?" said Carlton. "Cool! It would be a dream come true, Ma'am. I've only been outside Alabama twice."

"It's a long drive back to Montgomery, Leslie. Come in for a cup of tea first," suggested Mandy.

Leslie wished she could accept Mandy's invitation.

"Thank you, Mandy, that's a real tempting offer but it'll be totally dark soon. It won't be safe for those stranded back in Montgomery. I think I need to get back on the road."

Mandy impulsively hugged Leslie and Leslie hugged back. Carlton looked on, beaming.

"We'll be sure to be there Saturday, if it works out, although I'm sure you're hoping to be gone," said Mandy.

"What's one more day now?" said Leslie brightly.

Carlton cocked his head and asked, "Would it be OK if I go along with you, ma'am? You could drop me off at St. Jude and I could help with the final clean up, too."

"It's up to your Mother, Carlton. I'd love the company," Leslie said.

"That's a fine gesture, son," said Mandy. "Of course you may go my darling. Just be sure you stay close to your father and all leave together."

"I will, Mama," said Carlton.

"I'll make sure he finds them before I drive on," promised Leslie.

"See you later," called out Carlton as he and Leslie got back into the car and drove off.

Leslie wove her car back through town where traffic was thinning. They stopped for a red light.

Uncle Parker's black Cadillac rolled to a stop next to them. In the back seat, Sparky glanced over at Leslie's car and saw this cute white blond singing with her passenger, a black man.

"Well, looky there, bubba. Damn it all to hell!" All heads in the car turned just as Carlton turned his head away to look at a store window. His full black head of tightly curled hair was clearly visible but not his young face. Not that it might have made a difference.

Uncle frowned.

"They're probably headin' out to some hell hole to do it." The light changed and Leslie started up again. Uncle tried to keep abreast of her in the second lane but an elderly lady was in front of him and driving at a snail's pace. He fell behind.

An ice cream store on the left caught Leslie's eye.

"Boy," she said wistfully, "I sure could go for an ice cream cone."

"I got some money," said Carlton earnestly.

Leslie slowed. "It's not the money, sweetie. It's getting back to Montgomery." She suddenly made a quick U-turn and headed back to the store. "What the heck?" she giggled. "What's five more minutes?"

"What the sam hell?" Uncle said as Leslie's Ford disappeared. Uncle's car continued down the road. He checked his rear view mirror and saw Leslie had pulled off the road.

Leslie parked and she and Carlton got out and scurried toward the store entrance.

"You know, Carlton, my Justin really would love to meet you. I was serious when I told your Mom you should come and visit this summer. I think you'd like Michigan and we'll take a trip to show you where your Dad grew up."

"I know I'd like it. Dad's told me about all the lakes and how many cars they make there and stuff. I was there once but I was too small to know any difference."

They walked through the swinging door. Leslie was glad to see the store was empty so they could place their order quickly and get back on the road. A little ice cream wouldn't delay them that much. Carlton ordered Fresh Strawberry and Leslie had her regular—Rocky Road. She paid the server, a young high school girl who didn't seem to mind their races mingling, and strolled back to the car, licking their cones contentedly.

Leslie turned the car back around and headed out for highway 80. Uncle had pulled over to wait and see which way she went. He watched as she passed his car and pulled out behind her. As Leslie approached the open road she sped up. Uncle followed suit. His face set.

"We're going to take this car," he said.

Leslie picked up speed and was doing 50 mph. It was darker in the countryside and she turned on her high beams. She rounded a curve and the lights from Uncle's car caught her rear view mirror. Leslie took a last bite of her cone and sped up a bit. The car in back of her did likewise.

Choice began to sweat as Uncle pulled a revolver out from under his seat. He handed the gun back to Sparky who handed it to Choice. Rusty fished out another gun from underneath his seat and handed that one back to Sparky.

"We all get to have one," gloated Sparky. "Where's yours, Rusty?"

Rusty turned on the overhead light, unlocked the glove compartment, and removed a third gun. "Here!" He waved it in the air.

"Keep that damn thing down, stupid," commanded Uncle. "Don't be showing it off like a damn fool in case any cops are around." Rusty lowered the gun and checked to make sure the cartridge was loaded.

Leslie slowed back down. The car in back did likewise. She frowned. "I think we're being followed," she said.

Carlton twisted around and could make out four men in a Cadillac. Fear surged through his body.

They passed the sign for Lowndes County.

"Turn the damn light off, Rusty, for god's sake," demanded Uncle.

Rusty turned off the light.

"We're in the big time now!" shouted Sparky.

It was as if these men had been given an aphrodisiac. They were all high like they'd won the lottery and wanted to celebrate.

Swampland lay ahead. Leslie sped up again. Carlton kept watching the car behind them.

"They're keeping up with us," he reported to Leslie. He quickly finished his cone. "They're getting closer, Leslie!"

Leslie floored the gas pedal and the Ford began to shake. She maneuvered a sharp curve. Her wheels squealed. Uncle's car fishtailed but kept coming.

"Shall we run them off the road?" Uncle proposed. But Sparky quickly rejected that idea, having done too many auto paint jobs in his garage.

"Nah, bubba," he said. "If just a little paint from your car gets on theirs, we're caught!"

Uncle kept gaining on Leslie. Rusty hopped up and down in his seat. "Give it the gas! Give it the gas!"

Leslie rounded another curve and fishtailed. Her wheels screeched. She almost lost control but pulled it out by slowing ever so slightly. She screamed down a straightaway and Uncle pulled into the other lane. The cars were now drag racing side by side. Sparky and Rusty rolled down their windows. Choice's face was all sweat.

"Get along side me here, Choice," yelled Sparky.

Choice moved next to Sparky in the back seat. Rusty extended his arm in front. All three thrust their guns out the window.

"Get down, Carlton," Leslie ordered. Leslie looked straight into Uncle's car.

"OK!" Uncle shouted as he tried to keep the car steady and look at the same time. "SHOOT THE HELL OUT OF 'um!"

Rusty fired wildly. Sparky also fired. They emptied their guns, making polka dots on Leslie's door. Choice shot twice, a marksman hitting his target. Blood spattered Leslie's window and her Ford veered off the road and tumbled into a pasture. Carlton was screaming.

"LESLIE! MRS. COLE! LESLIE!"

The car plowed through a barbed wire fence, barely slowing it down. The pasture grass eventually rolled the car to a stop. Blood was splattered on the dashboard and on Carlton. He tried to pull Leslie's body away from the window and smeared even more blood on himself. "Oh, my god," he whimpered. "Oh, my god! Mrs. Cole? Leslie? Oh, my god!"

Leslie's body was motionless. Not so much as a moan passed her lips. Carlton reached for her lifeless hand and got no response. Her head lolled back and he saw the bullet wound.

Uncle's car stopped on the highway and slowly backed up until he was even with Leslie's car in the field. Both cars threw their headlight beams into the darkness. Sparky pushed Choice out the back door and Rusty handed him a flashlight.

"Make sure they're dead, big brother," said Sparky.

"Why me?" said Choice.

"Because you're the oldest except for Uncle and he's driving. Go!"

Choice slid down the embankment, the flashlight in one hand and his gun in the other. He approached the car warily, all the while shinning the flashlight ahead of himself, watching for any movement. He walked up to Leslie's window, now shot to hell and saw her slumped over the wheel. He shined the light across her to Carlton who was slumped over the gearshift. Blood was everywhere like so much splashed paint. Choice turned away quickly from the gruesome site and hobbled back to Uncle's car. They sped away.

Carlton finally exhaled and ever so slowly sat up. He peeked over Leslie's body. The car on the road was gone. He opened his door and ran up to the road and began to run toward St. Jude. Over his shoulder he heard a car approaching and turned to flag it down. Instead, the red sports car veered at him and he threw himself into the ditch to avoid being hit. He laid there a full minute, stunned, then stood up and began running again, half crazed with tears rolling down his face. A bigger vehicle came into view, driving slowly toward Selma. It appeared to be a truck. When he saw it was an open truck he guessed it was from the march. He jumped into the center of the road and began to wave his arms wildly.

"Stop!" he screamed. "Stop! Stop!"

The truck lurched to a stop and he ran up to the tailgate where people were looking to see why the truck had halted. When they saw Carlton, they reached down and helped him onto the truck bed. Elverse immediately recognized him and jumped over boxes to get to his side. Winnie followed.

"My god, son," said Elverse. "What's wrong?"

"Everybody down! Get out of here! Shooting!" He was frantic.

Another volunteer shouted to the driver to step on it. The truck pitched forward as the driver ground the gears and Carlton lost his balance. Elverse grabbed him and Carlton clung to him, smearing blood on his father's jacket. He was crying hysterically.

Moses slid over to them. "Get a hold of yourself boy," he said." "Catch your breath and speak to us! What's happened?"

Elverse put his arms around Carlton to comfort him. Carlton buried his sobs into his father's shoulder.

"You're with us. Shh. It's going to be OK," said Winnie, patting his back. "Can you tell us what happened?"

Carlton raised his head. Another volunteer with a flashlight shined it on Carlton.

That's when they all saw the blood.

"Oh, my god, Carlton, my boy!" said Elverse.

"Son?" said Moses. "Tell us what's happened. Where's my Elmira?"

Carlton looked imploringly at Moses.

"She home. It's Mrs. Cole... Leslie. Shot!" He eked out the words between his gulping sobs.

Winnie's body convulsed. Elverse stroked Carlton's head.

"What are you saying?" Elverse asked incredulously. "What do you mean? Is Leslie hurt?"

"Where's everyone else? Why are you out here alone?" Moses demanded. Carlton blurted out the news as he took in gulps of air.

"It happened… They're all home. Mrs. Cole, Leslie… and me… she's… in her car… in the field. Men pulled up next to us… and shot her up. She's… she's dead!"

Winnie fell back on a box, gulping for air.

Then they saw the car with its headlights resting in a field on the opposite side of the road. "Oh, my god," Moses whispered. He yelled to another volunteer. "Tell the driver to note his mileage from here to the police station. Tell him to drive directly to the police!"

Elverse pulled Carlton to his chest and rocked him as the truck tore down the road. Once inside Selma city limits, the truck drove to the Police Department. The policeman on duty called Baker who immediately called the FBI. Then Baker raced over to the station, called in a court reporter, and interviewed Carlton after giving him a glass of water. Elverse stood on one side of Carlton; Winnie stood on the other. Each kept a protective hand on his shoulders. Moses was in another room trying to reach Elmira but the phone was busy. When there were no more questions to be asked, the court reporter dropped off Moses and drove the Turners and Winnie home.

Elverse unlocked his front door and entered with Winnie and Carlton trailing behind. The blood on Carlton had dried but was still very evident. Elverse moved to shut the door.

"Hello?" Mandy called out from the kitchen. She entered the living room and screamed when saw her son. She rushed to clutch him in her arms. Carlton was calmer now, having told his story several times, but in his mother's arms, he began to cry again despite his best efforts to remain stoic. Mandy joined him with frantic tears of her own. Elverse encircled his wife and son in his arms and gently patted their backs.

"I wanted to be with you when you hear what's happened," said Elverse softly. "I didn't want to call."

"What have they done to my son?" implored Mandy.

"We picked Carlton up on the road when we were returning with the truck," said Winnie. "The worst kind of evil drove down that same highway and pulled up along side Leslie's car.

Men shot and killed her. Carlton was spared. We've already been to the police."

Elverse began to shake again as he could not process the facts. He couldn't fathom how Leslie was murdered in her car that his son was in, too, yet Carlton stood before him, alive. Not dead. Alive. Winnie put his hand on Elverse's shoulder to steady him.

They sat down, Mandy never letting go of her son. Carlton gained control of himself and his tears dried as he relayed his story once more. Mandy listened, hanging on his every word, desperately trying to comprehend what her child had been through. Then she took charge and rose, still holding his hand.

"Come with me, Carlton," Mandy said. We're going to get these clothes off you so you can take a long hot shower." Carlton rose and she took Carlton's arm and led him away, leaving the two men alone. They met each other's gaze, struggling to make sense of the senseless.

"Someone needs to tell Annie Lee," said Winnie quietly.

"Yes," said Elverse. "Immediately. I will go."

"Do you want me to go with you?" Winnie asked.

"No," said Elverse. "I'd feel better if you stay here with the family. I feel so vulnerable right now, it'll ease my mind if I know you're here. But please call Jackson and have him meet me at Annie Lees."

Winnie nodded and Elverse left.

There was a knock at Annie Lee's door. Annie Lee was in her bedroom and yelled from there. "Come on in, honey child. The door's unlocked!"

The door opened slowly and Elverse stepped inside. Annie Lee continued to shout from her bedroom.

"I was starting to worry about you. You won't believe how much I've already packed, sweet pea. I sure hope my suitcase will fit in your trunk next to yours. I have enough boxes to fill up the whole back seat."

Elverse stood there in the middle of the living room with clasped hands. He'd been in that room dozens of times before but now he noticed every single thing about it: the couch that could use reupholstering; a photo of Annie Lee and Jackson; a framed Christmas card photo of Leslie and her family; the neatly stacked Life magazines on the shelf underneath the wobbly coffee table; a framed picture of Dr. Martin Luther King accepting the Nobel Peace Prize; a framed nun's prayer for peace; a small electric clock that said it was almost nine o'clock; and a collection of figurines on a triple knick-knack shelf.

"It's me," Elverse called out. "Elverse."

"Oh!" came the voice from down the hall. "Thought it was Leslie May. Where could she be? Boy, what a mess I've made," Annie Lee chuckled.

Elverse could hear her walking down the hall. His body tensed.

"I must be crazy to be taking so much—" She stopped when she saw Elverse's face and how he still stood in the middle of the room. She frowned.

"What is it?" Annie Lee asked. "Something's wrong."

"Yes," Elverse agreed. "You better sit down. I have some terrible news."

"What?" Annie Lee demanded. "What's happened? Spit it out."

Elverse sucked in his breath.

"It's Leslie," he said. "She was shot in her car on her way back to Montgomery by men in another car."

"Oh, Lord, have mercy!" Annie Lee immediately jumped into action and rushed to fetch her coat from the coat closet. "Oh, god," she said. "Which hospital is she at?"

"She's not," said Elverse.

Annie Lee froze in her tracks. She turned back to Elverse.

"Annie Lee... Annie Lee, Leslie is dead." He spoke barely above a whisper.

"No!" Annie Lee cried. "No! She just left me a little while ago. She couldn't be. Who told you such a terrible, lying thing?"

"Carlton," said Elverse.

"Carlton?" Annie Lee sputtered. "What does he know? He's just a boy!"

Elverse reached out to comfort Annie Lee but she snapped her arm away and stepped back from him. She eyed him suspiciously and shook her head defiantly. She would not allow such things. A tear ran down Elverse's cheek. He stood there pleading with his eyes for Annie Lee to believe him.

"Carlton was in the car with her. They were on their way back to Montgomery to pick up any stragglers." Elverse's body gave a shutter and he had to pause. "A car full of whites pulled up along side them and shot at her. She took all the bullets. Carlton was in the passenger's seat. He wasn't hit." Elverse's voice cracked.

Annie Lee stood there unbelieving, his words bouncing off her like rubber bullets.

"I'm so sorry, Annie Lee. I'm so, so sorry. We all loved Leslie. None of us can believe it."

Annie Lee continued to shake her head in denial.

The front door flew open and Jackson rushed in. He halted when he saw Elverse and Annie Lee in a stand off. He locked eyes with Annie Lee. She read his face. Tears started to spill over her cheeks.

"Noooooooooo," whispered Annie Lee. She backed up from both of them until her spine hit the wall. Slowly she slid down to the floor. Jackson rushed to her side and Elverse kneeled down on her other side. A slow, deep wail rumbled in her chest and worked its way up to her throat and out into the room. It became a primal scream. She then began to heave great sobs. Jackson threw his arms around her and rocked her back and forth.

"Oh, sugar! My love, my sweetheart!" He cooed.

Elverse took her hand as tears streamed down his face in mutual pain and despair.

"It should have been me," Annie Lee whimpered between her sobs. "It should have been me. It should have been me. It should have been me. It should have been me."

"Shush my darlin'," said Jackson. "It shouldn't have been anybody."

⁊

SEVENTEEN

The next day David arrived at the Montgomery airport with Justin and Alex, courtesy of an outraged America. Little Annie remained home with Grandmother. Elverse was there to meet them and drove the longer, circular route back to Selma so they wouldn't have to drive past Leslie's car that still remained in the field on route eighty, surrounded by yellow tape and FBI investigators. Elverse took them to Annie Lee's home where Carlton and Winnie were already there, waiting to meet Leslie's family. It was a tearful meeting.

"Oh, David," Annie Lee blurted out as soon as they entered the house and took off their coats. She looked directly into David's eyes.

"She wanted to go home. She really did. It's all my fault. We just kept finding one more reason to stay a bit longer. I'm so ashamed I didn't save her from Alabama's wicked ways. Yesterday was such a jubilant day! We just plum forget there was still such vile hate stalking us."

David had nothing to say that could make Annie Lee feel better. It was never going to be better. His eyes were red and swollen from crying until he had no tears left, and still he could barely fathom that his wife was forever gone. His sons looked down at their shoes and took out tissues from their pockets and blew their noses. Carlton chewed his lip and glanced over at his father who had closed his eyes. David finally met Annie Lee's sorrowful gaze and muttered, "This is where she felt she had to be, Annie Lee. It's not your fault. Racism is."

It was decided Winnie would stay with David and Annie Lee to offer any support they may need while they discussed funeral arrangements. Elverse took all three boys and drove to the pizza parlor where they would pick up dinner. Alex sat up in front; Justin and Carlton sat in back. Awkward silence.

Justin glanced over at Carlton. "My Mom talked about how brave you were to march and all."

"I liked her a lot," said Carlton. "She was real nice."

Another silence.

Justin struggled to speak what was on his mind. "You were with her when she was shot." It was a statement rather than a question.

"Yes."

Justin regarded Carlton in wonder. "And... and you were spared."

"Yes," said Carlton softly. "I wasn't even hit."

Justin thought about Carlton's answer. "And there were lots of bullets?" asked Justin softly.

Carlton gazed out the window. "Yes," he said simply.

Justin frowned and turned to look out his window at the passing town of Selma.

"That's like some kind of miracle."

Carlton turned and studied Justin. "Maybe," he said.

With the boys gone, Annie Lee, Winnie, and David sat down, each in a separate chair, ignoring the cushy couch, needing their own separate space to breathe in oxygen and keep themselves from falling apart. David and Annie Lee knew they had to decide about Leslie's body but neither could bring themselves to speak the words. Winnie stepped in.

"I didn't know your wife for very long, David, but I can tell you she was an inspiration to this community. She had such energy and worked so hard. The first time I met her she was helping clergy find housing. We came pouring in to march with Dr. King the Tuesday before this last. She shuttled people back and forth as a member of the transportation team, not to mention how she visited Annie Lee every day in the hospital. She also planned meals and took over the phones when there were meetings."

David looked up desolately at Winnie.

"She was always a great organizer. She could do so many things at once. I loved her so much," he said weakly.

Annie Lee's body was shaking with her silent sobs. "I loved her, too," she offered softly. "She was always my favorite child."

"I know it's small consolation," Winnie said gently, "but your wife was an incredible, beautiful human being. You were very wise to have married her. She was that rare kind of woman who had real spirit yet was tempered by compassion."

David's eyes filled up with tears again. He bit his cheek. He could barely stand hearing his wife spoken of in the past tense. Winnie swallowed hard. He spied a Kleenex box atop a small cabinet and rose and brought it over to the coffee table. All three of them took several tissues and blew hard.

Finally, they faced funeral arrangements.

"I know Leslie's parents are buried here, Annie Lee," said David, "but I want to bring her home to Flint. Leslie hated Alabama. She shouldn't be buried in Alabama soil."

His words stung but Annie Lee only nodded.

"You need to listen to your heart," she said.

"I want her to be close. I want her so the kids and I can visit her often. Have a place where we can go when we're really missing her." Annie Lee nodded again and allowed for another surge of tears.

There was a gentle knock at the door. It was Moses. He was there to take them to the mortuary where David would have to positively identify the body. There were papers to be signed and arrangements to be made to fly the body home.

The mortuary had worked feverishly through the night to prepare the body for viewing. The mortician had created a lace-embellished skullcap that fit over Leslie's forehead and hid the bullet wound from view. Her yellow curls peeked out. Even so, David almost collapsed when he saw his wife's lifeless form. Winnie caught him and held him up until he could regain his composure. Winnie couldn't bear to look. He left and stood by the door to allow David to be alone with his wife.

Next, it was Annie Lee's turn. She and Moses entered but as soon as Annie Lee saw the body, she screamed. Immediately ashamed that she could not hold it together for David's sake, she smothered her cries with a fist to her mouth. Slowly she walked up to the casket. Moses hung back. Annie Lee leaned over and kissed Leslie's lifeless face.

"I'm so sorry, my precious child," she murmured into the casket. "I'm so very sorry. And I was wrong. You knew it in your heart. I knew it in mine. I just was afraid to lay claim. I just couldn't cross that line, I don't know why. May God forgive me. I love you, Leslie May. I love you."

Wilson Baker had arrived and signed off for the body to be transported. He introduced himself and then offered his condolences. David thanked him. Baker stood there, needing to say more. He cleared his throat.

"Today President Johnson announced the arrest of the men who were in the car that killed your wife. The Federal government will insure that justice is done."

"They caught them already?" David asked in disbelief.

"The FBI seems positive. It is a bit of a marvel," said Baker.

David thanked him for the news. They shook hands once more, and Baker left. Moses and Winnie exchanged troubled looks. It was confusing. Whereas they should have been ecstatic over the arrests, they felt this pronouncement was like a piece of a puzzle that did not fit. Knowing what they knew about Southern justice, it seemed too illogical and sudden to be true.

Hosea Williams arrived at the mortuary and offered his heartfelt condolences. He asked how Dr. King's organization could be of service to David.

"The funeral won't be here," said David. "We're taking her back to Michigan."

"I completely understand," said Hosea. "We've planned a candlelight service tonight to honor your wife, sir, if you would like to attend. People here are devastated by this violence. We are all truly so very sorry."

"Thank you," said David. "I don't think I have the strength to attend."

Hosea nodded compassionately. "Dr. King stands ready to deliver a eulogy if you so desire when you do have your service in Michigan."

So Selma held yet another tribute to a life that had been snuffed out because of the simple premise that all Americans have a right to participate in their democracy with their vote. The service was more subdued than usual as people found it hard to express their anguish at the depth of Alabama intolerance. Only the candles that were lit that night seemed to offer any rays of hope.

The next morning David, Alex, and Annie Lee caught the plane home that would also carry Leslie's body. Their tickets and transport were courtesy of the Teamsters.

Justin remained behind. He helped Elverse, Carlton, and Winnie load up the Rambler with their road trip supplies and Annie Lee's boxes. Elverse and Mandy agreed Carlton would learn more about life on a trip north than remain a week in school. Besides, Carlton needed time away from all the town gossip, and he and Justin had become close. The boys could support one another.

Winnie would share the driving with Elverse and then return to California from Michigan. They would drive Annie Lee's things to Flint where she would again be a… a what? Labels no longer mattered. What did matter was Annie Lee's resolve to keep Leslie Cole's memory alive, not just for the sake of her children, but for the sake of the nation to comprehend that a mother gave up her life for a cause. A very worthy cause.

And when Annie Lee finally returns to her home in Selma, Alabama? She will vote.

꿈

AFTERWORD

In 1965 I was barely aware of the Voting Rights struggle being fought in the South concurrently with the Vietnam War. I had recently moved from California to Ohio, and adjusting to my new state and the burgeoning war took all my attention. I knew of Dr. Martin Luther King, Jr., of course, and that there was civil unrest in the South, but I was woefully uninformed of the reasons beyond the obvious ills of segregation.

Many years later I read an article in the Southern Poverty Law Center (SPLC) Newsletter about a woman named Viola Liuzzo. KKK members and an FBI informant had murdered her after the triumphant Freedom March from Selma to Montgomery. They were in an automobile that pulled alongside Liuzzo's car and shot and killed her as she drove back to Montgomery. Viola's family sued the U.S. government since the FBI indirectly participated in her murder, and the SPLC article was reporting on the outcome of that case. The family had lost.

In ignorance I originally thought the informant was an FBI *agent* and was outraged he had been involved in such a violent act yet went scot-free and was placed in our government Witness Protection Program. I sympathized with the Liuzzo family that they had not received justice.

I began to research the period, reading all the old newspaper and magazine accounts written when the voting rights movement was daily big news. Soon I was confronted with the wider story of how thousands of everyday folks, black and white, had joined together to right a wrong: to make voting a universal right in our United States. Truly, protesters risked their lives to speak truth to power. Their acts of courage haunted me.

I found it hard to believe that the blatant, racist voter suppression practiced in the South existed in my lifetime. It was so un-American, so the antithesis of our values. I was compelled to write their story and bring to life these protesting citizens who fought so hard and gave up so much. They understood that the right to vote is the bedrock of our country. They helped propel our country forward toward a more just and equitable society.

Viola Liuzzo became the inspiration for my character, Leslie Cole. While the real Viola Liuzzo arrived a few days prior to the Freedom March, my own character, Leslie Cole, needed to arrive weeks before the final march in order to weave a narrative around the people who kept the movement alive and to pay homage to their selfless efforts. Leslie Cole's biography is complete fiction. There have been books written about Viola Liuzzo as well as an excellent documentary that tells her tragic story. She is also honored on the 54 mile Selma to Montgomery National Historic Trail in Alabama. But Leslie Cole is not Viola Liuzzo.

There are other fictional characters that were inspired by real persons but in no way do my fictional characters claim to represent them. Any resemblance between my fictional characters and real characters is meant only to convey the difficulties of the movement and the horrific calamities people endured, rather than portray the real persons themselves.

It is my hope that by personalizing this struggle through fiction, Americans will better understand what citizens went through to gain the right to vote that today we too often take for granted. Some eligible voters don't bother to vote, which I consider ignorance personified and shirking one's civic duty. Conversely, I consider any elected official who votes for any law that makes voting more difficult to be a Judas to democracy. All patriots need to take up the fight to preserve this precious right. Without the vote, we cease to be a republic, we cease to be equal citizens, and we cease to be America.

Many people encouraged me as I wrestled to tell this story. It was a slow, sometimes painful process and there were many periods when my manuscript took a back seat to daily life. Friends and family kept me going, as did the promise I made to the spirit of Dr. King to finish the work. As my muse, Martin and I struggled together over decades to give this story the respect it deserves.

To all the people who read my story through the years, both as a screenplay and then as a novel, thank you. Your suggestions made my writing better. I am grateful to all who supported me with their love and editorial help. I especially could not have completed this book were it not for Halie Rosenberg, Steven Rosenberg, Heidi Lesemann, Sharon Hildebrand, Guy Kervyn, Orloff Miller, Marsha Bryan, the Pettigrews, Gary Hansen, and most especially, Sharon Chatten and Michael Wilson.

When this novel first began as a screenplay, Sharon Chatten, with her vast and keen knowledge of Hollywood, helped me craft stronger characters and tighten the arc. I poured that effort into the novel.

Michael was responsible for giving me the courage to change the genre in which I was working from screenplay to novel. I majored in film, not English literature and was filled with self-doubt. But Michael never wavered in his faith that I would find a way to adapt the narrative. He always believed in my writing to tell this story that mattered and needed to be told. I am eternally thankful.

I have created a list of my novel's cast of characters, separating those who are fiction from those who actually lived and participated in this era. Of those actual people who were part of this struggle, I added a few, short bits of dialogue that were reported in newspaper accounts, particularly the New York Times. I am grateful that such a newspaper exists in our country and that it recognized the importance of documenting the voting rights movement in Selma, Alabama, which was to change our nation. I am also grateful to the Santa Monica library where I spent countless hours researching this subject and honor all libraries that strive to preserve our history through the written word.

While I was unable to secure permission to quote Martin Luther King, Jr., his heartfelt words are a beacon that continues to light our way to a better, more just future. Many books have been written that record his speeches and profound and inspiring words verbatim. I recommend you read one of them. Our country would be a better nation were we to heed his words of warning and encouragement.

And finally, I would like to acknowledge Tracy Martin, who kindly permitted me to use one of her father's remarkable photographs for my cover.

෨

CAST OF CHARACTERS

REAL PEOPLE

DR. RALPH ABERNATHY:
Dr. King's best friend and Vice President of SCLC.

WILSON BAKER:
Director of Public Safety for the town of Selma, AL. Also known as the Police Chief.

HARRY BELAFONTE:
Singer, actor, and human rights activist. Produced the entertainment shows for the five day Freedom March.

JAMES BEVEL:
SCLC Director of Direct Action and Nonviolent Education.

AMELIA BOYNTON:
One of the founders of DCVL in Selma, Alabama and a prominent movement leader.

JAMES (JIM) CLARK:
Sheriff of Dallas County, Alabama.

RAMSEY CLARK:
Deputy Attorney General, U.S. Dept. of Justice.

MAJOR JOHN CLOUD:
Commander of the Alabama State Troopers.

JOHN DOAR:
Asst. Attorney General for Civil Rights, U.S. Department of Justice.

REV. JOSEPH ELLWANGER
Lutheran minister from Birmingham who marched with and for the protesters.

ROBERT GARDNER:
Owner of the farm where marchers slept the third night of the Freedom March.

A.G. GASTON:
Owner of the farm where tents were pitched the second night of the Freedom March.

REV. DANA MCLEAN GREELEY:
President of Unitarian Universalist Association of Congregations. Led the Unitarian contingency involvement in the Selma marches.

DAVID HALL:
Farm owner where marchers camped the first night of the Freedom March.

JAMES HARE:
Judge who issued injunctions against DCVL and voting demonstrations.

JIMMY LEE JACKSON:
Participant in the Marion demonstration who was shot by a Deputy. He died a week later.

FRANK MINIS JOHNSON:
United States Federal Judge who enabled the Freedom March from Selma to Montgomery to legally occur.

LYDON BAINES JOHNSON:
President of the United States (1963 – 1969).

BILL JONES:
Alabama Governor George Wallace's Press Secretary.

NICHOLAS KATZENBACK:
U.S. Attorney General.

DR. MARTIN LUTHER KING, JR.:
World famous Civil Rights leader who founded SCLC and became its President. Led the Freedom March.

CORETTA SCOTT KING:
Dr. King's wife and active participant in the movement.

JIM LETHERER:
A social worker with one leg who walked the entire Freedom March on crutches.

JOHN LEWIS:
Director of SNCC and Voter Registration campaign leader. Played a major role in the movement throughout the South.

AL LINGO:
Director of the Alabama Dept. of Public Safety.

REV. JOSEPH E. LOWRY:
Civil rights activist and co-founder of SCLC with Dr. King.

FEDERAL MARSHALS:
Assigned to Selma, Alabama to keep order.

DR. ALFRED MOLDOAN:
NY physician who assisted the march that crossed Pettus Bridge the first time.

JAMES ORANGE:
Voter registrar who worked for SCLC.

FATHER HAROLD PURCELL:
Founded the City of St. Jude where marchers slept and supporters gathered the fourth night of the Freedom March.

F.D. REESE
President of DCVL during the time of the marches.

JOSEPH SMITHERMAN:
Newly elected Mayor of Selma, AL.

REV. C.T.VIVIAN:
An executive staff member of SCLC.

GEORGE WALLACE:
Governor of Alabama.

HOSEA WILLIAMS:
Southern Project Director for SCLC and Dr. King's right-hand man.

ANDREW YOUNG:
The Executive Director of SCLC.

FICTIONAL CHARACTERS

REV. HANK ANBERG:
A minister who fed the marchers during the Freedom March.

ALEX COLE:
Leslie Cole's second son.

ANNIE COLE:
Leslie Cole's little daughter.

DAVID COLE:
Leslie Cole's husband.

JUSTIN COLE:
Leslie Cole's oldest son who followed the events of the movement.

LESLIE CUMMINS COLE:
Raised by Annie Lee Jones in Selma. She returned to Selma during the voting rights demonstrations. (Her character was inspired by Viola Liuzzo.)

MELANIE VI DENTON:
Married to Rusty Denton.

RUSTY DENTON:
Youngest member of the KKK cell and Uncle's nephew.

SANDRA DE DENTON:
The Denton's baby daughter.

JACKSON DUPREE:
Annie Lee Jones' long time partner and friend.

REVEREND ANTON ENGEL:
A Unitarian minister who answered Dr. King's call to march in the second Selma Pettus Bridge march and was beaten afterwards. (His character was inspired by Reverend Orloff Miller.)

REV. JAMES FREY:
Unitarian minister who answered Dr. King's call to march in the second Selma Pettus Bridge march and was murdered. (His character was inspired by Reverend James Reeb.)

ANNIE LEE JONES:
Active in all voting rights demonstrations and a dedicated DCVL Board Committee member. She raised Leslie Cole from an infant in Selma. (Her character was inspired by activist Annie Lee Cooper.)

FBI MAN:
Agent assigned to the demonstrations in Selma. He handled the informant.

SISTER MARY:
Nun from Chicago who marched in the second Selma Pettus Bridge march and remained.

CARLA GRACE:
Small girl forced to march out of town by deputy sheriffs.

APRIL ALLIE PARKER:
Uncle Parker's wife.

UNCLE PARKER: Member of the White Citizens Commission and leader of his KKK cell.

REV. WINSTON (WINNIE) PHILLIPS:
Minister from CA who answered Dr. King's call to march in the second Selma Pettus Bridge march, was beaten, and became part of the support team for the Freedom March. (His character was inspired by Reverend Clark Olsen.)

JOSHUA JAKE RAWLINGS:
Construction yard owner.

SISTER STELLA:
Nun from Chicago who marched in the second Selma Pettus Bridge march and remained.

CHOICE THOMPSON:
Member of the KKK cell, on disability, and an FBI informant.

CARLTON TURNER:
Mandy and Elverse's fifteen-year-old son who became an activist and marcher.

ELVERSE TURNER:
Committed voting rights activist and DCVL Board Committee member. His entire family was deeply involved in the movement.

MANDY TURNER:
Elverse's wife who worked double shifts as a nurse so her husband could take time off from his store to demonstrate.

ELMIRA WASHINGTON:
Moses' wife and active DCVL Board Committee member.

MOSES WASHINGTON:
Beloved teacher and active DCVL Board Committee member, and Elverse Turner's best friend.

SPARKY WILKERSON:
Member of the KKK cell and owner of an auto repair shop.

ACCRONYMS

DCVL: Dallas County Voters League

KKK: Ku Klux Klan

SCLC: Southern Christian Leadership Conference

SNCC: Student Nonviolent Coordinating Committee

Peggi Menagh Chute lives in Lake San Marcos, CA. Retired from the fields of education and film **Soul Of A Nation** is her first novel.